Lady Gambit

Rogues of Fortune's Den
Book 3

ADELE CLEE

This is a work of fiction. All names, characters, places and incidents are products of the author's imagination. All characters are fictitious and any resemblance to real persons, living or dead, is purely coincidental.

No part of this book may be copied or reproduced in any manner without the author's permission.

Lady Gambit
Copyright © 2024 Adele Clee
All rights reserved.
ISBN-13: 978-1-915354-35-8

Cover by Dar Albert at Wicked Smart Designs

'The madness of love is the greatest of heaven's blessings.'
— Plato

Chapter One

Fortune's Den
Aldgate Street, London

"Including the vowels Tindell wrote last night, the man's debts run to ten thousand pounds," Aramis said, glancing at his ledger. "I shall visit him today to ensure he knows he's not welcome in the club until he's settled his account."

Delphine Chance sat at the dining table, observing her four brothers as she slowly sipped her tea. She rarely attended the family meeting held at ten o'clock each morning. She had no interest in business matters. Mr Tindell would find himself in the Marshalsea. Next week, they would sit discussing another faceless man addicted to the turn of the cards or roll of the dice.

But if she meant to attend her secret meeting with Mr Flynn this afternoon, she had to know her brothers' whereabouts. She could not outwit them. They were strong, intelligent men, a product of a life spent surviving on the streets. Now they were as rich as Croesus, with resources aplenty. A lady needed more than a strategy if she hoped to evade suspicion.

Her eldest brother Aaron—known as the King of Clubs to those who frequented the gaming hell—sat at the head of the table, scanning a page in his leather-bound diary. "Meldrum is late with his payment. We must remind the arrogant lords of the *ton* that they receive no special privileges here." He set his dark eyes on their youngest brother, Theodore. "Speak to Meldrum. Tell him he'll incur a five percent fee if he fails to pay within the next three days."

Delphine gave an inward sigh of relief.

Aramis would visit Mr Tindell near Chelsea Common. Theodore would be occupied with Lord Meldrum. Aaron had an appointment at the solicitors and the bank. That left Christian.

"You haven't forgotten I'm at the museum today?" came Christian's well-timed question. "It's Isabella's lecture on Egyptian mathematics. I'll not let those with a contempt for female scholars mock her work."

Christian would walk over hot coals for his wife.

Nothing would drag him away from the museum.

"And I'm at the modiste's at two," Delphine said, thankful there was no one to act as her chaperone. "I cannot miss the appointment."

She prayed the mysterious Mr Flynn would attend this time. One would expect a former Bow Street runner to be reliable.

Aaron arched a curious brow. "Today? I've no record of the appointment. You usually inform me two weeks in advance." He flipped to a page in his diary. The one where he noted all her movements. When she ate and slept and breathed. "There's no mention of a visit to Miss Darrow."

Delphine kept her composure. She'd spent the last two days standing before the looking glass, rehearsing her reply. "We had a slight disagreement at last week's fitting. I had to leave to arrange Aramis' wedding breakfast but agreed to continue the discussion today." She forced a frown. "I told you about it when you accused me of acting strangely."

Having sent word to Mr Flynn, informing him to enter Miss Darrow's premises via the yard, she had battled disappointment when he'd failed to show.

Aaron rubbed his chiselled jaw as he studied her. "When I asked what was troubling you, you said it wasn't worth mentioning."

"You have more important things to worry about than ladies' fripperies, but I said I needed to return today." Guilt flared. She hated lying to the people she loved. They were her brothers by choice, not blood. That made them all the more exceptional. The last thing she wanted was to hurt them, but she was beyond desperate for answers. "It was when Miss Lovelace arrived. Perhaps your mind was engaged elsewhere."

The lady had a profound effect on Aaron.

He denied it most vehemently, of course.

Indeed, the mere mention of the woman who owned the ladies' club across the road had Aaron firming his jaw. "Be assured, there isn't a woman alive who could distract my mind."

Aramis snorted. "I recall saying something similar once. Love has a way of catching a man unawares."

Quick to intervene before anyone else offered words of wisdom, Aaron said, "I consider Miss Lovelace our competitor. The less said about her, the better." He pinned Delphine to the seat with his intense gaze. "Theo will accompany you once he's dealt with Lord Meldrum. Send word to Miss Darrow and inform her you'll be late."

Late? Mr Flynn would not wait.

Her throat tightened.

Aaron's lack of trust in her was a bitter pill to swallow.

Yes, dissolute lords might take her hostage in the hope of having their debts cleared. Yes, men looked for ways to hurt her brothers. But she was almost six and twenty— well, she wasn't exactly sure how old she was. Aaron had guessed her age when he found her alone and injured in an alley all those years ago.

"I'm not a child anymore. I'm a grown woman." At times, he still treated her like a ten-year-old urchin with no clue as to her identity. "I told Miss Darrow I would be there promptly at two, and I intend to keep my word."

Aaron closed his eyes briefly. "As a grown woman, you know why I insist on taking every precaution when you leave the house."

The pressure of keeping his family safe was taking its toll. More so since both Aramis and Christian had married.

"Then I shall take Sigmund."

Their trusted man-of-all-work was as strong as an ox. Skilled in combat, he could ward off an army of rogues. He wouldn't linger in the shop but would wait on the street, guarding the front door.

Aaron was firm in his stance. "I'll visit Meldrum. The man needs a sharp shock. Theo will ensure you arrive at the modiste's on time." He covered his heart with his hand and softened his tone. "I'd never forgive myself if something happened to you because of the choices I have made. Power and wealth come at a price. One I refuse to let you pay."

She was already paying a hefty price.

She was like a helpless butterfly trapped in a glass jar.

Aaron sighed deeply. "Please understand the need for rules."

"You don't want Lord Meldrum ruining me to punish you," she said, yet wondered if he had another motive for keeping her prisoner.

No one mentioned the parents she could not remember. But what if Aaron had found them? Were they gin swiggers who'd sold their daughter to feed their addiction? Were they part of a criminal fraternity? Were they heartbroken, and Aaron feared losing the sister he'd raised?

Hopefully, Mr Flynn would find the answer.

She glanced at Theo. If anyone had to accompany her, she would rather it be him. His handsome looks and playful manner would have Miss Darrow tripping over her own feet. The modiste would keep Theo entertained, giving Delphine time to talk privately to Mr Flynn.

Aaron slammed his diary shut, a sign all conversation was at an end. "It's settled, then. Theo will accompany you to the modiste's. I'm sure he would rather engage in flirtatious banter with Miss Darrow than listen to a scoundrel's pathetic excuses."

The modiste was waiting at the door when the carriage stopped outside the fashionable shop on New Bridge Street. The sudden tinkling of the overhead bell echoed the woman's excitement.

Miss Darrow gripped Delphine's hands and drew her over the threshold, out of Theo's earshot. "You said you were hoping to come alone. You should have warned me you were bringing your brother. I'd have worn my best dress." She glanced at Theo's commanding figure as he stood on the street talking to their coachman. "I look like I've been dragged through a hedge by an errant donkey."

Delphine chuckled. It was the first time she'd laughed in days. "Theo is more interested in what lies beneath the creased muslin. Besides, his gaze rarely moves from your lips."

Miss Darrow patted her fiery red curls and grinned. "I might be flattered, but the King of Hearts collects them and breaks them. I would prefer to keep mine intact."

It was Delphine's cue to laugh again, but she knew a deep sadness lay beneath Theo's carefree facade. He didn't break hearts. He was always clear in his intentions. He simply refused to allow a woman to hurt him again.

"You must keep him occupied while I speak to Mr Flynn." She checked over her shoulder to ensure Theo was still outside on the street. "Theo cannot know I've hired an investigator."

Lady Gambit

If her brothers learned she was searching for her parents there would be hell to pay. They would caution her against such folly. Remind her she had been left alone in the rookeries. That no one had come forward to claim her.

Miss Darrow pursed her lips and said in her usual eloquent tone, "Are you sure this is the road you wish to take? I would sooner upset the devil than Mr Chance."

She referred to Aaron. The arrogant lords of the *ton* thought the devil was Aaron's protege, not the other way around.

"Given time, he will understand."

Guilt coursed through her when she thought of the sacrifices Aaron had made to protect his family. He would always be her brother, her hero, a man she trusted and admired. Nothing would ever change that. But the dreams were becoming more frequent and vivid. The desire for answers nagged her night and day. She believed Aaron kept her in a gilded cage because he feared the truth, too.

Was it not better to know than to live with uncertainty?

"Once Mr Flynn has gathered the evidence, I shall present it to my brothers. Then we will decide what to do as a family."

Miss Darrow gave a little shrug. "Let's hope they don't blame Mr Flynn for encouraging you. He takes no prisoners. It will be one hell of a war if they come pounding on his door."

Delphine's pulse rose a notch. She knew next to nothing about the ex-runner. He could be a beastly devil. A fat-bellied oaf who found answers in the bottom of his tankard. Professional men kept an office and had a clerk to deal with appointments. They did not do business from the corner table in the local tavern.

Still, Mr Flynn came highly recommended.

Aramis' wife Naomi had mentioned his name. Mr Daventry, a family friend and skilled investigator, had slipped Mr Flynn's card covertly into her hand and confirmed he could be trusted.

"Aaron cannot blame Mr Flynn for doing his job. A man must earn a living. Doubtless he has a wife and children to feed." And money to keep refilling his tankard at the Old Swan in Long Lane.

Miss Darrow gave a bemused grin. "So you've never actually met Mr Flynn? When you asked me to deliver a note to him, I presumed he must have had dealings with your brother. That you'd met before."

"No. I shall leave you to make the introductions." She gripped Miss Darrow's hand. "I cannot thank you enough for helping me with this problem. It's above and beyond what anyone would ask of their modiste, but I hope you see me as a friend. If I can return the favour, all you need do is ask."

Miss Darrow smiled and patted Delphine's hand gently. "You might invite me to tea." Her gaze moved to the door. "Preferably when your brother Theodore is at home. I might add a love potion to his beverage. Having such a man at one's beck and call must be thrilling. I'd wager there's never a dull moment in the day."

Delphine laughed, though she could not imagine Theo pandering to a woman's whims. "You'd need potions by the dozen to win my brother's heart." But if Aramis had found love, there was hope for them all.

Lady Gambit

The tinkling of the overhead bell drew their attention to the door. Theo strode into the modiste's shop with his usual confident swagger.

"Now I know why you're not paid by the hour, Miss Darrow. You spend more time gossiping than sewing on buttons."

"And what else have you to do, Mr Chance, but play nursemaid?" the modiste said in the same playful manner. "Perhaps you would prefer to wait in your carriage. I will escort Miss Chance out after her fitting. I wouldn't want you to die of boredom in the chair."

"You sound keen to get rid of me, madam."

Delphine's heart thudded in her chest.

She did not want to rouse Theo's suspicion.

"Miss Darrow is merely teasing you." Delphine linked arms with her brother and escorted him to the elegant sofa. The one with a view of the road, not the fitting rooms. "Make yourself comfortable. I shall be no more than half an hour. Then you can take me on a ride around the park. It's such a beautiful afternoon."

Hopefully it would remain that way.

Theo snatched the newspaper off the side table. "Today's edition of the *Herald*." He gave Miss Darrow one of his heart-melting smiles. "I'm impressed. You certainly know how to keep a man entertained, Miss Darrow."

The modiste arched a brow. "If you're so easily entertained, sir, one wonders why you're not married."

His smile died for all of a heartbeat. Was he thinking about the night Lady Lucille Bowman refused his suit and announced her betrothal to a man they all despised?

Quick to fill the awkward silence, Delphine said,

"Well, let's pray we can reach a compromise on the gigot sleeves." She moved towards the corridor leading to the fitting rooms. "Creating the sloped shoulder is à la mode this season, but I prefer a tailored style."

Miss Darrow looked on as Theo made himself comfortable and opened his newspaper. "Coffee, Mr Chance?"

Theo's gaze slid over the modiste's figure. "Indeed. A man might become accustomed to your hospitality, Miss Darrow."

"A lady must strive to keep her clients happy, sir. Now, if you'll excuse me, I have work to do." She turned on her heel and escorted Delphine into the narrow corridor, drawing the thick curtain behind her. "You should undress to your undergarments, or it will look suspicious," she whispered, pointing to the last door at the end of the hall. "There's a dressing gown on the chair. It will protect your modesty."

Her undergarments!

Had Miss Darrow lost her mind?

"I mean to greet Mr Flynn in a professional manner." She would not have a strange man ogling her stockings. "I want him to take my request seriously. Besides, if Theo finds me in a state of dishabille with Mr Flynn, there'll be a dawn appointment."

Miss Darrow appeared oddly disappointed but then jumped to attention as she remembered something. "I'll fetch the gown I'm working on. It should fit you nicely, though I'm still making alterations to the neckline."

With little time to spare, Delphine nodded. "Very well."

Lady Gambit

The gown in question was not her favoured blue but pale gold silk. It belted at the waist with a pretty diamanté buckle, accentuating her curves. The puffy gigot sleeves fell off the shoulders, the décolleté skimming the upper arch of her breasts.

She stared at her reflection in the looking glass, hardly recognising the woman staring back. Clothes were her armour—a means of protecting herself from criticism. A way of forging an identity when her lineage was questionable. Every pelisse had padded shoulders to create a strong silhouette. Every bodice synched her in, forcing her spine straight.

She studied herself again.

This was not the vision she usually presented to her peers. This was the gown of an optimistic woman. The dress of someone who believed the world was a magical place. A woman who knew men found vulnerability attractive.

Miss Darrow faffed with the skirts and puffed the sleeves.

"I'm not holding court," Delphine joked, trying to stem her tears. She had never looked so feminine, so unburdened. "One would think Mr Flynn is a member of the nobility."

"He is! His father is the Earl of Retford." Miss Darrow straightened the buckle, looking quite pleased with her efforts. "Mr Flynn was born on the wrong side of the blanket. He has no airs and graces. He's a straight-talking gent, much like your brothers."

Mr Flynn was the son of an earl?

Her throat tightened.

Panic fluttered in her chest.

A working man posed no threat. But her self-assured facade would falter when pitted against a gentleman of refinement. Like the pompous peers who graced her brothers' club, did Mr Flynn thrive on making a woman feel inferior?

She should cancel the appointment. Hire someone who would keep his disparaging remarks to himself. But before she could speak, Theo called Miss Darrow and made a teasing remark about the lack of hot beverages.

Everything happened quickly then.

Theo popped his head around the curtain as she entered the corridor with Miss Darrow. Shocked to see her wearing something other than blue, he gasped. "Good Lord. You look divine. Miss Darrow has excelled herself." He gazed at the modiste with glowing admiration. "How the devil did you persuade her to wear gold?"

Aware Mr Flynn might arrive at any moment, Miss Darrow acted quickly. "Shoo, you wicked devil." She chuckled and waved her arms, encouraging him to retreat. "It's supposed to be a surprise." Glad for an excuse to engage with Theo, the modiste ushered him back to his seat.

The light rap on the back door made Delphine jump.

Fearing Mr Flynn would enter the premises, she hurried to greet him. Oh, why had she concocted this harebrained plan? The strain would kill her long before she learned the names of her parents.

She opened the back door, slipping into the yard before closing it behind her. There was no time to gather her wits.

She swung around to face the gentleman and almost swooned.

"Mr F-Flynn?"

Good Lord! She'd been expecting a much older man, one who had to roll out of bed in the morning. One who spilled his dinner down his waistcoat because he functioned better when sotted.

The shock—and the sight of Mr Flynn's athletic physique—left her somewhat lightheaded. Swaying slightly, she gripped the man's forearm, which was another mistake. It was strong, like his powerful shoulders. Firm, like his sculpted jaw.

"Are you well, madam?" His tone was as smooth as fine wine. He clasped her upper arm to steady her balance, touching her where no man had ever touched her before. "Allow me to escort you inside."

She stared at him, mesmerised by the amber flecks in his confident brown eyes. A little lost in the fullness of his lips and the fact his unruly brown hair was in contrast to his pristine black coat.

"Miss Heartwood?" He called her by the name she had invented to avoid any association with her brothers. "I must ask you again. Are you well?" His thumbs shifted, the unintentional caress stealing her breath.

No, she was not well.

Mr Flynn was a handsome man of thirty.

An earl's ill-begotten son to boot.

If her brothers caught them together, they'd drag him to the altar, a pistol pressed to his back until he recited his vows verbatim.

"Let me help you inside." Like a gentleman of good breeding, he was guiding her towards the door, not mauling her like a drunken oaf who conducted business from a tavern.

"No! Wait! I assure you, I am perfectly well. But time is of the essence. It's imperative we discuss our business posthaste."

His gaze moved to her bare shoulders, his grumbles incoherent. "Before we begin, allow me to convey my terms." Aware they were still gripping each other like lovers about to part ways, he released her.

"Your terms?" She stiffened her spine and drew a calming breath, though she could still feel the imprint of his hand on her skin. "I was told the initial consultation was free."

His expression turned as sombre as a judge donning a black cap. "It is, though I demand honesty from my clients. You have lied to me, madam. I want your name, not an alias, and I want to know why we're conversing in Miss Darrow's yard. If I'm satisfied with your answers, you may explain your problem."

She was used to dealing with blunt men, so she replied with utter confidence. "I used an alias to avoid causing my family distress. We're conversing in the yard because my brother Theodore is reading the newspaper and drinking coffee a mere ten yards away. He cannot know you're here. The punishment will be worse than death if he finds us."

Unperturbed, Mr Flynn said, "What is worse than death?"

"Marriage, sir."

Doubtless many women dreamed of marrying a man as handsome as Mr Flynn. But good looks faded. Loyalty and kindness topped her list of desirable attributes. Wrinkles and a paunch did not destroy a lady's soul. Deceitful words and deeds did.

"Marriage! Yes, a swift death is preferable to a life spent in shackles." He glanced at the shop door but seemed distracted by the rapid rise and fall of her chest. "Perhaps you should explain your dilemma so I might consider your case."

"My dilemma?"

"Why you seek to hire me?"

"Oh. My dilemma. Yes."

Heavens! Her mind had turned to mush. She tried to focus on the reason she had lied to her brothers. That's when the chill of trepidation shivered across her shoulders. A warning to leave the past behind and not poke the snake's basket.

Aaron's sensible words echoed in her head.

The dream we conjure in our minds is often far removed from reality. It's human nature to seek happy endings. For most, the truth brings nothing but disappointment.

She should apologise for wasting Mr Flynn's time.

But the emptiness inside was profound. It was becoming harder to breathe by the day. All the rules and restrictions made home feel like Newgate.

"My story begins sixteen years ago, sir. When my *adopted* brothers found me injured and crying in the rookeries." Saying the words aloud to a stranger released a tidal wave of emotions. Gratitude for the men who treated her like kin. Sadness for the years spent mourning her parents. A fearful curiosity for a life she could not remember.

"Adopted brothers?"

"Four boys ousted from their Mayfair home by their wicked stepmother and left to perish on the streets. The oldest was fifteen at the time."

Even then, Aaron had learnt to bury his emotions. He was ruthless, brutal with others. Protective and loyal to her and his kin.

"The oldest being Aaron Chance?" Mr Flynn said, taking a small step back. Most men would run until their legs gave out.

Her shoulders sagged. Mr Flynn had every reason to refuse her request now. "You worked at Bow Street. I presume my brother's reputation precedes him."

Mr Flynn's mouth curled into a slow smile that softened his rugged features. "A friend, Lucius Daventry, informed me of the complexities of this case. Evading your brothers might prove more problematic than finding your parents."

She frowned, a tad annoyed. "If you know who I am and why I called you here, why not say so in the beginning?" It would have saved them precious time. "It's as if you've come for the pleasure of refusing my request."

He seemed to find her mild rant amusing. "Few men in London would pit themselves against your brothers. Only a fool answers a beautiful woman's summons. But I'm compelled to accept your case without hearing the evidence."

"You are?" Somewhat surprised he'd implied she was beautiful and that she'd hired his services so easily, she said, "But we haven't discussed your fee. Are you certain you can find my parents after all these years?"

Mr Flynn's weary sigh said he regretted his decision already. "There is no fee. A benefactor settled your account, along with all necessary expenses. As for finding your parents, the chance of locating them after all these years is slim."

A benefactor?

But few people knew of her forgotten past.

"Who paid the fee?" Who cared if she found her parents? Not Aaron. Otherwise, he would be standing beside her, a strong shoulder of support. "I demand to know his name, sir."

Mr Flynn smiled, the sight making her stomach flip. "Mrs Sybil Daventry," he said, shocking her to the marrow of her bones. "She believes you deserve to know the truth. She believes in happy endings."

Mrs Daventry? Good heavens! During their brief conversations, the lady's kindness had shone through. But to pay Mr Flynn's fee? It beggared belief.

"Why take the case if the outcome is grim?"

"Because Lucius Daventry once saved my life and has called in the debt. He believes I'm the only person who can help you."

Mr Daventry was right. She had warmed to the gentleman instantly. His cordial manner put her at ease. Then she remembered Miss Darrow's warning. Anyone who wasn't afraid to tackle her brothers must be dangerous indeed.

As if keen to prove the point, Mr Flynn hardened his tone and said, "Before we begin, there are a few things you should know about me, Miss Chance. I bow to no man. I'm no pretty lady's lackey. And I would rather die than admit defeat."

Chapter Two

Lucius Daventry would regret saving Dorian's life. If Daventry sauntered into Miss Darrow's yard, Dorian would throttle him with his own cravat.

The sleuth's urgent visit to the Old Swan this morning made perfect sense now. He had come to persuade Dorian to take the case. He had revealed Miss Chance's real name and explained her predicament, though had failed to mention the most obvious fact.

Delphine Chance possessed an inherent beauty.

A means to distract a man from his intended course.

She had appeared as a vision in gold silk. A goddess of Olympus in a gown that hugged her figure like a glove. He'd tried not to stare at her bare shoulders and imagine brushing his mouth over her soft skin. It had been so long since he'd held a woman in his arms. It was doubtless the cause of his body's fierce reaction.

Daventry had misled him. He had used the word *spinster* to imply the lady was beyond marriageable age. He'd not said she was undesirable or that she preferred to chase her independence. But few people spoke of Aaron Chance's sister, and so Dorian had assumed no one wished to cause offence.

"There are some things you should know about *me*, Mr Flynn." She spoke quickly, her gaze darting to the door of Miss Darrow's shop. "Confident men do not intimidate me. In theory, you might consider me worldly. There's nothing you could say that would shock me. In reality, I have very little life experience."

The lady was definitely chaste. It explained why she feared being caught alone with a man. Why her brothers would force her to marry. That said, Aaron Chance would likely kill Dorian before welcoming him into the fold.

"Is there anything else you need to know?" she added.

Yes, he needed to know why such a beautiful woman was seldom seen about town. Why had she not approached her brothers to ask for their help? They were powerful men. Dangerous devils. Why was Daventry so damned keen for him to assist her?

"In these cases, people rarely find what they're looking for." It was only right he cautioned her before she revealed sensitive information. Most women had unrealistic expectations. "The truth is often ugly."

The day he learnt the truth about his own tainted lineage was a memory he'd sooner forget. A child had no need to question his parents' relationship. He didn't wonder why his father came home late at night and left before dawn. Why his mother's favourite chair faced the window. Along with every punch, the pampered boys at boarding school were quick to offer explanations.

He's Retford's by-blow.

Lady Gambit

His mother is a common whore.

His mother had been Lady Retford's maid.

Miss Chance stepped closer, the seductive notes of her perfume waking him from his reverie. "You may be right, but ignorance won't stop the nightmares. Who am I, Mr Flynn?" She opened her arms, tempting him to examine every delightful curve and contour. "I have no notion."

"Our parents do not define us, Miss Chance."

If they did, he would be a weak man, controlled by his appetites. He'd be a philanderer who lied at every given opportunity. A pathetic creature filled with his own self-importance.

"That's easy for you to say. You know your parents."

Dorian snorted. "Trust me, I wish I didn't."

Undeterred by his cold response, she pressed her case. "One of your parents must have dark brown hair. Someone in your family must be tall and broad. From whom did you inherit your proud nose?"

With a bitter taste in his mouth, he said, "My father."

She gave a little huff. "You see my point? Is my mother's hair as dark as mine?" She pulled an ebony tendril loose and let it slip through her dainty fingers. "Are her lips as full?" Said lips formed a perfect pout. "Who in my family has long eyelashes?"

Whoever it was possessed a pleasing countenance. And yet, the kindness in her eyes and the determination in her voice held him entranced.

"I dislike mussels." She wrinkled her nose, ensuring he knew how much they turned her stomach. "There's no logical reason I should."

He found himself smiling. "Miss Chance, I cannot

begin an investigation with nothing more than a hatred of mussels."

"I'm a gifted horsewoman, though to my knowledge, I've never had a lesson. I'm quite pedantic when it comes to tidiness. I find beauty in small things—the shimmer of sunlight on the water, the first blooming buds of spring. The tragedy of Romeo and Juliet makes me weep inconsolably."

He raised a hand to silence her. "I'm not here interviewing for a wife." Though he could not deny she was adorable. Thank heavens he need only spend a short time in her company. She would test any bachelor's resolve. "We're the sum of our experiences. Traits aren't always inherited. Now. Tell me about the day you met Aaron Chance."

She nodded and was about to begin when a harried Miss Darrow appeared at the door. "Your brother is asking to see you in the gown again." The modiste spoke in frantic whispers. "He insists I finish it today and deliver it to Fortune's Den. He won't take no for an answer."

Miss Chance's breathing quickened. "But you can't. It's not my gown." Keen to offer an explanation, she turned to him. "Miss Darrow suggested I meet you wearing my undergarments and a silk dressing gown. I'm sure you agree that would be inappropriate."

"Most inappropriate." A picture formed in his mind. An erotic picture of gossamer and ribbons, of soft breasts and a sensual silhouette. A picture that would haunt him for days, weeks, maybe months to come.

"Just step into the corridor so he can see you." Miss Darrow flapped her hands and looked like a frightened bird about to take flight. "I told him we disagree on the neckline and that you'd rather the dress was blue."

Miss Chance faced him again. "Will you wait a moment, sir?"

The pleading look in her eyes made it impossible to refuse. He had no option but to take the case and wanted the matter dealt with swiftly. Still, she needed to know he was not a servant to be summoned.

"Be quick. I have an appointment across town in an hour."

Her grateful smile left him holding his breath. Cursed saints! He would strap Lucius Daventry to the rack for this and take pleasure in turning the crank.

Miss Chance hurried inside, leaving the door ajar.

Eager to learn more about the lady's relationship with her brother, he moved closer, hoping to hear their exchange.

"Miss Darrow said you're not sure about the gown," came the man's strong voice. "She said you're not struck on the neckline or the colour."

Through the gap in the door, Dorian could see Miss Chance in the corridor, wringing her hands and struggling to stand still. "It's not what I'm used to, Theo. You know I love blue. And where would I wear such an elegant gown? My social calendar begins and ends at the circulating library."

For some unfathomable reason, Dorian's heart constricted.

"You look exceptional in gold," Mr Chance said affectionately.

Being an honest man, Dorian silently agreed.

"We'll persuade Aramis to have a party. Another excuse to celebrate his wedding. He'll do anything to please his wife. Wear it then."

A mocking snort escaped her. "They prefer to spend time alone."

"We'll speak to Aaron and see if he'll permit you to attend Miss Lovelace's club for ladies." Theodore Chance was undeterred in his effort to please his sister. "The Burnished Jade is across the road from Fortune's Den. I can't see why he would refuse."

Miss Chance sighed. "You know why. We've been told to avoid Miss Lovelace at all costs. We're not to speak her name or look in her direction. Heaven forbid we were to pass pleasantries."

"Then we must persuade him otherwise."

She hesitated before shaking her head. The ebony lock she'd pulled from her chignon caressed her cheek. "The gown is awfully expensive, Theo. It seems such a waste if it's to remain in the armoire."

"We're not scavenging for crumbs anymore, Delphine." Resentment coated her brother's words, though it was not aimed at his sister. "She'll have the gown, Miss Darrow. Measure her for another in a similar style but in pale pink."

Two things became apparent in their brief conversation.

Theodore Chance loved his sister.

Beneath Miss Chance's cheerful facade lay a deep sadness that would tug on any man's heartstrings. Indeed, Dorian was keen to find the lady's parents. If only to prevent her from ruining her relationship with her brothers.

"Thank you. You always did know how to make me feel special," she said, sniffing and dabbing her fingers to her eyes. The tenderness in her voice spoke of love and admiration for the brother she'd been forced to deceive. "I promise I won't be much longer. Miss Darrow will fetch you more coffee."

"Take as long as you need."

Miss Chance disappeared behind a door. Seconds later, she slipped back out into the yard. "I'm sorry for abandoning you, Mr Flynn." A tear slid down her cheek, and he resisted the urge to dash it away. "Forgive me for wasting your time. I know it's extremely precious. Please tell Mrs Daventry I have had a change of heart. I no longer require your services."

Evidently, her brother's affectionate response had made her reconsider.

He should be relieved. He could put this woman from his mind and never think of her again. But there was one thing he loathed more than his father—injustice.

"You're certain?" he said, keeping an indifferent tone.

"Quite certain." A sob caught in her throat.

The tension in the air was palpable. He could see the strain on her face, the furrows of an inner conflict etched on her brow. More tears fell.

Hell, he didn't know what the devil to do.

He pulled his handkerchief from his pocket. "Allow me."

"Thank you." She took the linen square and dried her cheeks. "Heaven knows what you must think of me."

He thought she was a little broken inside. That this was

the most genuine display of emotion he had ever witnessed. "It's clear you're in a difficult predicament."

She stepped closer. The crackle of an invisible force charged the air. An obscure connection that made no logical sense. "Have you ever had a recurring dream? One so vivid you can recall it with absolute clarity?"

He used to daydream, invent the perfect life, the perfect parents. He used to imagine he was like the other boys at school. But he came to learn a valuable lesson. The things that set him apart were the things that made him excel.

"No, but dreams are often a doorway to one's destiny. The mind uses mysterious ways to guide us on our journey."

She didn't question his logic or suggest he spoke nonsense.

"Why in every dream am I compelled to follow a faceless man? What if it's my father, and he is brokenhearted? What if, in finding him, I make a dreadful mistake and lose those I care about most?"

Pain coated her words and had her reaching for him. A mere hand on his coat sleeve to steady her balance. But then her knees buckled, and she collapsed into his arms and wept.

Sweet mercy!

He'd demand double the fee after this.

Miss Chance cried on his coat while he tried to ignore the alluring smell of lilac in her hair. The delicate scent tightened the muscles in his abdomen. It didn't help that her breasts were squashed against his chest, that his palms

Lady Gambit

were hot against her back. That he thought about kissing away her troubles and tasting those luscious lips.

The Chance brothers were dangerous men.

Their sister's sweetness would be Dorian's downfall.

He set his hands to her upper arms and stepped away. Hell, he was struggling to suppress the first stirrings of arousal. "We could take things at a slow pace," he began but quickly clarified his meaning. "I could make discreet enquiries. Give you time to consider how you wish to proceed."

The sooner he put some distance between them, the better. Even the possessive way she clutched his handkerchief had an odd effect on him.

"Yes," she said, inhaling a calming breath. "There's no need to tell anyone. It could be our secret. But I don't want to cause you any trouble."

"It's no trouble." He needed to do something to appease Daventry and earn his fee. "What say we meet here at the same time next week? Send word to Miss Darrow if you change your mind and want to cancel the appointment."

She thought for a moment. "Very well."

"I'll need a lead to follow. A name, address, a prominent memory."

This was not how he usually conducted business. When taking a case, he demanded a detailed list of facts, a timeline of events. He asked sensible questions and remained impartial. He did not attend secret rendezvous with beautiful women or embrace them as if they were destined to be lovers.

She blinked tears from her long lashes. "I have no memory of my life before the night I met my brothers. But you might try speaking to a patient in Bethlem Royal Hospital. On a recent visit, a woman called to me through the bars. She seemed to think my name was Sofia."

What the devil was Miss Chance doing at Bethlem?

"Do you know this woman's name?"

"No. But she was in the last cell at the end of the gallery, opposite the day room. Her hair was white and lank, and her hands were shackled. I saw the irons as she gripped the bars."

There seemed little point questioning a madwoman, but he'd earned a reputation for being thorough, and after a visit to Bethlem, one always counted their blessings.

"When we meet again, you must tell me your story from the beginning." He prayed she didn't appear in the same fetching gown. "It might save time if you record anything you remember."

She nodded and edged towards the door. "It won't be much."

"Any insignificant detail might help."

Her smile carried the warmth of a summer's day. Yet he suspected storm clouds gathered beneath the surface. "It was a pleasure to meet you, Mr Flynn. If only all men were so approachable."

With that unexpected compliment, she left him standing alone in the yard, minus his handkerchief and the steely armour he'd worn since being locked in a chest at school barely able to breathe.

Dorian made his way to Bethlem Royal Hospital in St George's Fields, south of the Thames. It wasn't difficult to gain admission, not as a visitor or a patient. Half the people housed in cells or taking air in the ornate gardens were a burden to their families, not insane. People often said the only lunatics in Bethlem were the staff.

That was Dorian's current opinion of the Superintendent, Mr Powell. The thin, long-legged fellow had a menacing look in his eyes. One could imagine him slipping through the shadows at night to cause mayhem. A real monster. Not a figment of the patients' nightmares.

"What do you want with Nora Adkins?" Powell drummed his bony fingers on the desk and glanced at the mantel clock.

Dorian kept his temper. "It relates to a missing person's case. One I've been asked to investigate." He handed Powell the letter given to him by the magistrate at Bow Street. It was from a previous case but wasn't dated. "Sir Malcolm Langley grants me permission to question anyone I deem relevant to my enquiries."

He watched Powell squirm as he read the missive. The glow of satisfaction was akin to what he'd felt upon pummelling his tormentors at boarding school.

Powell mumbled his displeasure. "You'll get no sense from her. The woman is as mad as a March hare. She's been a patient at the hospital for over sixteen years. She yanks out her hair and nibbles her nails until they bleed."

Sixteen years?

The length of time Miss Chance had lived with her brothers.

Was it a coincidence?

Dorian shrugged. "Then I suspect the interview will be brief."

Like a petulant child, Powell threw the letter across the table. "I'll have Peters show you to her cell. For your own safety, I must insist you speak to her from the corridor. She's liable to scratch out your eyes and carve her name into your soul."

Dorian gave a humourless snort. The patients needed the man's compassion, not his contempt. "I'll need to see the physician's report." He didn't need to see the report but wished to unsettle Powell. "What is the nature of Miss Adkins' condition?"

"She's tuppence short of a shilling, that's what."

"Who had her committed?"

Powell retrieved a silver flask and two glasses from the desk drawer. He was stalling. "We lost the paperwork when we moved from Moorfields to the new premises," he said, handing Dorian a tot of brandy.

How convenient.

"Is Miss Adkins a pauper, or is someone paying for her keep?" He knocked back the liquor and met Powell's gaze. "No doubt the Board of Governors demand you examine the accounts regularly. The Select Committee on Lunacy assesses the welfare of all paupers. There must be recent records."

Lady Gambit

A muscle in Powell's cheek pulsed. "I can't answer that without trawling through the files. Such things take time."

"You can't, or you won't?"

"Now listen here." Powell snatched the empty brandy glasses and shoved them back in the drawer. "That woman is a raving loon. The only thing between her ears is wool. Trust me. You'll leave here with nothing but a barrowful of nonsense."

Dorian stood, keen to interview Nora Adkins before Powell threw him out. "My visit is a mere formality. A means of leaving no stone unturned. I'll ask her a few questions and be on my way. I'll wait outside for Peters."

Itching to get rid of him, Powell sent for the guard.

Peters arrived and barely spoke as he led Dorian along the women's gallery. Vile bodily smells clung to the air. Cries and groans and angry protests filled the silence. Rattling chains and high-pitched rants explained why Bedlam—the nickname for Bethlem Hospital—was now a word meaning chaos.

Amid the crazed cacophony, Peters clutched his ring of keys like a weapon. The tubby man was a gaoler tasked with keeping the unruly patients chained to their rickety beds.

Peters stopped at the end of the corridor and banged on a locked door. There was no reply, not a grunt or groan from within.

Dorian stepped closer and peered through the bars in the small window. An elderly woman lay on a crude metal bed, her eyes wide open, her shackled hands covering her heart. She was so frail and thin her grey dress was lost amid the coarse grey blanket.

"Rise and shine," Peters barked. "You've a visitor, Nora."

The woman ignored him.

Dorian feared she was dead—then she released a weary breath.

Peters gritted his teeth. He hit the metal ring against the bars, his temper barely caged inside his bulky frame. "Wake up, you old witch, before—"

"Leave us." Dorian placed a firm hand on the man's arm. "I will return to the office once I'm satisfied she's incapable of answering my questions."

"But she'll have your—"

"I'm not in the habit of repeating myself." Dorian met the gaoler's gaze, hoping he knew not to anger the spawn of the devil. "Move, or I'll shove those keys so far down your throat you'll be spitting metal filings for weeks."

He did not need to tell Peters twice. The man grumbled and stomped away, gripping his keys as if primed for an attack.

Dorian moved closer to the bars, hoping to coax Nora from her bed, but she was at the door in seconds, her haggard face pressed to the iron rails, her beady eyes fixed on him.

"If I had a guinea, I'd give it to you, sir." Nora smiled, revealing a mouth of rotten teeth. "About time someone put that beggar in his place. He's a mean devil. One day, he'll come a cropper."

Though Dorian agreed with her assessment, he wasn't about to criticise Peters. The patients had probably assaulted the gaoler on countless occasions. "If you'd answered him, you might have avoided a verbal altercation."

Nora laughed, the sound bitter. "Riling him is my only pleasure."

"According to the Superintendent, you enjoy carving your name into men's souls." He observed her, anticipating the moment her inner demon revealed itself, and he learned why she was truly here.

"Do you know what happens to timid women here, sir?"

He knew what happened to timid women in gaol cells; hence, he no longer worked at Bow Street.

"I'm keen to know why you're here." She'd been a patient for a long time. People rarely survived a year, let alone more than a decade.

"What's it to you? He sent you, did he? Wondering if I'd kicked the bucket. Tell him he'll be dancing on my grave soon enough." She hummed a folk tune and did a little jig. "*Da de, di da, da diddly dum.*"

"Someone is paying for your keep?"

She motioned to the dank room and cackled. "Happen he meant for me to stay at the Pulteney Hotel but got in a muddle."

"Who?" Dorian pressed. The information might not relate to Miss Chance's case, but it might support the theory that this woman wasn't entirely mad. "Do you know his name? Can you describe him?"

The basic questions caused her to stare strangely.

Her sly smile made her look oddly sinister.

She shrugged. "Big black hat. Big shiny shoes. One

ruby eye on a stick. He strokes it round and round and makes a girl dizzy."

Again, Nora Adkins was keen to show how dizzy.

"Get up! Get up!" she cried, having an odd conversation with herself. "Run. Run, Caterina. Let the night swallow you whole."

She began acting out roles.

Someone weeping, their outstretched hand grabbing at the air.

Someone running, their eyes wide in terror. "*Mama!*"

Someone looming, a mouth curled into a baleful grin.

"He came for the Jubilee and got lost in the whispers. And here I am, sir, in the belly of the beast, hoping it might belch."

Dorian drew a notebook and pencil from his pocket and scribbled down the woman's ramblings lest he forget. He wasn't sure why, but his thoughts turned to Miss Chance. That said, it was hardly surprising. He'd thought of little else since they'd parted ways in Miss Darrow's yard.

Nora's cries had prompted the other patients to shout and jeer and mimic her mindless rants. The din was deafening. Worn out from her grand performance, Nora returned to her bed, where she stared at the ceiling in a trance-like state.

"A friend was here recently." Dorian caught himself. He was a professional man. Miss Chance was his client, not his friend. A fact he would do well to remember. "You spoke to her through the bars. She said you called her Sofia."

Nora did not move, speak or blink.

Dorian tried to coax a response but to no avail.

He returned his notebook to his pocket and moved to walk away. That's when he caught Nora Adkins' faint whisper.

"Sofia is dead. Find the girl. Find Caterina."

Chapter Three

One long week had passed since Delphine had met Mr Flynn in Miss Darrow's yard. She had spent endless hours fretting over their conversation, deciding what to do. But her sleepless nights were consumed with thoughts other than guilt and betrayal.

Why did she feel oddly connected to a stranger?

Why had his warm embrace left her craving his company?

She looked out the carriage window as the vehicle trundled along Ludgate Hill. Mr Flynn's handkerchief was not in the blue reticule she clutched in her lap. It was wrapped in silk and tucked in the back of her drawer. The musky scent of his cologne diminished by the day. All remnants of the man would soon be lost, along with these precious moments of freedom.

"Why so glum? Anyone would think we were bound for debtors' prison." Theo chuckled and brushed an errant blonde lock from his brow. He wore his new blue coat and the bergamot and rosewood cologne ladies loved. "I thought Aaron's compromise would lift your spirits."

Aaron had summoned her to his office and spent silent seconds watching her from behind his imposing desk. She feared he knew about Mr Flynn. Knew the man had held her close and whispered soothing words against her hair.

Aaron had not asked what she thought about parties, gowns or visiting a ladies' club. With deep furrows marring his brow, he had issued a blunt statement. The words were still ingrained in her memory.

Purchase what you desire and send me the bill. Your sisters-in-law will take you to dine at Mivart's and to the theatre. You'll not visit The Burnished Jade. There's no way of knowing who Miss Lovelace permits in her club.

Aaron would be at Mivart's, watching from the shadows. He would hide in a theatre box, pistol at the ready to shoot anyone who dared approach her.

She had smiled and thanked him for his generosity.

How could she tell the man who'd saved her life that he fell short of her expectations? How did she explain she was slowly dying inside, withering away like a rose starved of sunlight?

Perhaps it was foolish to find hope in a square of linen.

Perhaps it was wrong to think the wearer of such an enticing cologne might be the answer to her prayers. The person with the key to her prison.

"Give Aaron time to adjust," Theo said with his usual optimism. It was a means of hiding his own disappointment in a life that had gone awry. "We should trust him. He's stubborn to a fault but always does what is right for our family."

Knots of guilt twisted in her gut. She had tried to talk to Aaron this morning and had begun by asking what he remembered about the night they first met. His reply had helped her reach a decision.

You looked so lost, so helpless. I swore you'd never look that way again. I've done everything in my power to keep you safe.

She was still lost.

She was still helpless.

She was a frightened child trapped in a woman's body.

Ignoring the problem had not made it go away.

"Sometimes it's hard to breathe at home," she confessed. With Theo being her youngest brother, surely he understood. "Sometimes I feel like an ornament in a cupboard." A useless knick-knack kept out of sight.

Theo reached for her hand and gripped it tightly. "There are times I wish we still lived above Mrs Maloney's bookshop. Life was much simpler then." His smile brimmed with compassion. "Let me talk to Aaron. What say we keep pushing the boundaries a little?"

She had done more than push the boundaries.

She had taken a mallet to the dry stone wall.

Perhaps it was pointless worrying. If Mr Flynn had any sense, he would fail to attend the meeting. One could not find answers without evidence, and Aaron would throttle him for prying into family affairs. The only saving grace was Mr Daventry knew both men and would act as a mediator.

"I think Miss Darrow likes you," she said, hoping the change of subject might settle her nerves. What if Mr

Lady Gambit

Flynn had learned something from his visit to Bethlem Hospital? What if he had grave news to impart?

Theo gave a playful wink. "Most women do."

"Oh, conceit is thy middle name."

He shrugged. "Can I help it if I'm charming?"

"I'm beginning to think Aramis is the most charming of all. Have you heard the beautiful things he says to Naomi?" And the way he looked at her. What must it be like to feel so cherished?

Theo tutted like he found affection a dreaded inconvenience. "Aramis is suffering from temporary amnesia. He'll be back to his grumpy self soon."

She begged to differ, and might have said true love stands the test of time but did not want to remind Theo of Lucille Bowman's treachery.

Miss Darrow was waiting at the door when their carriage stopped outside the modiste's shop. The lady wore a fashionable green dress and a smile capable of lighting the heavens.

Theo perused her figure as he alighted, his hum of pleasure audible. "Are you so desperate to see me, Miss Darrow, you've taken to loitering in the street?"

"I'm not loitering, sir. I'm looking for the barrow boy."

"In the hope he may have something to satisfy your appetite?" he said, handing Delphine down from the vehicle.

"Yes, something that hasn't been mauled by a dozen women's hands." Miss Darrow turned to Delphine. "I don't mean to rush you, but do you mind if we begin right away? I have a pressing appointment at three."

Miss Darrow's meaning was abundantly clear.

Mr Flynn was waiting for her in the yard.

"Of course not. I shall begin undressing while you feed my brother's coffee addiction." She tried to sound jovial, but her thundering heart left her breathless. Was Mr Flynn as handsome as she remembered? Would his cologne still have such a profound effect? "I'm excited to see my new gown."

Miss Darrow had hired another seamstress to help with the workload and had persuaded the lady who'd commissioned the gold gown that peacock blue would suit her better.

While the modiste tended to Theo's needs, Delphine left her outdoor apparel in the room at the end of the corridor and hurried outside.

Mr Flynn stopped pacing the second he saw her. He appeared relieved though somewhat anxious. "Miss Chance. I was beginning to wonder if you'd show."

She managed a smile. Something about this man always left her flustered. "I would have informed you if I'd had no intention of meeting you today."

"Do I detect a veiled reprimand?" he said, alluding to his failure to keep their first appointment. "Forgive me. I was stuck in Winchester. I should have offered an apology when last we met."

What had kept him in Winchester, she wondered?

Family? Friends? A mistress?

Someone soon to be his betrothed?

"Missing person cases must take you away from home quite often." A week spent thinking about a man she hardly knew had left her distracted. Having a husband who

Lady Gambit

was rarely at home would be hard to endure. "I imagine your presence is missed."

His narrowed gaze said he was surprised by the personal nature of her comment. His slow smile said he was intrigued to know her thoughts. "I live alone, Miss Chance. I'm free to roam the length and breadth of the country without admonishment."

His reply piqued her interest. The notion that he might be lonely fuelled her growing obsession with him. "Then I won't feel guilty for making you work long hours." Before she began waffling, she focused on the purpose of their meeting. "Did you speak to the woman at Bethlem Hospital?"

"Yes, though the man in charge tried to persuade me it was pointless." He stepped closer, and the butterflies in her stomach took flight again. "Her name is Nora Adkins. Is it at all familiar to you?"

Had she spent years attending society functions, she might have trawled her mind to put a face to the name. "Sadly, no."

"She has been a patient at Bethlem Hospital for sixteen years. You would have been a child when you knew her."

Sixteen years?

The same length of time she had been under Aaron Chance's care?

Was it a coincidence, or did Nora Adkins know the secrets of her past?

"I remember nothing about my childhood. Whenever I try to recall places, names or faces, it's like trawling through dense fog." It proved so frightening she always turned back.

Mr Flynn's brown eyes softened. "Daventry said you were wandering barefooted through the rookeries when you stumbled upon Aaron Chance. That you had a large lump on your head but cannot recall how you came by it. What do you remember about that night?"

She'd woken to find herself curled up in a doorway. It was cold and dark, the noises of the night terrifying. Dogs prowled the streets, vicious in their hunt for scraps. Drunken men cursed each other, brawled and vomited in alleyways. The pained cries of hungry babes wrenched at one's soul.

"I'd been sleeping in the entrance to a baker's shop, though I don't know how I came to be there. My head hurt. The pounding like a hammer on an anvil. Dried blood coated my fingertips and my matted hair." She bent her head and parted her locks. "If you look closely, you can still see the scar."

Had someone hit her?

Had she fallen?

How could she not know the answer?

Mr Flynn examined the scar. He stroked the silvery line gently with the tips of his fingers, feeling the remnants of the wound Aaron had tended long ago.

"You're lucky you hit the hardest part of your head," he said, his voice warm with compassion. His breathing deepened as he slid his fingers back and forth through her hair. Then he suddenly whipped them away and straightened.

Their gazes met, and though she felt a little giddy whenever she looked at him, she explained how Aaron had taken her under his wing and found them lodgings above

Mrs Maloney's bookshop. That her adopted brothers called her Delphine because that was the name sewn into her dirty dress.

"Delphine?" Her given name slipped effortlessly from Mr Flynn's lips.

"Yes. Mrs Maloney was surprised. Most people sew initials into garments."

Mr Flynn glanced at the door to the modiste's shop. "I need to speak to you privately. Somewhere we can sit, and I can probe your mind. Where I can make notes and discuss the possibility Nora Adkins does indeed know you."

A gasp caught in her throat. She had expected him to say the woman was deluded, to look remorseful and confirm there was no hope of her discovering her true identity.

"I believe we should sit with your eldest brother and have him work with us. Your safety must be the priority." He covered his heart with his hand to show he spoke in earnest. "I cannot be your protector, Miss Chance, and I fear you may need one desperately."

Her pulse skittered.

None of this made sense.

What had he learned at Bethlem?

"Aaron will be furious. He will hide the truth from me. He'll push me aside and attempt to solve my problems." He'd gather her in his competent hands and return her to the perch in the gilded cage. "He will never forgive me for seeking help elsewhere." She would forever be at fault when all she'd wanted was answers.

"I fear the last thing you need is a war between me and

your brother." Concern marred his tone now. "We must dig deep to discover the truth, not squabble amongst ourselves."

He'd omitted to say this was men's work.

That she was a liability.

A burden to him and her kin.

The sudden need to flee rose in her chest. Familiar words echoed in her head as they always did during times of stress.

Run! Run, my darling. Save yourself. Don't look back.

"I'm such a fool," she said, tears of despair choking her now. Why had she believed she could trust this man? "I thought you understood my dilemma. I thought you knew what I've risked to learn the truth." Water filled her eyes, blurring her field of vision. "Thank you for your time, Mr Flynn. But I wish to proceed no further. Good day to you."

She moved to leave, but the gentleman captured her wrist.

"Wait! In visiting Nora Adkins, I fear I have opened Pandora's box. A man asked for me at the Old Swan last night. He'd sat in the tavern all day, awaiting my arrival. The landlord heard him harassing the punters, asking if anyone knew my direction."

She blinked away her tears. "Perhaps he means to hire you."

Mr Flynn pulled her closer and firmed his jaw. "You're in grave danger, Miss Chance. I have a sixth sense about these things. I urge you to speak to your brothers and have them visit me at Daventry's office."

She suspected Mr Flynn was not easily spooked and

Lady Gambit

was exaggerating the threat. "When you visited Bethlem Hospital, did you mention my name?"

"Of course not."

"Has this mystery man visited you at home?"

"No, but—"

"Then what is there to fear?"

His mocking snort said she was being naive. "You visited Bethlem with your brother and his wife two weeks ago. Daventry said you were moving a patient to a private institution."

"Yes." Naomi's sister had relocated to Merryville, an asylum with an excellent reputation. "That's when Nora Adkins saw me and called me Sofia."

"You were all required to sign the register. The Superintendent and his staff have access to that information. Your brother gave his address when signing the release papers."

Her heart skipped a beat.

Should she take his warning seriously?

"Someone is paying to keep Nora Adkins at Bethlem Hospital," he continued, his grave tone sending an icy shiver down her spine. "That someone may know you. Now they have your name and your direction."

She remained silent. Mr Flynn was right. The devil could be sitting at the card table at Fortune's Den. He could be planning to sneak upstairs and lie in wait in her room. Worse still, he could force his way into Aramis' house and hurt Naomi.

What had she done?

Had she placed her family in danger?

"I should never have hired you." She should have

listened to Aaron, not Mr Daventry. She looked back at the shop door. Doubtless Theo was teasing Miss Darrow, unaware of the impending threat. "I've ruined everything. It's all my fault."

Mr Flynn captured her elbow and forced her to face him. "It's not wrong to want answers. But your problems have nothing to do with hiring me. The instant Nora called you Sofia, the die was cast. Whoever is paying to keep her in Bethlem will have bribed the staff for information."

She didn't shirk out of his grasp but drew comfort from his touch. "What can I do to make this problem go away? Please tell me, Mr Flynn. I'll do anything to keep my brothers safe."

Before he could utter a word, the back door flew open with such force it almost came off its hinges.

Theo appeared, his charming smile giving way to a menacing snarl. "Get your damned hands off my sister before I break your bloody neck." He covered the distance in a second, shoving Mr Flynn hard in the chest. "You devious bastard. I should have known something was amiss."

Mr Flynn stood firm. "This isn't what you think."

"I'm not blind. I saw you mauling her."

Theo threw a powerful punch that whipped the air.

Mr Flynn proved agile enough to deflect the blow.

Theo stripped off his coat and tossed it to a terrified Miss Darrow. "Hold this. It's the last thing you'll ever do for me, madam." He faced Mr Flynn and bared his teeth. "You'll fight me now or in Green Park at dawn."

She tried to step between them. "Theo! No! This isn't Mr Flynn's fault." He did not deserve Theo's disdain. He

Lady Gambit

did not deserve to make an enemy of her brother. "He's not to blame. I arranged the meeting. I called him here."

Mr Flynn remained unruffled. "I have no argument with you. My business is with your sister, though I'll not break her confidence by explaining why."

"She's my responsibility, damn you. Your business is with me."

"Miss Chance is old enough to make her own decisions," Mr Flynn countered, his courage quite impressive. "I answer to my client. No one else."

Theo pulled back his arm, but she grabbed it before he let his fist fly. "Mr Flynn is an ex-runner. I've hired him to find my parents."

Her brother jerked as if reeling from a slap. Confusion and pain marred his blue gaze. Darkness passed over his handsome features—shadows of betrayal and mistrust.

"I asked Mr Flynn to discover what he could. Then I intended to sit with you to decide what to do. I saw no point upsetting everyone unless I had solid evidence they were alive."

A shroud of sadness fell over him. "You trusted your secret to a stranger? You should have told me. I'm on your side, Delphine. You should have had faith in me, believed I would help you."

If only this was a horrible nightmare and she could wake to make different choices. "Theo, I'm not allowed to visit Miss Lovelace to take tea. Do you think Aaron would permit me to scour the rookeries looking for my parents?"

She didn't want to argue with him, not here, not now, but once someone lit a fire in her brother's belly, no amount of water could douse the flames.

"I would give my life for you," Theo cried, thumping his chest instead of hitting Mr Flynn. "I would do anything you ask of—"

"I have tried talking to Aaron. He won't listen."

"Then we will try harder," he countered. "We'll call a meeting as soon as we return home. We'll find the answers you seek. You have my word." He gestured to Mr Flynn, who stood silently watching their exchange. "Though the less said about this dubious arrangement, the better."

Once home, her brothers would take control of the matter. They would keep her in the dark and share half-truths to spare her feelings. They would make swift judgements to protect their family.

"We have no need of your services, Flynn." Theo scanned the man's athletic physique and scoffed. "I'll forward your fee. I demand your silence in this matter, else there'll be the devil to pay."

Mr Flynn looked at her, concern etched in his dark eyes. "I must hear it from you, Miss Chance. As you know, my fee has been paid. Do you still require my services?"

"Perhaps you're hard of hearing, Flynn. I said—"

"Enough, Theo! I can speak for myself." She faced Mr Flynn, feeling a pang of regret that they would have no cause to meet again. "Thank you for taking the time to assist me, sir." Her brothers would not permit him to pry into her affairs, so this was the last time she would gaze upon his handsome face. "And for agreeing to meet in this unconventional manner. I never meant to cause you any trouble."

"You haven't," he said in a soothing voice. "Should

you need my services in the future, you know where to find me."

"She won't," Theo snapped.

Mr Flynn ignored her brother. His gaze drifted over her face. "Tell them what we discussed. You need their protection. You must take every precaution while searching for the truth."

"I will. Thank you."

Their eyes locked for a heartbeat.

Then Mr Flynn bowed and left the yard.

She stared at the empty space—a genuine ache in her chest.

How strange she should miss a man she hardly knew.

How odd she was glad to have his handkerchief at home.

Miss Darrow cleared her throat. "Your coat, Mr Chance."

Theo snatched the garment from the modiste, his displeasure evident. "I can tolerate many things, Miss Darrow, but never deceit. I'll not trust a word from your lips again. Send me the bill for your work thus far. My sister will find a new modiste."

Tired of being deprived of a voice, she said, "I shall see you next week, Miss Darrow. You're not at fault here and merely followed your client's instructions." She faced her brother. Mr Flynn's courage had given her the strength to be bold. "If you'd rather not pay her bill, I shall find work to cover her fees. Don't challenge me on this, Theo. It is not open for debate."

Before he could reply, she returned to the fitting room

and dressed in her outdoor apparel, dreading the thought of going home.

Miss Darrow was waiting in the corridor. "Mr Chance stormed through the shop without saying a word. I believe he's sulking outside on the pavement."

"Pay him no mind." She took a moment to embrace Miss Darrow. "He's never annoyed for long. Despite his volatile reaction, Theo is a loving brother. He worries about me. That's all."

"Men and their pride. He's lucky you were here. Mr Flynn can kill a man with his bare hands but would never brawl in front of a lady."

The mention of Mr Flynn brought a wave of guilt. "Will you send word to him? Offer another apology for what occurred today. It was foolish to think I could keep my brothers in the dark."

Miss Darrow gripped Delphine's hand. "Of course."

"I shall see you next week at two o'clock."

The modiste hurried to open the shop door. "I doubt I'll be welcome to tea, but I'm sure we'll have much to discuss at your appointment."

"I shall be here promptly at two."

Miss Darrow was her only friend. She would wage war with her brothers rather than find a new modiste.

Theo was pacing in a bid to cool his temper. He threw the modiste a disapproving glare before opening the carriage door. "It's one thing to keep a confidence. It's another to trick a man into believing a lie."

Delphine might have spoken up, but two burly men dressed in black appeared on the pavement behind Theo. A beast of a fellow stepped around the front of the carriage, a pistol in each hand, his mouth a menacing sneer.

He cocked the hammers simultaneously and aimed one muzzle at their coachman, Godby. "Move a muscle, and I'll put a lead ball in your chest."

Theo stiffened and stepped forward to shield her. "I suggest you move along. You've picked the wrong person to rob." He spoke in a sabre-sharp tone that would make anyone consider their position. "You have until the count of three. Don't let me find you standing there. You'll not get a second warning."

The fiend grinned. "Give me the girl, and no one will get hurt."

Theo transformed from angel to demon in an instant. Gone was the inviting smile that made ladies' hearts flutter. His eyes turned ice blue, cold and dangerously chilling. His face twisted into a grotesque mask of the devil's own making. "Who sent you? Tindell? Meldrum? Whichever fool hired you, I'll triple the fee."

"Give me the girl, or I'll shoot you where you stand."

Though fear had her heart thumping hard in her chest, she gripped Theo's arm. "I shall go with him." If the villain wanted her dead, he would have shot her already. He certainly had no issue waving a weapon in broad daylight. And the distraction might give Godby and her brother time to disarm him. "Let me go, Theo."

"Over my dead body," her brother cried.

That's when the blackguard fired a shot.

That's when her beloved brother collapsed to the pavement.

When her world came crashing to the ground.

Chapter Four

The loud crack of pistol fire was unmistakable. A woman's ear-piercing scream rent the air. Not any woman. Dorian would stake his life Delphine Chance was in trouble. Panic seared through his chest. Without thought, he instructed his coachman to wait on Water Lane, then took to his heels and sprinted the short distance to Miss Darrow's shop.

He saw Miss Chance crouched on the pavement beside her brother's lifeless body, shaking him and begging him to wake. A thug had a pistol trained on their coachman. Two other rogues loomed over her. One grabbed her arm roughly and yanked her to her feet.

"Let go of me," she cried, swinging around and punching the beast squarely on the jaw. "You monster. I'll see you hanged for this."

Miss Darrow burst out of the modiste's shop, wielding an iron skillet. She struck the other fiend, whacking him on the shoulder and back while calling to the crowd to intervene. Some onlookers hid in shop doorways while others

Lady Gambit

fled. Amid the chaos, the armed thug didn't know where to aim his pistol.

Dorian covered the distance quickly, kicking the blackguard to the ground to prevent him from shooting Miss Chance.

The devil scrambled to his feet, and the men took flight, barging through the few bystanders who were too craven to offer help.

Miss Chance fell to the pavement again, crying and stroking her brother's cheek. "Theo? Can you hear me? Don't die. Please don't die."

"Move aside, Miss Chance. Allow me to check for a pulse." Dorian crouched beside her and pressed his fingers to Theodore's neck. The weak pounding brought a sigh of relief. "He's alive. We need a physician. He's been shot in the shoulder. We must remove the lead and stitch the wound. Miss Darrow, fetch a needle and thread."

Miss Chance gripped Dorian's arm. "Please, Mr Flynn. You must save him. This is all my fault. He cannot die because of me."

"I'll do everything I can." He hauled Theodore into his arms and stood, steadying himself under the strain of the man's weight. Then he turned to their coachman. "Cross Blackfriars Bridge and head south past Walworth Common. I shall direct you from there."

The coachman didn't straighten or take up the reins. "In the event of trouble, I've instructions to return to Fortune's Den, sir. It ain't far to Aldgate Street. Mr Chance will send for his own physician."

No doubt Aaron Chance would throttle Dorian for

disobeying his orders, but protecting Miss Chance and saving her brother were his only concerns.

"Fortune's Den may be under attack," Dorian countered. The devils must have followed Miss Chance from the gaming hell or paid someone to search Miss Darrow's diary. "We need to move out of the city until the threat can be determined. If it eases your conscience, return to Aaron Chance and explain what happened. I shall contact him before the day's end."

Dorian considered treating Theodore's wound in Miss Darrow's shop, but instinct said it was a mistake. Only hardened criminals shot a man in broad daylight. The thugs were determined. It was only a matter of time before they returned to finish the task.

"Follow me, Miss Chance," Dorian said, desperate to be on his way. "My carriage is waiting in Water Lane. We will tend to your brother en route."

Miss Chance sniffed back tears and nodded before addressing her coachman. "Reassure my brothers. Tell them they can trust Mr Flynn. Mr Daventry will vouch for his character."

Miss Darrow reappeared carrying a small wooden box, not an iron skillet. "I'm coming with you. I've brought needles and threads." She locked the shop door and slipped the iron key into her pocket.

He didn't waste time questioning her motives. "Hurry. There's not a second to lose."

They raced to Water Lane. Once the ladies were safely inside the vehicle, they helped Dorian lay Theodore on the leather seat.

"Home, Briggs."

The coachman frowned. "To Walworth, sir?"

"Yes. Take the usual precautions." While his associates knew of his lodgings above the Old Swan in Long Lane, only a privileged few knew of his private abode. "Drive like the devil."

Dorian closed the door, and the carriage lurched forward. Despite the cramped conditions, he shrugged out of his coat and handed it to Miss Chance. "There's a flask of brandy in the pocket. Find it."

He drew Theodore's arm from his coat with care, then unbuttoned his waistcoat and ripped open his bloodstained shirt. The shot had missed his heart and a main vein and was embedded in the soft tissue beneath his shoulder.

"I have the flask." Miss Chance's eyes widened when Dorian pulled a small hunting knife from his boot.

"Remove the stopper and coat the tip of the blade."

With a shaky hand, the lady obeyed, her eyes flicking between him and the sharp point. "Can you save him, Mr Flynn? Tell me you can. Save him, and I shall be forever in your debt. I shall do anything you ask of me. Anything."

His mind would have run amok if not for their grave situation. "The next twenty-four hours are critical." He refused to lie to her but was careful to soften his tone. "Let us pray he doesn't take ill with a fever."

Only a fool would allow a Chance brother to die on his watch. But this situation demanded a logical approach. Emotion clouded one's ability to think, and the incident proved that the secrets hidden deep within Miss Chance's memory might get her killed.

"Reach under the seat, Miss Darrow. You'll find a wooden box. I need bandages, tweezers, a pair of clean gloves and a tincture of opium. Miss Chance, when I expose the damaged flesh, you're to flood the wound with brandy. Then you must both hold him down firmly while I remove the lead ball."

Thankfully, the ball was intact. Stray fragments would likely cause an infection. Theodore would need to rest and recuperate, not lead a charge to find the culprit.

"Hold him!"

Both ladies obliged and proved quite capable.

He wasn't sure how Miss Chance occupied herself at home, but she was intelligent and had a backbone of steel. No wonder she felt trapped by her brother's rigid rules.

The moment Dorian dug the tip of the blade into the torn flesh, Theodore regained consciousness. The man writhed and winced in pain. All colour drained from his face, leaving him as pale as a ghost.

"Damn the devil!" He gritted his teeth as blood gushed from the wound. "Just get the blasted thing out."

"Hold still. I'll be as quick as I can."

Miss Chance brushed her hand through her brother's golden hair. "Can you ever forgive me? Please know I love you and never meant for this to happen. You might have died because of me."

"We don't know why the men shot your brother," Dorian said.

Aaron Chance had many enemies.

Dorian had more than a few himself.

"They came for me, Mr Flynn. I should have gone with them."

"Had you been foolish enough to do so, we'd have found you floating in the Thames." What did a band of thugs want with Delphine Chance? Why had they not shot her in the street? "Did they mention you by name?"

"No, but—"

"It's not the first time someone has planned to kidnap her," Theodore mumbled, his face twisting as he battled the pain. He tried to speak again, but the effort proved too much for him.

"I need to remove the lead and close the wound," Dorian said, steadying his hand. "We can discuss the incident later. Feed him the opium tincture, then use brandy to clean the wound. Hold him down, Miss Darrow. Keep all your weight on his legs."

"I shall do my best." A blush touched the modiste's cheeks as her dainty hands settled on the man's muscular thighs.

Miss Chance ignored her brother's sharp hiss as she poured liquor on the wound. "Be brave. You'll be up again in no time."

The man's pride had likely taken the brunt of the damage. Such a dangerous fellow would need to prove he could still pound his opponents to a pulp. The wound would heal. The assault on his character might do irreparable harm.

Dorian braced himself as the carriage bumped through ruts in the road. He inhaled deeply, digging the blade into the torn flesh and using the tweezers to free the ball.

Theodore cursed. "Damn you to Hades!" He jerked violently. "Get the damn thing out! I swear, I'll kill you for this, Flynn."

"Hold still."

"He's trying to help you," Miss Chance interjected. She met Dorian's gaze. Even amid the strife, something warm and enticing swirled between them. "I assure you, Mr Flynn. He is most grateful for your efforts. He will tell you so when he's of sound mind."

He smiled to reassure her. Nothing would be the same after this. The Chance brothers would go to war. She would return to her impenetrable tower, the guilt a heavy burden to carry.

He pulled the lead free and used the bandage to soak up the blood. Miss Chance watched while Dorian set to work with the needle and thread.

"One might wonder where you gained such a skill, sir." Miss Chance's large brown eyes seemed to drink him in.

"Chasing the truth comes at a price." He had been in many scrapes since school. "When one finds blackguards for a living, it pays to be prepared. Daventry could tell you a tale or two about our escapades."

Her gaze moved over him as if she could see the scars beneath his clothes. "Aaron almost died once. His body is like a journal of his life. Each mark and blemish tells the story of his endless battles."

Everyone knew of Aaron Chance's pugilistic skills. He began fighting at the tender age of twelve when his disreputable father forced him to brawl with men twice his age. Being the sons of selfish prigs, they had something in common. In siring a bastard, Dorian's father bore some responsibility for the ugly scars on *his* body, too.

"Most women disapprove of violence." He took

another bandage from Miss Darrow. "Yet you speak with a semblance of pride."

"Along with honour, courage is the greatest quality of the mind."

"You quote Aristotle." He was equally well-versed in the ancients. When a man had a buffoon for a father, he sought guidance elsewhere.

She gave an embarrassed shrug as she watched him secure the bandage over the neat stitches. "I could quote many philosophers. Their message is often the same. My brothers refused to be defeated. Against the odds, they built an empire. That takes courage, Mr Flynn. How could I not be proud?"

He studied her for a moment, compelled to discover what else lay hidden behind those intelligent eyes. What delights lay beneath her fashionable blue dress?

He became aware of how close she was. So close he felt the soft breeze of her breath on his cheek, warm like summer air and just as enticing. He could smell her lilac soap, feel lust's undercurrent coursing through his blood.

Miss Darrow's discreet cough broke the spell. "It seems the opium is taking effect. Do you have a blanket, sir? We should ensure Mr Chance is warm while he sleeps."

"Sadly, a blanket is the one thing I don't have." He glanced out the window and noted they were passing the alms' houses in Newington. "We'll reach our destination soon. We'll see to his every comfort while awaiting a physician."

Miss Chance stroked her brother's forehead. "I'll never

forget what you've done for him, Mr Flynn. I'm sure you know to expect Armageddon when my eldest brother arrives. But you've saved Theo's life. As silly as it sounds, I shall be your protector."

The comment slipped through a chink in his armour. It stole the breath from his lungs. He'd have staggered back were he not crouched on the carriage floor.

I shall be your protector.

She didn't know what those words meant to him. His entire life, he'd had no one. No one to fight his corner. No one to save him from the wolves. No one but a white-haired Greek man who lived long ago urging him to strive for greatness.

Sensing his discomfort, she added, "I will ensure my brothers know none of this is your fault."

"I appreciate the gesture, Miss Chance, but your brothers do not intimidate me." She intimidated him. She made him imagine things he shouldn't. Feel things that had no place in his ordered world. She made his body ache and his cock throb. Her perfume drove him to distraction. Now she would enter his home and touch his private things.

And when she was long gone, when he was ambling through the manor's empty rooms and corridors alone, those five simple words would haunt him. A painful reminder that, for one brief moment, someone cared if he lived or died.

"Few men could make such a claim." She looked at him with a kind of fascination. "My brothers can be quite terrifying."

"I pride myself on being unique." Which was better

than saying when a man had nothing to live for, he had nothing to lose.

The conversation came to an abrupt end when the carriage turned into the narrow lane hidden amidst a thick copse—the long drive leading to Mile End.

Miss Chance's hand rested on her brother's arm, though her eyes remained fixed on the window. "You live here?"

"I stay mostly at the Old Swan."

The coachman climbed down from atop his box to open the wrought-iron gates. As the vehicle charged along the tree-lined drive, she faced Dorian and frowned.

He knew what she was thinking. The Earl of Retford had purchased the house for his only son. That despite being a bastard and a working man, he'd led an entitled life. That he had no idea what it was like to sleep in a baker's shop doorway or spend restless nights fearing for his life.

He rarely cared about other people's opinions and surprised himself when he said, "Lord Carstairs paid me to find the captain of *The Conquest*. He stole the ship and its valuable cargo. The reward for retrieving the goods paid for this house."

Miss Chance looked relieved. "Anything worth having comes as a result of hard work. It's why I admire you, Miss Darrow."

"Me?" Miss Darrow drew her worried gaze from their patient. "Independence comes at a price. We're all trying to escape something," she said cryptically. "And please, call me Eleanor."

Miss Chance's smile could warm the coldest heart,

brighten the darkest days. "And you must call me Delphine. Well, until I discover if that is indeed my given name."

After the shocking attack outside the modiste shop, it was imperative he discovered the lady's identity. There were many reasons why thugs would attempt to kidnap the sister of a gaming hell owner, but that was for Aaron Chance to determine.

Briggs parked the vehicle outside Mile End Manor. He climbed down and opened the carriage door. "I'll let Kingsley know we're here, sir."

"Tell him to alert Mrs James." Dorian struggled to stand without brushing his body against Miss Chance. He gripped the seat, but his thigh touched hers as he stood.

They gasped in unison.

The lady scrambled onto the seat, giving him room to alight.

"I keep a small staff, Miss Chance." He offered his hand to assist her descent, though he wished he had the manners of a sewer rat and had no cause to be polite. "They will attend to your needs where possible, but you should expect to handle basic tasks yourself."

Having both removed their bloodstained gloves, Miss Chance slipped her bare hand into his. "We k-keep a small staff at home, too, Mr Flynn," she said, her cheeks turning an alluring shade of pink.

His knees almost buckled. Her hand was soft and small and warm. The instinctive need to protect her rose in his chest. But he was quick to remind himself it was not his job to keep her safe.

"My eldest brother trusts few people," she added,

Lady Gambit

holding on to him a second longer than she should. "Many are too scared to work for him. He can be a hard taskmaster."

"Privacy is important to me. As a working man, I cannot afford to be frivolous." He could never be as wasteful as his father.

"You don't need to explain, sir." The corners of her mouth curled into a weak smile. "I'm not interviewing for a husband."

He smiled. "If you were, I suspect you'd be more interested in a man's heart than his purse."

Her eyes widened upon hearing his compliment. "One can survive with little money. We did so for many years. But love ... To be starved of love is to be starved of air."

The comment sliced through his defences. Memories he'd tried hard to forget burst into his mind. He could hear his mother's needy voice echoing in his head.

Don't send him to school, Augustus.

The boy can have a tutor.

She had selfish reasons for keeping him at home. When Augustus tired of her, he still had a reason to visit.

The boy needs an education, Martha.

Oh, he'd learned many hard lessons in that hellhole.

Kingsley appeared, his panicked tone dragging Dorian to the present. "Briggs mentioned an accident, sir. A shooting in town." The thin man's gaze moved from Dorian to the beautiful woman with blood on her dress, and he stared, somewhat dumbstruck.

"We have guests, Kingsley." His butler had never had to deal with visitors, let alone a beautiful woman of marriageable age. He needed to brace himself for Aaron

Chance's arrival. They all did. "Miss Chance's brother has been shot. Briggs will take you into Walworth to fetch Dr Skinner."

Briggs returned. "Mrs James is heating the water, sir."

Dorian instructed Briggs to help him carry Theodore Chance upstairs to the largest bedchamber and then sent him on his errand. The room was decorated in a soft pink, the bed hangings a sage green velvet that matched the chairs in the adjoining salon.

Miss Chance scanned the decor with an appreciative eye. "Are you sure you're not looking for a wife, Mr Flynn? This would be a perfect room for a new bride."

"I've not decorated the room since I purchased the property. I've been too busy to make any changes. And I'm not wasteful."

Mrs James arrived with a pitcher of water for the washbowl. "Sir, if I'd known to expect guests, I'd have aired the room."

He made the introductions and assured the middle-aged woman she was not at fault. "Mr Chance will sleep for the most part. I doubt he'll notice a speck of dust on the nightstand."

Miss Chance took the heavy pitcher from the housekeeper's shaky hands. "Thank you, Mrs James. I know what a terrible inconvenience this must be. If there is anything I can do to assist you, please ask."

Mrs James glanced at the lady's fine clothes and kind brown eyes. "I thank you, miss, but I'm more than able to cope. Tending to a sleeping man will be no trouble."

Miss Chance's teeth grazed her bottom lip. "I'm not sure you understand. The doctor will insist my brother remains in bed until there's no fear of a fever. I couldn't possibly leave him, which means I shall need a room here, too."

Dorian froze.

His mind ran wild.

He'd spent the last few minutes considering how he'd become embroiled in this mess. He could deal with Aaron Chance. An attempted murder investigation didn't faze him. With the help of Nora Adkins, he could discover Miss Chance's true identity in less than a week.

But to have the woman reside in his home?

Have her roaming about in a scanty nightgown?

Dine with her at a table permanently reserved for one?

For a man used to living alone, it would be pure torture.

"You're an intelligent woman, Miss Chance," he began, desperate to put paid to this foolish notion. "Your brother will not permit you to stay in an unmarried man's home."

The lady placed the pitcher on the washstand and looked at the golden-haired man sleeping on the bed. "I'm not leaving him." Her tone was so firm and determined the devil himself would concede. "He's here because of my dithering. He almost died because I was afraid to tell the truth."

"You couldn't have known this would happen." Of all the children abandoned on London's dangerous streets, why should she be a target? Did she hold a valuable clue in the hazy depths of her mind? "I understand why you bear the burden of guilt, but I cannot permit you to stay here."

She met his gaze, pinning him to the spot as she

stepped closer. "Are we not friends, Mr Flynn? In the short time I've known you, I feel like we are. I've confided in you, told you things I've never told another soul."

Something stirred in his chest when he recalled their conversations in Miss Darrow's yard. There'd been a moment when he thought they were the only two people in the world who spoke the same language.

"As I told you, I value my privacy. I can count my friends on one hand. You're my client. That's where our association must end."

Having spent a lifetime deprived of affection, a man built walls to keep people out. He convinced himself love was like a pot of gold at the end of a rainbow. A thing of fancy that did not exist. The only thing accomplished from forming deep connections was a wealth of misery and pain.

She moved closer and touched his upper arm, the contact awakening something primitive inside him. "Please, Mr Flynn. Don't dismiss me. Don't push me aside because I'm a woman. I shall be no trouble. You'll not know I'm here."

He almost chuckled at her last remark.

She'd not left him since the moment they'd met.

"This is a pointless discussion. I'm certain your brothers will want Theodore moved to Fortune's Den." He stepped back, her hand slipping from his arm, bringing temporary relief. "Now, if you'll excuse me, I must send word to Daventry while we await the physician."

He left the room and closed the door, though remained on the landing, inhaling deeply and pinching the bridge of his nose.

Lady Gambit

The sooner Aaron Chance arrived, the better. There would be raised voices, vile threats, and maybe punches thrown. Displays of aggression and violence were an everyday occurrence. Only kind words, warm brown eyes and a gentle touch could bring Dorian crashing to his knees.

Chapter Five

Delphine gazed at the ominous clouds looming in the distance. Tension charged the air. There would be a storm. The heavens would grieve. Angry raindrops would lash the ground like her plump tears.

She felt the same intense sorrow.

The same need to unleash an inner fury.

She hugged herself as a mother would, with the reassurance all would be well. Except she didn't know her mother and could not recall feeling the comfort of a parent's unconditional love.

She turned from the window and looked at Theo asleep in the comfortable tester bed. Nausea roiled in her stomach. Nothing would ever be the same again. Soon, Aaron would arrive needing someone to blame. She could cope with his curses and angry outbursts but not the cold dread of fear in his eyes. Not the pained grimace that said his worst nightmare had come to fruition.

"Forgive me," she whispered.

You trusted your secret to a stranger?

You should have told me.

Theo's words entered her mind.

Guilt was the punishment for her deceit.

"I love you." Sniffing back tears, she sat beside her brother on the bed and drew the coverlet a little higher over his injured shoulder. "You were right. I should have told you."

Fond memories of Theo surfaced. Him running errands for one of Mrs Maloney's customers so he could buy her new ribbons. He would pass notes to her under the table. Comforting words to help her cope with Aaron's gruff temper. In those early days, when Aaron was fighting in the pits to put food on the table, Theo would read her stories at night to keep the thoughts of faceless monsters at bay.

He did not deserve to be shot in the street like a feral dog. Dr Skinner said he was lucky to be alive.

The sudden creak of the door drew her gaze from the bed to the plush seating area. Mr Flynn appeared, dressed in a smart black coat and grey waistcoat. He'd shaved, and his hair was damp at the ends.

He took one look at her and froze, his dominant stance faltering. "Forgive me. I didn't mean to disturb you. Mrs James said you went to lie down. I came to check on your brother."

He'd been avoiding her since she insisted on staying.

She managed a smile. "It's hard to rest when there's a storm brewing. And I cannot banish the thought of impending doom."

"Perhaps keeping busy is the answer. Miss Darrow is

making broth. A family recipe handed down that's said to aid healing. She is most keen to help."

The stilted conversation was far removed from the honest way they'd spoken in Miss Darrow's yard. He didn't want her here, disrupting his life and disturbing his peace—a fact he had made abundantly clear.

"Like me, Miss Darrow feels guilty for deceiving my brother." She stood, conscious her hair was a little wild and unkempt, and that spots of dried blood stained her bodice. Her cheeks were red and blotchy from the copious tears she had shed. "I suppose I should bathe. Hopefully, Aaron will bring clean clothes when he arrives."

Mr Flynn drew his gold watch from his fob pocket and peered at the face before tucking it away. "I doubt there's time. Daventry and your brother will be here shortly. I can ask Mrs James for soap and a brush if you'd like to wash your face and tidy your hair."

She tucked a stray lock behind her ear. "Before today, I would rather die than let a man see me in this sorry state. Now it hardly matters." With Mr Flynn, she didn't have to hide behind a facade.

He took a hesitant step back and beckoned her to join him in the seating area. "If I may be so bold, you should make yourself presentable. It doesn't matter to me. I fear you would look lovely in a grain sack. But one is better equipped to deal with difficult situations when looking one's best."

She tried to focus on his logical statement but could think of nothing other than he thought she looked lovely. "Perhaps you're right. I'll need my wits when I see Aaron."

"We all will," he said with a humourless chuckle.

While alone, she'd been consumed with the notion of vengeance. Someone would pay for hurting Theo. But who? And how might she achieve the impossible? How might she persuade her brothers to allow her to help?

"I shall protect you, sir."

His gaze fell to her lips. "You don't need to do that."

"It's the least I can do after all you have done."

Ten feet separated them, but the magnetic pull of attraction was too strong to ignore. They both took a step forward. Unspoken words hung in the air. The need to understand why some people passed through one's life unnoticed. Why, on a rare occasion, a stranger sent one's world spinning.

Her cheeks grew warm. "I should attend to my hair."

He stiffened as she closed the gap between them. "I shall send Mrs James to your room and await your brother in my study."

She stopped a mere foot away from him, close enough to catch one last whiff of his shaving soap. "You were right. Aaron will not permit me to stay here." For all the will in the world, how could she argue with a grieving man? "I doubt we will see each other again, Mr Flynn. Not alone, at any rate."

His dark gaze moved over her face as if locking the image in his memory. "It's unlikely our paths will ever cross," he agreed.

A deep regret filled her chest. "I wish you every happiness."

The lady who captured his heart would want for nothing.

"Have faith, Miss Chance. Life is never as bad as it seems. Out of discord comes the fairest harmony."

"Heraclitus," she said, recognising the quote.

His eyes widened in surprise. "Yes. I'm impressed."

"I spend an awful lot of time at the circulating library." Books were her solace. A place where she might live many lives without ever leaving Fortune's Den. "Perhaps one day the catalogue of tragedies will make sense."

He held her gaze, the power of it sending her pulse soaring. "I tell myself the same thing often. Misfortune must count for something."

"Let's pray there's a glimmer of hope on the horizon soon." She stole one last look at his muscular physique, knowing she had to leave before she said something foolish. Something she could not take back. "Goodbye, Mr Flynn."

His breathing quickened. "Goodbye, Miss Chance."

She had taken no more than a step towards the door when he wrapped his firm fingers around her wrist to stall her. His piercing brown eyes were upon hers again, searching, seeking, for what she had no clue.

When he spoke, his voice was deep and husky. "Despite all thoughts to the contrary, I find I cannot let you leave. Not yet. Not without knowing the taste of your lips."

She blinked, wondering if she'd misheard. "Oh!"

He exhaled deeply and seemed annoyed with himself. "This is where you tug your arm free. Where you tell me no respectable man would say such a thing to a lady. Where you refuse to speak to me again and race out of the room, affronted."

She did nothing. Said nothing.

How could she?

This was the most thrilling moment of her life.

"Heed my warning. You have three seconds to refuse me, madam. Three seconds before my resolve snaps and I feed this damnable craving."

She counted silently, but curiosity got the better of her before she reached two. Unable to wait, she gripped his coat lapels and pressed her mouth to his.

They both inhaled sharply and froze.

Her heart pounded so hard it might burst through her chest.

She wasn't sure which one of them moved first. Had she brushed her lips softly over his? Had he moulded himself to her mouth as if they were made to fit together?

One thing was certain. Everything about this moment felt right—the warmth of his lips, the enticing scent of his shaving soap, the desperate hunger in every ragged breath.

He wrapped his strong arms around her, one hand settling at the small of her back, one sliding around her nape. He held her tight to his body, the heat chasing away the cold, the guilt, the fear.

Nothing mattered but the taste of Mr Flynn.

With slow, teasing strokes, he coaxed her lips apart. Sweet mercy! He knew how to kiss. Perhaps ladies were supposed to remain pliant in a man's embrace, a passive participant, hypnotised by his touch. This man caused a fire in her blood. A pulsing between her thighs that had her returning his kisses like a wicked wanton.

He pulled away, his mouth curling into a sensual smile. "You're my one weakness, Miss Chance. A dangerous distraction. A delightful diversion." He was panting. His eyes roamed over her and she felt it like a soft caress on bare skin.

"Every man has a vice. Presently, I'm yours, Mr Flynn." She moistened her lips, silently willing him to devour her mouth again.

Don't stop.

Don't let this be over.

He must have heard her plea because he was on her in a heartbeat, his kisses demanding, urgent, his tongue sweeping through her lips.

The tempo reached fever pitch when she slid her tongue over his and deepened the kiss. He was suddenly everywhere, cupping her buttocks, drugging her senses, surrounding her with his powerful aura.

A knock on the door had them jumping apart.

"Who is it?" He was breathless.

"You have visitors, sir," Mrs James called, though it was strange she didn't enter. "There's a carriage trundling up the drive."

"Thank you, Mrs James. I'll be down in a moment."

While listening to the retreating footsteps, she stared at Mr Flynn. His flushed cheeks and mussed hair drew a smile. She was more than a little infatuated with the man who'd lost control of his steely resolve.

He scrubbed his face with his hand and sighed. "There is no excuse for my behaviour. Please know I meant no disrespect."

She brushed a stray lock behind her ear and straightened her shoulders, though the potent thrum of lust still coursed through her veins. "It's fair to say we both lost our heads. I'm sure we'll refrain from succumbing to our appetites in future." Yet she would devour his mouth in a heartbeat.

"Perhaps it's just as well this is goodbye," he said, the comment causing her discomfort. He was everything a woman wanted in a man. Strong. Loyal. Dependable. So ridiculously handsome she could hardly breathe.

"Because you fear you cannot exercise restraint?" Such a powerful attraction was fraught with danger. They would have to fight it whenever they were alone.

"Because one thing is apparent." He stepped back, an air of sadness about him now. "I doubt I would ever tire of kissing you, Miss Chance."

They both fell silent.

Neither of them dared to discuss what that meant, probably because Aaron's imminent arrival had them hurrying from the room.

There was no time to tidy her hair or dwell on the strange emotions that left her dazed and dizzy. She was hot, so hot she could barely breathe. The pulsing between her thighs proved a dreadful distraction. Guilt joined the fray. Keen to chastise her for kissing a man while her brother lay injured in bed.

She raced downstairs.

Mr Flynn followed, his proximity stirring the hairs on her nape.

She stood in the hall, brushing creases out of her dress and patting her hair—dreading the moment she locked eyes with Aaron.

Kingsley opened the door, and her heart wrenched in two.

Aaron strode into the house. He looked pale, shaken, nothing like his usual domineering self. The news had rocked him to his core. She could see panic in his eyes, fear marring his brow.

He reached her, his cold hand cupping her elbow. "Where is he?"

"Upstairs. The chamber door is open. He's sleeping."

Aaron glanced at Mr Flynn, coldly assessing the man who'd saved their brother's life, but said nothing before mounting the stairs two at a time.

Mr Daventry appeared, his expression equally grave, though he managed a smile for her before addressing Mr Flynn. "How is he?"

"Dr Skinner is confident he will make a full recovery," Mr Flynn said calmly. He wasn't breathless and panting as he had been mere minutes ago. Gone were the throaty moans of pleasure he had struggled to contain. "He lost a fair amount of blood. Miss Darrow is making broth. We're focusing on letting him rest, keeping him warm and well nourished."

"The coachman said Theodore may have died had you not come to his aid. He said the blackguards would have taken Miss Chance hostage."

"I acted as anyone would under the circumstances," Mr Flynn said modestly.

"We owe Mr Flynn a great debt," Delphine said, quick to ensure Mr Daventry knew what the gentleman had sacrificed to help her. "I'm sure he never expected to be embroiled in a case of attempted murder." Or to have to deal with her brother's wrath.

Mr Daventry gave Mr Flynn a friendly pat on the upper

arm. "Flynn has dealt with worse things. You're lucky he was there to intervene."

Tears gathered behind her eyes. "I was wrong to pursue personal goals." Mr Daventry had a way of drawing a confession without saying a word. "I don't know how to put this right, sir, but I want to try."

Mr Daventry hit her with the truth. "After this, Aaron will lock you in an ivory tower with no means of escape. Uncovering the secrets of the past is the only way forward. Getting your brother to agree will require the utmost courage and determination."

Amid the chaos in her mind, it was impossible to think clearly.

Mr Daventry had a sixth sense because he offered a pearl of wisdom. "In battle, one must never lose sight of the goal, else what is the point of war? The suffering has to count for something."

Her thoughts turned to the other men she loved. "I cannot risk another casualty. Do Aramis and Christian know about the shooting?" She assumed not as the devil himself couldn't keep them away. But they needed to know their lives were in danger, too.

"Aaron wished to determine the facts, and we cannot risk anyone following them here." Mr Daventry glanced at the man whose mouth had the power to make magic. "Flynn prefers a private existence. Mile End is his solace, a haven from troubling investigations."

And now his two worlds had collided, which explained his obvious frustration at having houseguests.

Mr Flynn pressed a gentle hand to her back, the intimate gesture reminding her of their fervent kisses. "Let's retire to the drawing room and take refreshment. We'll wait for Mr Chance to join us. I'm sure he'll want a detailed account of events."

Mr Daventry agreed. "Aaron will need time alone to process what has occurred. Be patient with him. He's spent a lifetime trying to avoid such a tragedy."

They entered Mr Flynn's drawing room. It was a warm, masculine space with mahogany furniture and burgundy leather sofas. Like the man himself, the room was immaculate, everything pristine and in its place. Yet she pictured their crumpled clothes strewn about the floor, cushions scattered on the rug near the hearth, him trailing burning kisses over her skin.

Mr Flynn rang for tea but poured himself a brandy and tossed it back quickly, hissing to cool the burn. He returned to the seating area, passing Mr Daventry a large dram.

"While we wait, perhaps I should explain one theory." Mr Flynn sat in the chair opposite the sofa, his black trousers gripping his muscular thighs, and told Mr Daventry about his visit to Bethlem. "In all likelihood, Nora Adkins is a little deranged. Sixteen years spent in Bethlem will do that to a person."

"Do you know who had her committed?" Mr Daventry sounded excited by the possible mystery.

"Not yet, but it should be easy to find out." Mr Flynn met her gaze, his dark eyes softening briefly. "I believe Nora knows Miss Chance. My visit to Bethlem may have led to the attack outside Miss Darrow's shop."

Her heart sank to her stomach.

It *was* her fault.

"What makes you so sure, sir?"

He would have explained the facts in Miss Darrow's yard had Theo not charged in like a bull at a gate. Then she might have taken every precaution.

"Nora acted out a scene for me." He gave a detailed recount of the woman's ramblings. "I'm convinced she witnessed an altercation between a man, woman and girl. Whatever happened was so terrifying, the girl was told to run, to disappear into the night."

Silence descended.

A familiar voice rang through her mind.

Run! Run, my darling. Save yourself. Don't look back.

Her heart pounded against her ribcage, so fast she could hardly breathe. "Did she name the girl? Did she say what happened to her? Did she return to her family? Was she lost?"

Mr Flynn shook his head. "This is only a hypothesis, but I think the woman's name was Sofia, and the child was Caterina. The gentleman's identity is a mystery." He went on to describe the person Nora believed was keeping her at Bethlem. Something about big boots and a ridiculous red eye on a stick. "Are the names familiar to you, Miss Chance? Does anything I've said spark a memory?"

She scoured the dark recesses of her mind.

You're Delphine Chance.

Never forget it.

I'll kill anyone who says otherwise.

Aaron had repeated the statements so many times they were etched in her brain. And she so desperately wanted to belong to someone.

"No." She hesitated, unsure whether to mention her

secret. But lies were the reason Theo had been shot in the shoulder. She would not be the cause of another mishap. "Whenever I'm afraid or facing difficult decisions, I hear a woman's voice telling me to run." She repeated the words verbatim. "Perhaps it's a coincidence."

Mr Daventry and Mr Flynn exchanged curious glances.

In the stillness, she heard the thud of footsteps on the stairs. She braced herself, waiting for Aaron to storm into the room and throw daggers of disdain in her direction, but the front door opened and slammed shut.

Was it Aaron?

Was he leaving without speaking to her?

She was on her feet and at the window in seconds.

Aaron marched back and forth on the drive like a caged animal, the gravel crunching beneath his booted feet. His clenched fists hung at his sides like heavy mallets. His eyes were as dark as the bowels of hell. He was priming himself to attack. But then he gazed heavenward and roared like a beast baying for blood.

"It will be hard to control him," Mr Daventry warned. "If you hope to solve this case, you'll need to appease Aaron Chance. He'll want to tear every suspect limb from limb."

Mr Flynn cleared his throat. "Miss Chance has changed her mind. She is no longer interested in pursuing the truth."

She glanced over her shoulder. "I'll not be responsible for someone else getting hurt. The past no longer matters."

"I'm afraid the decision is not yours to make, Miss Chance." Mr Daventry swallowed a mouthful of brandy. "A man was shot in broad daylight on a London street. I've been tasked with overseeing the case. Flynn has already received his fee and will lead the investigation."

Mr Flynn's handsome eyes widened in surprise. "I'm not an enquiry agent. Yes, the attempted abduction may be linked to Miss Chance's search for her parents. What if it's related to a gaming debt or a disgruntled mistress?"

While she listened, stunned by the turn of events, Mr Daventry said, "You worked at Bow Street and are more than capable of dealing with whatever problems arise. I've no available agents, and you're skilled at uncovering the truth." Mr Daventry waved nonchalantly in her direction. "Miss Chance will assist you. I'm convinced the key to the past lies trapped within her mind."

"Me?" She locked eyes with Mr Flynn. They had dared to kiss because there was no hope of them being alone again. How could she spend time in his company without recalling the warmth of his lips?

"Miss Chance is not equipped to deal with cutthroats," he said, for he looked just as perturbed by this shocking proposal. "I cannot be responsible for her safety."

"On the contrary," she began, desperate to impress him. "I'm an expert shot with a pocket pistol. Under my brothers' tutorage, I can throw quite a decent punch."

It was a pointless argument. Aaron would never permit it. After this debacle, he would not let her out of his sight. And a woman who barely left home did not possess the skill to find villains.

The drawing room door swung open and Aaron appeared, looking ready to tackle a heathen army. He stared at her, ignoring the other people in the room, and slowly closed the gap between them.

Tears filled her eyes.

She wasn't afraid of him.

He would never hurt her.

He stopped when they were a foot apart but remained as silent as the grave. His dark, unreadable eyes searched her face. There was no flicker of disappointment. No flare of anger. No flash of blame.

"This is my fault," she said, her voice a ghostly whisper.

"None of this is your fault." Aaron reached for her, hauling her into his muscular arms and embracing her tightly. "You're not to blame."

In this rare display of affection, she rested her head on his broad chest and let her love for him chase away her fears. This was the first time she'd felt the physical warmth of her brother's love. It would likely be another sixteen years until she felt it again.

"I've done everything in my power to keep you safe, to make you happy, but it's not enough," he said, inadequacy marring his tone.

She looked up at him, about to bury her feelings and wear her usual mask, but she could not lie to him anymore. "You did what you thought best. You're the man I admire most in this world, but sometimes it's hard to talk to you."

Aaron's heavy sigh echoed through the room.

"I needed to know if my parents loved me," she confessed, not caring if the men watching thought it sounded pathetic.

"I was only trying to protect you."

She held his gaze, her throat tightening. "I need to

know who I am. I need to know why they abandoned me. Was I not good enough to keep?"

Mr Flynn stood abruptly and went to pour himself a drink. He stared at the row of crystal decanters, lost in his own thoughts.

Aaron released her, straightening to his full height. "You're my sister. You are Delphine Chance. Nothing will change that. But I'm losing control of our family and don't know what to do."

"You can begin by being honest," Mr Daventry suggested from his comfortable seat on the sofa. "You can hope that the love and respect you've earned over the years will always keep those you care for close."

She cupped Aaron's cheek. "We will always be kin. I merely seek answers. A way of bringing an end to the confusion."

He closed his eyes briefly. "Then I pray you will forgive me for what I have done. I pray you will understand why I never told you the truth."

A chill shivered through her. "The truth?"

"Do you think I'd risk your parents returning to ruin our lives? Do you think I'd raise you as my sister knowing someone might steal you away? Would I let you live this life if I knew a better one awaited you elsewhere?"

She blinked rapidly, scared to ask the most obvious question. "What are you saying?" Somehow, she knew the answer would change things irrevocably.

Aaron covered his heart with his hand. "I know who you are, Delphine. I know where you came from. Trust me. You would rather die than return to that viper's pit."

Chapter Six

Amid the stunned silence, Dorian cradled his brandy goblet and stared at the amber liquid in the glass. Despite being in the company of three people, the chill of loneliness found its way into his heart. The profound bond that connected Delphine and Aaron Chance was palpable. The power of love thrummed in the air. It forced a man to dwell on his own tragic past. To wonder if life might be different if he'd had a sister to love.

Not that he saw Delphine Chance as a sister.

Far from it.

The woman had stolen his breath.

She'd crept into his mind and robbed his sanity.

Kissing her had done more than feed his curiosity. It had left him wanting and wondering. What was this strange connection that existed between them? Why had a simple kiss rocked him to his core? Why had the thought of never seeing her again made him behave like a reckless rogue?

He might have trawled his mind for the answer had

Aaron Chance not confessed to knowing the truth about her parentage.

Miss Chance stared at her brother, her face a mask of hurt and confusion. "You met my parents and never told me? You know who I am but left me in the dark?"

"We will discuss this at home," Aaron said abruptly.

"We will discuss it now."

Daventry coughed to gain their attention. "While my opinion counts for little, you cannot allow Miss Chance to return to Fortune's Den. Fifty men pass through there nightly. Let us not forget why your brother was shot."

Aaron Chance swung around, his temper flaring. "Do you think I will ever forget seeing my brother lying helpless in that bed? This has nothing to do with Delphine's parents. This isn't the first time a peer has hired thugs to kidnap her. Trust me. I shall have my hands around the culprit's neck before dawn."

Miss Chance gasped. "So there has been a plot to kidnap me before. An actual plot, not a fear or suspicion. Not tittle-tattle or ballroom gossip."

"Just verbal threats from debt-ridden fools," her brother countered. "This was another such incident. Once I've dealt with the problem, no one will dare approach you again."

The lady paled as if her life had just flashed before her eyes. Was she imagining days locked in her bedchamber? Was she thinking how cold and long the nights were when one sat alone?

"Aaron, I'm not going anywhere until you tell me about my parents." Perhaps her brother's revelation had given her the confidence to be bold. "You will treat me the way you do our brothers and allow me to form my own opinions. I'll not go back to how things were."

The man firmed his stance. "I'll not leave this godforsaken house without you. Do you understand?"

Tired of watching from the sidelines, Dorian joined the battle. "Perhaps you should remember whose godforsaken house this is. I've been forced to take a case I don't want. To creep about in yards and alleys and conduct secret meetings. I have risked my life to save a stranger. Now you test my patience and take advantage of my hospitality." He hit Aaron Chance with a steely glare. "As I'm charged with solving this case, you will sit down and answer my questions, or you'll get the hell out of my house."

Daventry failed to hide a smile.

Miss Chance's eyes sparkled with admiration as she scanned his physique. "Please accept our sincere apology, Mr Flynn. It's extremely rude of us not to consider your wishes."

With obvious reluctance, Aaron Chance inclined his head. "What case? What could you possibly want with me?"

Daventry explained. "I'm afraid this is now an official matter. Either Flynn investigates the shooting or Sir Malcolm Langley will appoint a man from Bow Street to act in his stead."

"The men from Bow Street can go to hell. Half of them are corrupt. I'd sooner trust an alley cat."

"Then unless you want them prying into your private affairs, I suggest you sit down and allow Flynn to do his job."

Lady Gambit

Miss Chance sat in the leather chair. "Do you have sherry, Mr Flynn? If I'm to hear my brother's confession, I will need something soothing to drink."

"I have port or brandy, madam."

"Anything strong will suffice. I am only permitted to drink sherry at home."

Her brother looked at her and cursed under his breath. "Can we get to the matter at hand? I'm taking Theo home tonight."

"That's out of the question," Dorian snapped. If he was to solve the case and be rid of Aaron Chance, he needed to show the King of Clubs he was not intimidated. "He's a key witness in an attempted murder enquiry. And to move him would hinder his recovery."

Aaron Chance firmed his jaw. "I'm taking my brother home."

"He will receive the utmost care and attention. Your family is in grave danger, Mr Chance. We must focus on what's important. We must find the culprit before someone else you love is shot."

Dorian strode to the drinks table and poured two glasses of brandy. He gave one to Aaron Chance, who sat beside Daventry on the sofa, his mood as black as a thunderous sky. His heart galloped as he handed Miss Chance her drink and their fingers touched. She met his gaze, the jolt of attraction hitting him hard in the chest.

Mother of all saints!

His mild infatuation with his client only added to the complexity of the case. Perhaps his obsession was more than mild but it would pass. He needed to focus on the facts. Investigating a crime of this magnitude required his undivided attention.

Dorian sat in the wing chair next to the hearth. "Before we begin, I believe you have something to say to me, Mr Chance. You strike me as a man who always pays his dues."

Aaron tossed back his drink. He pinned Dorian to the seat with his intense gaze. "I'm in your debt, Flynn. While I regret I cannot throttle you for meeting secretly with my sister, your swift action saved my brother's life."

Dorian inwardly smiled. "Then permit me to call in that debt. You already know I will do everything in my power to protect your family. Consequently, you will work with me and abide by any decisions I make."

Aaron fell silent.

"We are on the same side," Dorian reminded him.

Miss Chance shot her brother a challenging look and answered on his behalf. "He agrees, Mr Flynn. I am equally in your debt. Heaven knows where I would be if you had not intervened."

Aaron sat forward, resting his arm on his knee. "If I place my faith in you, Flynn, you had better deliver. Cross me at your peril."

He took the threat seriously.

Aaron Chance would kill to protect his family.

"Here are my terms." Dorian swept his hand between them. "There will be no lies, no skirting around the truth. If you must take matters into your own hands, you will inform me first. You'll not tell a soul where I live." He'd not have wolves scratching and howling at his door. He'd

Lady Gambit

not suffer his father's interference. "You'll not arrive here unannounced."

"And *you* will treat my sister with the utmost respect."

Their passionate clinch flashed through Dorian's mind.

It's just as well this is goodbye.

I doubt I'd ever tire of kissing you.

"Miss Chance is my client and a witness in an investigation. I shall treat her accordingly." He daren't look at her. He had overstepped the mark, but the sadness in her bewitching eyes tugged at his heartstrings. "Let me begin by explaining why you're wrong about who arranged the attack on your family."

Aaron Chance listened intently while Dorian described meeting the exuberant Nora Adkins. He mentioned her silly dance and the parting words that had sent a shiver shooting down his spine.

"She sounds like a loon," Aaron replied.

"Whether you believe her ramblings is immaterial. Allow me to give you the facts. Someone is paying to keep Nora at Bethlem. In front of witnesses, Nora called your sister Sofia. Within a week of me questioning the woman, thugs attempted to abduct Miss Chance from outside the modiste's."

Miss Chance shuffled forward in the seat. "You think I am the child who fled? That Sofia was my mother? That I am Catcrina?"

Before Dorian could reply, Aaron Chance scoffed. "You're not Caterina."

"Perhaps someone thinks she is," Daventry said.

"Then who am I, Aaron." The lady's hands shook as

she gripped the brandy glass. "Is my past so terrible you would deny me the right to know my parents?"

Aaron scrubbed his face with his hand and glanced at Daventry. "I blame you for this. In future, keep to your own affairs."

"She deserves to know the truth," came Daventry's stern reply.

"The truth will get her killed."

"She is already in grave danger. You knew this day would come."

Aaron hung his head, the strain of keeping the secret taking its toll.

The silence stretched, the incessant ticking of the mantel clock like the drum of a death knell.

It took Aaron a moment to gather himself before he said solemnly, "You're an orphan. Your parents perished and are buried in a pauper's grave. I'm sure they loved you. How could they not?"

It wasn't the whole truth. He hadn't touched on the damning fact that placed her in jeopardy. Indeed, why would he keep such an unremarkable tale to himself all these years?

"You're hiding something from me." Miss Chance's intelligent eyes narrowed. "How did they die? What were their names? Why was I not sent to the workhouse?"

Aaron shuffled in the seat. "I don't know."

The lady downed a mouthful of brandy, almost choking as the fire scorched her throat. "I can forgive you for trying to protect me. But your reasons make no sense. How did I hurt my head? How do you know my parents are dead if you don't know their names?"

Lady Gambit

Tense seconds passed.

"Why won't you trust me?" she pressed.

Aaron gritted his teeth. "If one word of what I'm about to say is repeated outside this room, I'll kill the man responsible." He pointed to Daventry and Dorian in turn. "Before I reveal the details, I want your solemn vow, your promise to protect her. No matter the cost."

Dorian glanced at Miss Chance, wondering what was so awful her brother would demand their fealty. "You have my word. I shall protect Miss Chance as if she were my own sister." He would do an excellent job of convincing himself he should treat her as kin. Yet every time he looked at her mouth, his blood rushed to his loins.

Daventry gave his oath.

After a visible wrestle with his conscience, Aaron confessed to knowing how the lady had found herself in the rookeries. "When your parents died, a woman took you in. She fed you, clothed you, kept a roof over your head. You were with her for almost a year before you stumbled upon me."

Hope sprang to life in her eyes. "Someone kind like Mrs Maloney?"

"Someone so cruel and selfish she would make Satan look like a saint." The malice in his voice sent a chill down Dorian's spine. "She hacked off your hair, dressed you in breeches and put you to work with her *boys*, determined you would earn your keep."

Daventry inhaled sharply. "Her boys? Where was this?"

"Seven Dials."

"Tell me she didn't work in Mrs Haggert's hen house."

Dorian braced himself, praying Aaron Chance would correct the misconception. Most of the boys who worked for Mrs Haggert found themselves dangling from the hangman's noose.

"Who is Mrs Haggert?" Miss Chance said.

"She's a notorious criminal who uses children to line her pockets." Dorian had encountered her during his time at Bow Street. Despite being an ageing woman of sixty now, she commanded an army of louts keen to do her bidding. "Her charitable work and the children's fear of speaking out means she remains a free woman."

Aaron Chance looked pained when he said, "The dress you wore when we met was probably stolen. It's likely you were involved in criminal activity when you received the blow to your head."

Miss Chance shook her head vigorously. "No! I would have remembered committing a crime. You must be mistaken. I can be terribly clumsy. I would have made a useless thief."

Dorian listened intently.

All the rules and secrets made sense now.

They explained why Miss Chance was encouraged to remain at home. Why her brothers had not helped her to find her parents. It was a testament to the men's dangerous reputations that their sister had not encountered trouble before.

"Mrs Haggert would not let you take one of her *chicks* without a fight." Dorian had heard that Mrs Haggert would kill a boy if he threatened to leave. No one escaped the coop. Not when they were party to her wicked deeds.

Aaron clutched his hand to his chest. "I almost died

fighting for Delphine. But I won the wager. Mrs Haggert agreed to let Delphine go as long as I agreed never to seek vengeance. Our blood pact has remained binding ever since."

Miss Chance buried her face in her hands and sobbed.

It took every effort for Dorian to remain in his seat.

Aaron crossed the room and knelt before his sister. "Please understand why I didn't tell you. The risks were too great."

She rubbed her eyes and sniffed. "I do understand. And I don't care where I came from. I care that you almost died to save me. I'll never forget that dreadful night. We all thought we'd lost you."

Dorian was forced to watch another outpouring of love. Despite a silent wrangle with his thoughts, he envisaged Miss Chance holding *his* hand, not her brother's. She was stroking *his* cheek, telling him nothing would ever come between them, that they would always have each other.

Bloody hell!

He shot daggers at Lucius Daventry.

Damn the man to Hades.

He would have taken any case but this one. He would have repaid the debt tenfold to avoid the rush of unwanted emotions.

Then Daventry drove the metaphorical blade a little deeper between Dorian's ribs. "If I might offer my expert advice." He waited until he had everyone's attention before making a shocking suggestion. "Aaron, you should establish if a peer was brave enough to arrange the abduction. I will visit Mrs Haggert with Flynn. We need to know if she is involved. Hopefully, she will tell us where she found Delphine."

In the stunned silence, Dorian considered the plan.

The first task in finding a missing person was to trace their last steps. The second was to question anyone in the known vicinity at the time of their disappearance. For the right fee, Mrs Haggert might provide answers to many important questions.

"Agreed," he said, knowing they should plan for every eventuality before venturing into the hen house. "We'll need a bargaining tool. Something to appease Mrs Haggert."

Mischief twinkled in Daventry's eye. "I know just the thing. Meet me in Hart Street at noon tomorrow, and we'll travel to St Giles together."

Aaron Chance stood slowly. "I'm taking my sister home to Fortune's Den. She'll have no part in your scheme."

"You cannot protect her while trying to solve the case," Daventry urged. "I would trust Flynn with my life. No harm shall come to her while in his care. Who wouldn't want their sister left in the hands of such a capable man?"

"Let me remain here with Theo." Miss Chance spoke as if it were a simple solution, not a damnable inconvenience. "With his help, I can make a sketch of the man who shot him. I can help with the case while tending my brother."

Dorian might have argued against such folly but they were going round in circles. The sooner he solved the case, the sooner he would be rid of them all.

"I shall have my coachman Gibbs act as her personal

Lady Gambit

guard," Daventry said by way of an incentive. Upon hearing a light knock on the door, and Miss Darrow's faint call, he frowned. "Who else is here?"

Dorian explained before inviting the lady to enter. He made the introductions. "Miss Darrow has spent the last hour making a healing broth. She is quite the nurse." A blind man could see the modiste held some affection for the patient.

Miss Darrow smiled. "Forgive me for snooping, but I was passing and heard raised voices. I should like to offer my services. I shall tend to Mr Chance and act as Delphine's companion."

"What about your clients?" The last thing Dorian needed was another guest at his dining table. On a positive note, it meant he would have no cause to be alone with Delphine Chance.

The modiste paled. "I won't feel safe until the thugs are in custody."

It made sense, but he suspected the lady was not being entirely honest. "Perhaps you fear they came for *you*," he said, testing a theory. "They didn't mention Miss Chance by name."

The lady shrugged. "What would they want with a simple modiste?"

Somehow, he suspected the lady knew.

Determined to have his way, Aaron Chance said, "I'll agree, but only if Gibbs and Mrs Maloney remain here with my sister. The woman is like a mother to me. I trust her implicitly. She took us into her home when we were mere street urchins and is firm of mind and opinion."

"This isn't Mivart's Hotel," Dorian countered.

"Those are my terms."

He might have dug his heels in and refused the King of Clubs' request, but Miss Chance looked at him through large brown eyes, her soothing voice like a siren's song as she said, "I pray you agree, Mr Flynn. I know you were coerced into taking this case, but I cannot help feeling this is fated."

He should have disputed the claim. Put paid to any notions of a mysterious force at play. But he could feel the hands of destiny guiding him on this treacherous journey. And though he longed for peace and solitude, an inner voice told him to hunker down and prepare for one hell of a storm.

Chapter Seven

Mr Flynn had dined alone in his study last night. He'd taken his breakfast a little after dawn before riding to Walworth to collect a tincture from Dr Skinner. He strode briskly through the corridors this morning, barely stopping to exchange pleasantries. While Delphine couldn't help but admire how splendid he looked in his dark blue coat, he stared at the gilt-framed paintings and wall sconces, too preoccupied to hold her gaze.

Was he avoiding her?

One might think so.

He had sent a note saying he was leaving to meet Mr Daventry in Hart Street. That he would return with Mrs Maloney and Gibbs but had other affairs to attend to this evening.

Perhaps Mr Flynn was used to dealing with timid women. Perhaps he had forgotten she'd been raised by Aaron Chance.

The gentleman had one foot inside the carriage when

he noticed her sitting demurely in the seat. "Miss Chance?" He froze, his shock evident.

"Good morning, Mr Flynn." Had she been wearing gloves, she would have tugged them firmly to show she would not be intimidated. But Mrs James was attempting to remove the bloodstains, and Aaron had failed to bring a clean change of clothes, believing she was returning to Fortune's Den. "I wasn't sure what time we were leaving and thought it best to wait in the carriage."

He inhaled deeply but said nothing.

"Ordinarily, I wouldn't dare make a house call without gloves and a bonnet." She had lost her hat in the scuffle with the blackguards outside Miss Darrow's shop and hoped someone in need had found it. "Though I don't suppose Mrs Haggert cares about etiquette."

"Mrs Haggert? What the devil? If you think I'm taking you to the hen house, you're sorely mistaken." The determination in his voice said he was not a man to cross. "You should remain at Mile End and tend to your brother, as we agreed."

"Theo is sleeping, and Miss Darrow barely leaves his bedside."

"You have the library at your disposal." He stepped down onto the gravel and gestured for her to alight. "There's paper and ink in the desk drawer if you'd like to see to your correspondence."

A hollow chuckle escaped her. "Who should I write to, Mr Flynn? Besides Miss Darrow, you're my only friend."

"You're my client," he corrected, though his tone lacked conviction.

Lady Gambit

She bit back a smile. "Do you make a habit of kissing your clients?"

Perhaps he was worried his coachman might hear their intimate conversation, because he climbed into the conveyance and slammed the door shut. The vehicle rocked on its axis as he dropped into the leather seat. "I'm not in the habit of kissing anyone."

Oh!

How strange that he should find her lips irresistible.

"Yes, I took you for a man in control of his appetites." So why had he been unable to tear his hot mouth from hers? "As you never kiss your friends or your clients, it makes our encounter yesterday a little confusing."

He removed his hat and dragged his hand through his dark hair. "Forgive me. I cannot explain the desperation that came over me, but there is no excuse for my—"

"Display of unbridled lust?"

His gaze fell to her buttoned pelisse. "For my ungentlemanly manner."

"Is that why you're avoiding me?"

"I'm not avoiding you."

"You let me dine alone last night."

"I needed time to think."

"You cannot think when we're together?" Her mind and body did odd things in his presence. Her heart skipped beats. Blood pumped wildly through her veins. Erotic daydreams pushed logical thoughts aside.

"My unforgivable actions yesterday would suggest so." A knot formed between his brows. "I pride myself on being nothing like my father. It came as quite a blow to discover I have inherited his disregard for propriety."

She could sense his internal struggle. The disgust he felt for surrendering to his desires. He had probably spent the night whipping himself with a birch as punishment for succumbing to a whim.

"You're mistaken. You had every regard for propriety." The need to soothe him overcame the need to prove a point. "You were honest and gave me fair warning. But one cannot fight fate. And if we're being pedantic, I kissed you first, Mr Flynn."

"I was a breath away from kissing you, madam."

Her pulse skittered. If only she had been patient. "Trouble yourself no longer. It's not the first time I've been kissed. I pray it won't be the last." Surely that snippet of information would settle his war with his conscience.

Strangely, it roused his temper.

"You rarely leave Fortune's Den. Who dared to take advantage?"

He sounded desperate to know.

"Aaron permitted me to visit Bath with Mrs Maloney. It's the only time I've been allowed to leave London. A dear friend of hers was sick."

She had not cared that they'd gone to nurse an ailing woman, to clean and prepare food and run errands. The rare moment of freedom had nourished her soul like the warmth of a summer sun.

"During a walk in the garden, the lady's nephew lost his wits and kissed me on the lips." It had left her aghast, her hands trembling, her stomach churning. She'd been repulsed and hadn't devoured him the way she had Mr Flynn. "I informed Mrs Maloney, and she had a discreet word with him." Though she had probably whacked him with her walking stick.

"Ah, now I know why your brother insisted Mrs Maloney act as chaperone. I understand you lived above her bookshop when you were children."

Her heart softened as she recalled the loving bond they shared.

"Mrs Maloney has never married and has no family. She's been like a mother to us all." She was always there with caring words and sound advice, a pillar of strength when their faith crumbled.

A darkness passed over Mr Flynn's rugged features. "I assume you mean she is kind and loving. Not all mothers are so inclined."

Those brusque words held a hint to his own troubled past.

Indeed, the icy chill of loneliness clung to the air.

"I have no recollection of the woman who nursed me, sir, but I assume instinct encourages a mother to love her child."

A heavy silence fell over them.

Keen to lighten the mood, she said, "I mention it merely for comparison, but kissing Mr Harper was like being assaulted by a wet fish. It was nothing like the kiss we shared."

It hadn't fired her blood. It hadn't left her with an undeniable ache. It hadn't stolen precious hours of sleep or had her yearning to feel the heat of his mouth again. The memory of kissing Mr Flynn stirred something sinful inside her. A desire to cast off her restraints and indulge in every wicked pleasure.

Perhaps he was plagued by the same salacious thoughts because he said, "I've not felt tempted to kiss a woman in years. Work has been my only focus." He glanced out of the window at the manor's elegant facade, the reward for his efforts, and gave a satisfied sigh. "Securing my independence has always been a priority."

"It's a beautiful house." Despite the plush furnishings and an abundance of exquisite paintings, the rooms felt empty and cold. Mrs Maloney's home was littered with paper and books, but love lived within the pages.

"It's mine. That's all that matters." His proud tone reminded her of Aaron's speech when he'd saved the money to purchase Fortune's Den.

It told her everything she needed to know.

Like Aaron, Mr Flynn hid behind a robust persona, a barricade to keep people out. He thought happiness lay in acquiring possessions. That love was fickle, and security soothed the soul.

"The kiss we shared was quite exceptional." So exceptional it had fed her obsession and left her wanting more. "But in the interests of the case, let us credit your lapse in judgement on the strain of saving a man's life."

"That seems the most probable cause," he agreed, though the flash of hunger in his eyes said otherwise.

"You were merely seeking comfort after a harrowing few hours." She straightened her skirts and smiled. "Good. Now we've established I am merely your client, I instruct you to take me to Hart Street. I want to discuss the case with Mr Daventry."

That knocked the wind out of his sails.

He stiffened. "You're no longer my client but a witness

in an attempted murder case. As Daventry said, this is no longer a personal matter but one of public safety. Therefore, I must insist you remain here."

She had sat nibbling toast this morning, anticipating his response. "Mr Daventry did not hire you, nor did he pay your fee. He merely persuaded you to take my case. Sybil Daventry paid you to find my parents. In that regard, nothing has changed. I am your client. If you decide to conduct an investigation for Bow Street, that is a separate matter."

She arched a brow, challenging him to argue.

He did not.

"You're a man of honour, Mr Flynn, a man of your word. Will you renege on an agreement made in good faith? Will you ignore the wishes of my benefactor?"

The corners of his mouth twitched. He seemed impressed and annoyed in equal measure. "Your brother put paid to any enquiries I might make on your behalf."

"My brother is not your client. But I will have the same conversation with Mr Daventry." She tapped the roof twice. The flick of the reins and the coachman's gruff command preceded the carriage rolling forward. "Forgive me, but we mustn't be late for our appointment. As Mr Daventry is overseeing the investigation, he can instruct you to ignore his wife's request."

She had spent the night thinking about what she should do. Sit like a stuffed goose waiting for men to solve her problems? Or become the master of her own destiny? The latter was not without risk. But if the incident outside Miss Darrow's shop proved anything, a thug could abduct her at gunpoint without warning. And she refused to watch another brother suffer as Theo had.

Mr Flynn stared at her as the carriage rumbled along the tree-lined drive. "Now I know why your brothers keep you prisoner in the attic. You have a man's grasp of logic and a woman's skill for manipulation."

"And only your passionate kisses can disarm me. What a shame I am merely your client. You have the wherewithal to silence me, sir, yet seem loathe to bend me to your will."

He breathed deeply and rubbed his jaw. "Don't tease me, madam."

"I am simply stating a fact." One that would get them into a wealth of trouble should they dare to lock lips again.

"A fact we should put far from our minds."

"I fear the moment will be forever ingrained in my memory. I must admit, your ragged pants and wandering hands led me to believe you were equally enamoured. I'm struggling to understand how you managed to fool me."

He grumbled to himself, his frustration apparent. "What do you want me to say, Miss Chance? That I'm disturbed to find I'm anything but a gentleman? That the need to ruin you for any other man simmers in my blood? That it took every ounce of resolve I possess not to seek you out last night and finish what we started?"

The raw passion in his voice had heat pooling between her thighs. Mr Flynn was a strong, virile man, a wolf in sheep's clothing. How fortunate she was accustomed to running with the pack.

"I lost my head yesterday and beg your forgiveness."

Lady Gambit

He sounded a fraction calmer now. "You have my word it won't happen again."

It would.

Something powerful existed between them.

Something both were too weak to fight.

"You're forgiven, Mr Flynn. Let us not mention it again."

She turned her attention to the passing scenery. Summer fields gave way to a quaint row of shops. A lady who rarely ventured to pastures new might press her face to the window and study the world with eager enthusiasm. But the man in the opposite seat dominated her thoughts.

He remained equally subdued.

Doubtless he was hoping Mr Daventry would squash her idea like one did an ant beneath their boot. But the master of the elite group of enquiry agents had one weakness—his love for his wife.

That proved the case when she arrived at his business premises in Hart Street and explained her dilemma. "There is some confusion surrounding Mr Flynn's appointment, sir."

Mr Daventry invited her to sit in one of two chairs opposite his desk in the study. "I'm not sure why? I believe my intentions were quite clear."

She glanced at Mr Flynn, who was leaning against the wall, his arms folded firmly to convey his objection. "Your wife paid Mr Flynn's fee. An amount he accepted to find my parents. Your need of his services in a criminal investigation is a separate issue."

Mr Daventry leaned back in his leather chair and

studied her over steepled fingers. "The suspect tried to abduct you, which—"

"May have nothing to do with me seeking my parents." She gave a half-shrug. "If Mr Flynn can no longer take my case, he should return the fee. That way, I may hire someone else to question Mrs Haggert and Nora Adkins. I shall visit Mrs Daventry this afternoon in the hope she might recommend another man for the task."

"You'll find no one as capable as me," Mr Flynn countered.

No, he was exceptional in every regard.

A confused hum left Mr Daventry's lips. "I don't see why we cannot tackle both cases together. I thought we'd agreed to question Mrs Haggert this morning. Isn't that why Flynn is here?"

She cleared her throat. "I wish to assist in the investigation."

It was ludicrous to think they would permit a woman to act as a sleuth, but Mr Daventry had employed female agents before, and she was invested in the outcome of this case.

Mr Flynn snorted. "I cannot solve a crime while protecting Miss Chance. She should remain at Mile End with her brother."

"Am I the only one who can see that wasting my days at Mile End is illogical?" She recalled a comment Mr Daventry had made only yesterday. "The answers lie within my mind. Visiting old haunts might trigger a memory. I see no issue as long as I avoid contact with my family and stay away from Fortune's Den."

Lady Gambit

"What of Theodore's recuperation?" Mr Flynn challenged.

"I trust Miss Darrow to take care of my brother." The modiste blamed herself for Theo being at her shop under false pretences and refused to leave his bedside until the threat of fever had passed. "I would rather draw the villain out than place my brother in danger. My assistance might prove invaluable."

A mischievous smile touched Mr Daventry's lips. "I suspect my wife would agree with you. She's never been one to sit idly while men do her bidding."

"Please tell me you're not considering her outlandish proposal?" Mr Flynn pushed away from the wall. "We gave Aaron Chance our word. We swore to protect her at all costs."

"And we will," Mr Daventry said casually.

"I won't be kept in the dark, Mr Flynn. I'm determined to discover the truth about my parents with or without your help."

Instinct said it was the only way to protect the men she loved. Her brothers would die for her and she had to do everything in her power to prevent that from happening.

Mr Flynn closed his eyes briefly. "It seems I'm left with little choice in the matter. I made a vow to keep you safe. A vow I mean to honour. I have no option but to remain at your side until you have the answers you seek, Miss Chance."

Mr Daventry braced his hands on the desk and stood. "It's settled then. We shall venture to St Giles together."

Not wishing to gloat or give a jubilant grin, she merely

nodded. "Is there anything I should know before we leave? Anything that will help in our endeavour?"

Mr Daventry reached into his desk drawer and removed a pocket pistol, powder and shot. "Keep these in your reticule. I'm told Aaron taught you how to use such a weapon."

"Until I could hit a bottle from ten yards."

"Anyone can hit a target, Miss Chance. Can you fire at a villain when your partner's life depends upon it?"

She glanced at Mr Flynn, her heart clenching as a vision of his blood-soaked body flashed before her eyes. The thought of losing him left her nauseous. "I owe Mr Flynn my life. His safety is of personal importance to me." She would fight with her bare hands, tackle a gang of hardened thugs.

Mr Daventry seemed appeased. "Excellent. Oh, before I forget, just one word of warning. There are wolves in the hen house. Never look Mrs Haggert in the eye and call her a liar."

Seven Dials
St Giles

The five-minute walk from Hart Street to Seven Dials was not without incident. They had stopped to help a barrow boy with a broken wheel. Ladies lingering near an alley had called to Mr Flynn, offering lewd ways to wipe the scowl from his handsome face. Perhaps that's why he insisted she take hold of his arm as they navigated the crowded streets.

She settled her fingers above the crook of his elbow, resting them against his bulging bicep. Heavens. He was a spectacular specimen of a man, spectacular in every regard, even when in a gruff mood.

"Our working relationship will be much easier if you accept my appointment," she said, attempting to ease the tension between them.

"You know why I raised an objection," he whispered.

"Yes, because you're worried you might kiss me again?" She brought him to a halt in the heart of Seven Dials, where a mob had once destroyed the sundial pillar. "There's really no need for concern. There are more important things to consider. I doubt either of us will make the same mistake."

While Mr Daventry spoke to a blind man begging outside the saddle shop and dropped a coin into his grubby hat, Mr Flynn wished to correct any misconception.

"My reticence has nothing to do with our *mistake*. Do you know how dangerous it is for a woman on these streets?"

Not wanting him to glimpse fear in her eyes, she kept her gaze fixed on the blind man, tapping Mr Daventry's boots with his stick. Nor did she wish to look at Mr Flynn's mouth and remember how wonderful he'd made her feel.

"I lived here for a year with Mrs Haggert." She had no memory of the hardships she'd suffered and had likely stolen more reticules than she'd eaten hunks of bread. "And we were on the streets for two weeks before Aaron secured lodgings with Mrs Maloney."

None of them would have survived had it been the dead of winter. Then, a mere week after they'd found a safe haven, Aaron had almost died in a fight with one of Mrs Haggert's thugs.

"That was sixteen years ago."

"Crime was just as rife."

Mr Daventry called to them. He pointed to Little Earl Street and beckoned them to follow as he fell into step beside the blind man.

"I'm used to working alone," came Mr Flynn's next excuse.

"I'm not used to working at all. This is new to us both."

He ground his teeth. "What part of this is hard to understand?"

"None of it. As colleagues, we're required to show restraint." She looked at him as they avoided the street seller, determined to sell them a broom. "It's only natural we're finding it difficult. You've not kissed anyone for years. A slimy peck from a fool with rotten breath is the limit of my experience."

He gave a mocking snort. "I trust you're referring to Mr Harper."

He had remembered the man's name.

"Of course. You taste divine and kiss like you've mastered the art. Indeed, you have filled my heart with hope. The law of averages says I may encounter another man who appeals to me as much as you do."

Lady Gambit

He fell silent, which was just as well because the blind man stopped at the entrance to Monmouth Court—a passage leading deep into the warrens of St Giles. Two boys wearing smart clothes and clean caps stood blocking the entrance, looking as proud as the King's guards.

Mr Daventry removed a pencil from his pocket and scribbled on his calling card. He shoved the card and a gold coin into one boy's hand. "Take this to your mistress."

While the boy scampered away down the alley, Delphine studied her surroundings. Nothing seemed familiar. Not the rowdy drunkards gathered outside the inn. Not the barefooted children clinging to their mother's dirty skirts. Not the hungry mites with their noses pressed to the baker's shop window, inhaling the smell of freshly baked bread.

Guilt flared as she said a silent prayer of thanks to the Lord. But for the grace of God, this would have been her home.

There were charities to help the needy. Ways she might make a difference to people's lives instead of wasting her days tidying her armoire.

She gripped Mr Flynn's arm a little tighter. "When this is over, I shall find more useful ways to spend my time. Aaron rescued me from a fate worse than death. I must repay the debt and help as many poor souls as I can."

He covered her hand with his own, an innocent gesture that caused a quickening deep in her core. "Walking these streets would make anyone count their blessings."

"You would make an excellent mentor for orphaned boys." There were lost children all over the city. "They need hope, and a purpose that doesn't involve stealing food to survive."

Ideas burst into her mind. Each one of her brothers had a skill that proved invaluable. She could start a charitable foundation. First, she needed to gain her freedom by uncovering the secrets of the past.

The boy returned and beckoned them into the alley.

Fear fluttered in her chest as she entered the narrow walkway. The hairs on her nape prickled to attention. Faint memories slid into her mind as she passed the bow windows of various shops.

Look what I've found, Mrs Haggert.
Well. Well. Ain't you the little magpie?

She concentrated on following Mr Daventry, putting one foot in front of the other, her sights fixed on the black paint-chipped door at the end of the passage—the gateway to hell.

"We don't have to do this," Mr Flynn whispered.

"There's no other way to ensure my brothers' safety." She did not hide her growing apprehension. In Mr Flynn's company, buried emotions found their way to the surface. "Though the truth will set me free, instinct says I have every reason to be afraid."

"No one will hurt you on my watch, Miss Chance." He spoke with a lover's warmth and tenacity. "Colleagues, friends, whatever we are to each other, I'll kill the first man who lays a hand on you."

She resisted the urge to throw herself into his arms and hug him for his unwavering loyalty. "I pray it won't come to that. I doubt my declaration will count for much, but I'd die before I'd let you risk your life for me."

Lady Gambit

Their eyes remained locked for a heartbeat.

But then the black door creaked open, and her breath caught in her throat. Not even the heat of Mr Flynn's gaze could chase the chill of fear from her bones.

A stick of a man beckoned them into the four-story house with one bony finger. "This way. You'll wait for Mrs Haggert in the drawing room." His skeletal features and sunken eyes would make any child believe in monsters.

A group of boys appeared on the landing, gawping and whispering amongst themselves. A stern voice barked at them from the shadows, and they scurried away like terrified rats.

The drawing room was like Mrs Maloney's sitting room, a cosy place with a stoked fire, dark walls and comfortable velvet chairs. A portrait hung above the mantel. The young, dark-haired woman looked almost regal in bearing.

Nothing seemed familiar until she noticed the iron fire tools with the gold ormolu handles.

Whine again, and I'll take that shovel to your bare arse.

The door opened, and an old woman with white curly hair appeared. She wore a fashionable black dress, red rouge on her cheeks and lips, though it failed to warm her pale complexion or soften her stern features.

The woman took one look at her, and though her wide mouth formed a grin, her black eyes were as cold as glass. "Well, well. What have we here? Foolish chit. Have you learnt nothing? No one returns to the coop. You know that, Caterina."

Chapter Eight

Mrs Haggert captured Miss Chance's chin between her gnarled fingers. "You always were a pretty little thing. As dainty as a spring bud. I knew this day would come, though I never thought Aaron Chance would be stupid enough to let you set foot in my house again."

Dorian froze.

The air crackled with tension.

He'd known this was a mistake.

Like the gorgon Medusa, Mrs Haggert looked at Miss Chance through unforgiving eyes. "Where is he? Aaron? He ain't dead. And he ain't the sort to hide in the shadows. Don't lie to me now."

Miss Chance's bottom lip quivered. "Aaron doesn't know I'm here." Her voice carried a childlike quality, as if she instinctively knew how to appease the crone. Before Mrs Haggert could bombard her with questions, she uttered, "You called me Caterina. May I ask why?"

Mrs Haggert cackled. "Ain't that your name? I know you took a knock to the head—happen that's why you don't remember—but when Davey found you, that's what you said."

"Davey?" Miss Chance looked baffled. "May I speak to him?"

Mrs Haggert released her. "The clodpole got caught swindling the chandler on Tower Street years ago. Good riddance. I'll not have a grubby little thief disturbing my boys' education."

The woman liked her victims to think she had a charitable heart.

They soon discovered it was rotten to the core.

"One of your boys is locked in a cell in Bow Street," Daventry said.

"And the rotter can stay there." Mrs Haggert clicked her tongue. "I try to run an honest house, and that's how these ungrateful mites repay me. When a boy is hungry, it's hard to tell if he's the Lord's child or the devil's spawn."

Daventry gestured to the sofa. "May we sit? We're here on an official police matter, though whatever we discuss today won't be relayed to Bow Street."

"Always the gentleman, Mr Daventry. You know just what to say to win a lady's heart." Mrs Haggert rubbed her bony hands together, thrust two fingers into her mouth and whistled loudly. "But nothing in life is free, sir. You know that better than anyone."

Upon hearing the shrill sound, two men burst into the drawing room. Their necks were as thick as the average man's thigh. Their squashed noses said they were used to taking punches. They stood like marble statues, blocking the doorway.

"It's like paying the boatman," Mrs Haggert continued with a mirthless chuckle. "If you want information from the underworld, you must show me the blunt." She gestured to Daventry's onyx cufflinks. "A man used to rolling up his shirt sleeves don't need fancy adornments."

Daventry stiffened. "My wife bought me these cufflinks as a wedding gift. I would rather slay everyone here than part with them."

Mrs Haggert met his challenging stare but knew not to provoke the devil. "Perhaps it's best I hear what you want before we negotiate a price. I'll not have blood on my new rug."

Miss Chance wasn't listening.

She was studying the room, staring at the men, trying to remember.

A knock to the head might affect a person's memory temporarily, but not for sixteen years. Dorian wondered if she had unwittingly chosen to forget the traumas she had suffered before becoming Delphine Chance.

"Let's hear from you, Mr Flynn." Mrs Haggert's soulless eyes were upon him, boring through his defences. "Happen you've been scouring the shadows, looking for boys who ain't lost. I'm surprised you'd show your face here. You know we shoot dogs that come sniffing around the coop."

Dorian wasn't afraid of this woman or her louts. She used gossip and intimidation to maintain her frightening persona. But what she knew about Delphine Chance might see the lady hanged. As such, he had every reason to fear her.

"Someone tried to abduct Miss Chance. In the process,

the blackguard shot her youngest brother." He was wasting his breath. From Mrs Haggert's passive expression, she already knew. "I'm charged with solving a case of attempted murder. Miss Chance has also hired me to discover her parents' identities."

A strange emotion passed over the woman's wrinkled face—something akin to dread or unease. "Aaron has many enemies. You've enough work to keep you busy for a month. Happen you feel more at home in the rookeries than in your father's fancy Mayfair residence."

He inclined his head. "You're right on both counts, madam."

"I hear he's arranging your wedding." She noted Miss Chance's sudden gasp and grinned. "Ah, and there's the truth of why you're really here, Mr Flynn. You're looking for an excuse not to marry the Marquess of Bexley's beloved by-blow."

His pulse quickened.

He was forced to acknowledge the problem he had been avoiding. "Forgive my coarse language, but it would take more than a pretty face and a large dowry to have me bend to that bastard's will. I'm my own man, Mrs Haggert. I choose my own fate. As I'm sure you're aware."

Mrs Haggert turned to Miss Chance. "What do you say, Caterina? Should Mr Flynn marry for money and acceptance? Or do you think he prefers getting his knees dirty?"

The lady raised her dainty chin. "It's not for me to say, Mrs Haggert. I am merely Mr Flynn's client. He is hard to read and shares his private thoughts with no one."

From the pained look in her eyes, Miss Chance thought

he'd kissed her as part of a rebellion. A way of secretly objecting to his father's demands.

"My father's plans for me are irrelevant," he interjected. "Hence I see no need to discuss a selfish man's motives."

Mrs Haggert shifted her weight to her left hip. "Age is a dratted curse," she said, urging them to sit so she might relax in a comfortable chair, too. "Tell me what you want to know and what you have to barter."

Daventry chose the leather chair, leaving Dorian to sit beside Miss Chance on the small velvet sofa. They exchanged glances as their knees touched. Mistrust swam in her brown eyes. It didn't help that she believed he'd been avoiding her since sharing a magical kiss.

Daventry waved for Dorian to offer terms.

"We need to know where Davey found Miss Chance and what she told you about her family." He made no mention of her parents being buried in a pauper's grave. Nor was he foolish enough to suggest Mrs Haggert was involved in their deaths. "We need to know how she came by the injury that stole her memory."

Mrs Haggert shook her head. "Why should I help you? When a chick leaves the coop, it's dead to me. Aaron Chance won the wager. She's his responsibility, not mine."

Yet two facts revealed an inconsistency.

Mrs Haggert never took girls into the coop.

If Mrs Haggert had cut the girl's hair and dressed her in breeches, why was she found wearing a dress belonging to someone named Delphine?

"Flynn spent the evening trawling through witness statements," Daventry said, revealing the reason Dorian had not dined with Miss Chance last night. "He acted on information that led him to a missing person. A criminal leading a secret life to escape his wicked past."

Mrs Haggert gripped the arm of the chair. "Who?"

"Someone stupid enough to cross you."

Anger flared in the woman's black eyes. "If it's that spawn of Satan, you'd better tell me now." She clutched her throat, blind fury making it hard for her to swallow.

Daventry nodded. "The information is worth a king's ransom. I know of no other man who's betrayed you and lived to tell the tale."

"Your husband is not dead," Dorian added, dangling the metaphorical carrot. "I happened upon his secret location at dawn this morning and can confirm he is alive and well."

Miss Chance looked at him.

When they were next alone, she would demand to know why he had kept her in the dark. Why he'd let her think he was avoiding her when, in truth, he had been working. Emotions would run so high he'd be tempted to kiss her again.

"Anything said here is confidential," Daventry assured Mrs Haggert.

Hungry for information, Mrs Haggert spoke quickly. "Davey was out stalking foreign coves near the Pulteney Hotel. It was a few days before the Jubilee. He saw her hiding in the shrubbery near Green Park and brought her home."

Miss Chance hung her head. "I don't remember."

"And she told you her name was Caterina?" Dorian pressed.

"It was the only thing she did say. The poor mite was frightened out of her wits. It took days before she found her voice and begged me to keep her safe."

Dorian suppressed a mocking snort.

No one was safe in the hen house.

"And so you cut off her hair and passed her off as one of your boys." He was careful not to accuse Mrs Haggert of being a criminal mastermind. "Was she literate?"

"She could read, write and play a decent tune on the old pianoforte. It took months to rid her of her faint accent."

Miss Chance spoke up. "What sort of accent?"

Mrs Haggert shrugged. "Foreign. I ain't no expert."

The snippet of information was like an elixir reviving her flagging spirit. "You told Aaron my parents died and are buried in a pauper's grave. Did I tell you that? Is it true?"

"It was sixteen years ago," the woman said impatiently. "Of course your parents are dead. Who'd leave such a sweet little treasure on the streets?"

Keen to ensure Miss Chance had the answers she needed, Dorian said, "I can do more than give you your husband's address. I can tell you where he went when he betrayed your trust and disappeared like a dawn mist." He paused. "But I shall say no more until you've told Miss Chance whatever she needs to know."

The crone's shrewd gaze turned sinister. "No one issues orders in the hen house. Lucky for you, you have something I want." She demanded her louts leave the room and waited until the door clicked shut before speaking. "She said her parents were dead. That someone had hired a man to kill them. I told her if she wanted to live she had to forget where she came from. We never spoke about it again. She did what she was told and earned her keep like the rest of my boys."

"And you didn't attempt to discover her real identity?"

The woman chuckled. "I ain't got time to go knocking on people's doors. Besides, if she had any hope of surviving, I knew it was best left alone."

Daventry was in complete agreement. "We won't mention the year Miss Chance spent here. The truth may place you both in danger."

The woman's hard features softened. "Something spooked her the night she fled. I don't know how she hurt her head."

Dorian wasn't sure why, but he believed her.

There was still one fact gnawing away at him.

"You have eyes and ears all over St Giles. Why give Aaron Chance the option to raise her as his sister? You had the power to take her back."

The woman looked at Miss Chance and sighed. "Having her here would have put all our necks on the chopping block. She'd have brought trouble to my door, Mr Flynn. And when Aaron Chance offered to fight for her, the purse was large enough to keep my boys indoors that winter."

Silence descended.

Miss Chance's shoulders slumped. "Aaron is a man of his word. He knew the truth would hurt me and put me in harm's way. He's done everything he can to keep me safe."

Mrs Haggert snorted. "I'd sooner cross the devil than Aaron Chance. He's grown more powerful over the years.

I've often thought it was so I'd be forced to keep my vow. Every sacrifice he's made, he's done for you, gal, and those other men you call brothers."

Miss Chance took a calming breath. "Regardless of your motivations, I want to thank you, Mrs Haggert. You could have thrown me out onto the street. Had you not helped me, I might have perished that night."

Tears filled the woman's eyes but she blinked them away quickly. "Sentiment is for fools, Caterina. The world is ruled by cruel people. You join the pack or die. That's the way of it." She faced Dorian, her temper returning. "I want everything you have on Harold Haggert. It best be worth my while, or you'll not leave here without a fight."

Dorian explained what he'd learned by studying the witness statements from a spate of highway robberies on the Kent Road. The fool had made the mistake of stealing his last victim's hat—a signature Harold Haggert had used as a footpad in his youth.

"He's working at The Bell coaching inn on the Kent Road." He explained that the landlord had moved from Peterborough, where there had been a spate of similar robberies.

"Working?" Mrs Haggert turned up her nose as if she'd smelled something foul. "What's he done with the jewels he stole from me?"

He shrugged. "You'll have to ask him yourself. I checked his likeness against the sketch Daventry sent with the statements last night. Your husband may be a partner in the business but wishes to remain incognito."

Mrs Haggert gritted her teeth and hauled herself out of

Lady Gambit

the chair. "If what you say is true, Mr Flynn, I'll be in your debt."

He merely inclined his head.

The crone whistled for her louts. "Gather the men. As soon as the sun sets, we're going out." She ushered Miss Chance out of her seat. "Time to go. Just one thing before you do. I heard Lord Meldrum ain't got the funds to pay his gambling debts. He's been spouting nonsense. He said if he married you, it would solve all his problems. He might have hired the men who tried to snatch you off the street."

Miss Chance gripped the woman's gnarled hand. "Thank you. I'm grateful for any information that might help me find the man who shot my brother."

"You mind yourself. They'll be slinking out of the shadows now they know you ain't invincible. When your life's on the line, you remember what I told you."

And with that parting message, Mrs Haggert shooed them all out into the alley and slammed the front door shut.

During the subdued five-minute walk back to Hart Street, Daventry suggested they visit Nora Adkins again. "Dig deeper. There's some truth to the woman's mad ramblings."

Miss Chance walked silently beside them, lost in thought.

Dorian wasn't sure which piece of information had affected her most. The fact she should be in fear of her life. That, in all likelihood, she was the mysterious Caterina who had been told to run and hide in the darkness. That men were scheming to see them both married to people they didn't love.

"I forgot to ask Mrs Haggert if she'd told Aaron my name was Caterina," she said softly when they entered Daventry's study. "I never asked why I was wearing a dress belonging to a girl named Delphine."

Daventry gestured to the row of decanters on the drinks table. "Miss Chance requires a glass of sherry. I must visit Bow Street but will be no more than twenty minutes. There's paper and ink at your disposal. Make a list of suspects and potential witnesses. When I return, we'll devise a plan."

He left them in the study and closed the door.

Dorian's fingers trembled when he tugged the stopper from the decanter and filled the lady's glass. Nothing fazed him but his desire to ease this woman's troubled mind and the knowledge he would kiss her again in a heartbeat.

"I'll make a note of any relevant questions," he said, handing her the glass. "Do you remember anything about your time with Mrs Haggert?"

She sat in the chair and sipped her sherry. "No, but when she spoke to me directly, I wasn't afraid."

He perched on the desk beside her. "You don't remember her. Perhaps life wasn't so bad there." Despite everything Mrs Haggert had said, he was convinced she had omitted certain aspects of the story.

"Some people come into our life for a reason. To teach us a lesson. To help us grow." Like a lover's sensual caress, her gaze fell slowly from his face to his thighs. "After the trouble I've caused you, a simple existence is all you'll long for."

He knew where this was going. "I live a simple existence."

He rose at dawn each morning and worked until dusk. Until the last vestiges of daylight disappeared beyond the horizon. He dined alone, the clatter of cutlery on china the only sound. He slept alone in a cold bed and kept to the same routine daily.

"Mr Daventry once explained the importance of balance. By day, he walks through the bowels of hell. By night, when he returns home to his beloved wife, he said it's like bathing in the splendours of heaven."

Dorian had tasted heaven once. When he had dared to grasp Miss Chance's wrist and make a scandalous suggestion. No matter how hard he tried to fight it, he needed to sup from her heavenly lips again. "What has that to do with me?"

She struggled to meet his gaze. "Perhaps you should consider your father's proposal and marry a woman befitting your station. I cannot help but feel something is missing at Mile End."

What could be missing?

He'd catered for every comfort.

A mocking chuckle burst from his lips. "An illegitimate son has no station. My father means to see me elevated from working man to lazy lout. He's happy for me to repeat his mistake and marry for money. The man knows nothing about love."

Miss Chance swallowed hard. "Is she beautiful?"

"Who?"

"The lady he wants you to marry."

"Miss Montague? Most men think so." Though he doubted his heart would ache if he kissed her. He didn't wake at night wishing she was sprawled naked beside him in bed. He didn't long to gather her close, keep her safe and chase her demons away. "It's not enough for me."

"Perhaps you should kiss her the way you kissed me. Beneath your stony facade, you're a passionate man. You might be surprised to find you share a similar connection with Miss Montague."

He stared at her, wondering why she would suggest he lock lips with another woman when it was obvious they wanted to kiss each other. "Our kiss was unique. As you said, I was suffering under the strain of having saved your brother's life. It's the reason for my fervent attentions."

"Yes, it's doubtful we would share such a powerful experience again." Her tongue grazed her bottom lip, the sight firing his blood. "And I cannot help but wonder if you kissed me to defy your father."

Everything he did was to show his disdain for the Earl of Retford's schemes. Everything except for that one unbridled moment when he'd lost sight of the war. When he'd dared to surrender to the curious whispers of his heart.

"We were alone. My father thinks I live above the Old Swan." And by God, it had better stay that way. He would rather call Mrs Haggert a liar than deal with the earl's unwanted visits. "We're the only ones who know what occurred in that bedchamber. The only ones who know what it meant in that moment."

The pleasure of that memory was evident in her gentle sigh. "The unconscious mind has its own agenda. Perhaps yours is seeking to reclaim control."

"And yours is on a quest for freedom."

She placed her empty sherry glass on the desk before

Lady Gambit

her eyes found his. "Or perhaps I see a hero in you, Mr Flynn. A quality I find as attractive as your handsome visage."

What happened next would baffle him for hours.

Why did her simple statement have him reaching for her? What made her jump to her feet and fall into his arms? Why had their mouths clashed with a force that defied logic?

They were kissing so rampantly they could barely catch their breath. He was perched on Daventry's desk, Miss Chance's hips wedged between his open legs. She gripped his thighs, her dainty hands mere inches from his throbbing cock.

Touch me!

The words echoed in his mind. Words that would shock any man who had built an impenetrable barricade. He didn't need affection. He didn't need love. He didn't need a tender touch or the warmth of a woman's lips.

But by God, he needed her.

A growl rumbled in his throat as he drank from her like a dying nomad at an oasis. He couldn't drink deeply enough to quench his thirst. His blood pumped too quickly through his veins. He ached to cover her body and plunge long and hard into her wetness.

Saints and demons!

He was a master at guarding his emotions.

So what in the devil's name was this?

If they didn't rein in their lust, they'd be making love on Daventry's desk, Themis, the goddess of justice, looking over them.

"This is madness," she breathed when he found the

strength to break contact. "The most exquisite form of torture." She slid her hands into his hair, her mouth finding his again.

He was lost.

Lost in the softness of her lips.

Lost in her natural scent, as potent as any aphrodisiac.

He'd likely pay with his life for this. Even the prospect of death by Aaron Chance's powerful hands proved a feeble deterrent.

Then the front door opened and slammed shut.

Daventry called to his housekeeper.

Dorian dragged his mouth from hers. In a frantic few seconds, they straightened their clothes and tried to calm their ragged breathing. Even then, they kissed briefly, like it might be their last.

When Daventry entered the room, Miss Chance was sitting demurely in the chair before the desk. She held the empty sherry glass as if they'd not moved a muscle since Daventry had left.

But the skilled investigator spotted every insignificant detail, and perhaps the sweet scent of arousal still clung to the air.

"I see the sherry hasn't helped to calm your pulse, Miss Chance." Daventry gestured to the lady's trembling hands. "It's only natural you would feel the cold chill of fear after visiting Mrs Haggert."

"I'm not afraid of Mrs Haggert." Miss Chance looked up from her glass, though the uncertainty in her eyes said she was afraid of something.

Perhaps of how quickly they'd devoured each other's mouths. Perhaps the power of their mutual attraction was a thing to fear. Next time, there might be no one to stop them succumbing to their desires.

"Good, as we may need to question Mrs Haggert again." Daventry straightened the ink well and the pile of papers on his desk but did not ask how they came to be askew. "Did you make a list of suspects?"

Dorian cleared his throat. "Not yet. We were busy discussing Mrs Haggert's revelations." That much was true. "What did you need from Bow Street?"

"On your advice, I asked Sir Malcolm to provide me with a list of foreign guests staying at the Pulteney Hotel during the summer of 1814. It's unlikely the hotel keeps records dating back seventeen years, but it was the Jubilee, and the long-serving staff might recall something important."

Miss Chance sat bolt upright in the seat. "You think I may have fled from the hotel? That my parents weren't English?"

Mrs Haggert had mentioned Miss Chance's faint accent.

Or had she meant to throw them off the scent?

"I don't know what to think. After all these years, checking the facts will be almost impossible." Daventry's tone turned grave. "Sadly, we must presume your parents are dead."

Miss Chance hung her head and nodded.

"Mrs Haggert wouldn't have kept her if there was a chance she'd be accused of kidnapping or abduction," Dorian said, knowing there was more to the story than the crone had admitted. "And she would not have risked Aaron Chance's wrath by lying to him."

Daventry pursed his lips. "Agreed." He thought for a moment. "Visit Bethlem Hospital tomorrow. Question Nora Adkins again. My coachman Gibbs is trained in all manner of combat. He'll be your driver for the duration of the case."

A shiver of trepidation ran over Dorian's shoulders. "If it's a matter of gathering evidence, wouldn't it be better if I went alone?"

Was it wise for Miss Chance to enter Bethlem? Her problems began shortly after his last visit, and he would rather there were no witnesses when he questioned the Superintendent.

Daventry grinned. "You're not going to Bethlem to collect evidence. You're going to lure a snake out of its basket. Miss Chance will be the bait."

Chapter Nine

"You've been holding that teacup for five minutes and haven't taken a sip." Mrs Maloney's smile carried the warmth of a winter blanket. Her presence helped soothe everyone's woes. "I've never seen you so out of sorts, dear. There's no need to worry about Theo. The doctor said he's making excellent progress. He always was a strong boy. Never a day ill in his life."

Delphine returned the cup to the saucer, grateful for Mrs Maloney's support and that they were the only two people left at the breakfast table. She'd defy any lady to concentrate when sitting opposite the enigmatic Mr Flynn.

Staring at his mouth had become her new hobby. Her heart raced whenever she recalled their passionate kiss in Mr Daventry's office. Every muscle in her body grew tense, anticipating the moment they would indulge themselves again.

"Guilt is a hard emotion to master," she admitted.

With every illicit kiss, her list of sins grew by the day.

"You're not to blame for what happened to Theo." Mrs

Maloney snatched the silver tongs and dropped another lump of sugar into her tea. She was sweet by nature and infinitely wise. "I told Aaron years ago, nothing good grows in the dark. But that boy is as stubborn as the emperor Caligula. Now he's learning that you can't control fate."

Her brothers were strapping men, not boys, but Mrs Maloney liked to dwell on the days when she took a damp cloth to their dirty faces and tucked them into clean beds. She'd done her best to guide Aaron, but his pain ran deep.

"Aaron is convinced one of his patrons is to blame. He spent yesterday trying to locate Mr Tindell, but the gentleman has vanished into thin air."

All three brothers had arrived with Mr Daventry last night to have supper with Theo and discuss which peers might be suspects. It was the first time they had closed the doors to Fortune's Den.

Nothing mattered more than family.

Aaron had scoured the corridors of Mile End looking for her, desperate to question her about her visit to Mrs Haggert's house. He'd waited until Aramis and Christian had stopped hugging her before ushering the men out of the library and closing the door.

I don't trust that woman.

Everything she does is self-serving.

She mentioned the rumour that Lord Meldrum wanted to marry her to force Aaron to tear up his vowels.

I'd no sooner let you marry that fool than I'd let you marry Flynn. You need a husband who won't gamble with your future. A husband who won't end up dead in a ditch over some damnable missing person's case.

Lady Gambit

Her obedient nod was at odds with her body's demands. The more time she spent with Mr Flynn, the more she longed for his company. But he spent long periods away from home. Work was his focus. He had said so himself. Why would she abandon her family to spend endless nights alone?

"Perhaps Mr Flynn can find him?" Mrs Maloney said.

"Find who?"

"Mr Tindell. Our host has a skill for finding missing people, does he not?"

"He does." He had excelled at helping her find the passionate woman hidden within. "Though Mr Flynn refuses to believe a peer would be foolish enough to have my brother shot."

To avoid an argument, he had made himself scarce last night, though both Aramis and Christian had spent time alone with him in his study.

"I hope someone told Mr Flynn about the other possible suspect," Mrs Maloney said before sipping her tea. "Perhaps the attempted kidnapping was a ruse to shoot Theo. The earl would sooner see my boys rotting in a shallow grave than disgracing his family."

She was referring to the men's estranged uncle, the Earl of Berridge—or the Earl of *Arsedom* as her brothers called him when cursing him to Hades. No one had saved the boys from the gutter. They'd been left shouldering the blame for their father's mistakes.

"I agree with Mr Flynn. Why would a peer risk his neck or make an enemy of my brothers? It makes no sense."

"A man can be born to privilege and still be a dolt, dear."

They ate their breakfast, the conversation turning to how long Theo might remain at Mile End.

"Mr Daventry thinks it's best to wait until the villain is in custody." She was of no mind to argue. Not because Theo's safety was a priority. Not because she relished the idea of spending time alone with Mr Flynn. But she sensed a change in her brother's mood. An inner anger had stolen the sparkle from his blue eyes. The notion he had something to prove had robbed him of his playful grin.

"Let's pray it's soon, dear. Mr Flynn must have the patience of a saint to suffer us all living under his roof."

Yes, he'd taken to muttering under his breath quite frequently.

"He's used to spending time alone and rarely has company." A mirthless chuckle escaped her when she thought about the years she'd spent staring at the bedchamber walls. "He says he enjoys the solitude."

He enjoyed kissing, too, but what did it all mean?

Mrs Maloney nodded. "Like Aaron, he spends a lot of time brooding in his study. He was there until midnight last night."

Had her brothers not visited, she might have sought Mr Flynn out. They might have kissed again without fear of interruption.

"Sorry I didn't come to say goodnight to you." She had planned to take a glass of sherry to Mrs Maloney's room and sit talking like the old days. "I was with Theo until quite late."

She'd crept into Theo's room once her brothers had

left. She'd cleaned his wound, mopped his brow and told him about her visit to Mrs Haggert.

I was frightened the night I hurt my head.

And Mrs Haggert doesn't know why?

She says not.

Perhaps she knows but doesn't want to incriminate herself.

She had sat thinking about the last comment long after Theo had fallen asleep. "It was so late. I don't recall climbing into bed."

"You wouldn't." There was a mischievous glint in Mrs Maloney's gaze. She reached across the table and gave Delphine's arm an affectionate pat. "Miss Darrow found you asleep on Theo's bed. She couldn't rouse you without disturbing him so summoned help."

"Oh." It was not surprising. She had not slept properly in days.

"We had to fetch Mr Flynn from his study."

Her pulse skittered. "Mr Flynn?"

Mrs Maloney covered her heart with her hand and smiled like all was well with the world. "He appeared like an errant knight, though he stared at you for so long we thought about calling the butler. Then he hauled you into his strong arms without waking you or poor Theo."

Delphine froze. "Mr Flynn carried me to bed?"

She'd been wearing nothing but a nightgown.

"Yes, dear. I know it might be inappropriate, but we didn't want to wake Theo. We can't have him relying on laudanum to sleep. And while we're all living together under one roof, we must make allowances."

Suspicion flared.

She might have pressed Mrs Maloney for more information, suggested she had taken to playing matchmaker, but the man in question entered the dining room and her heart skipped a beat.

"Forgive the interruption. We need to leave for Bethlem Hospital soon." He'd chosen to wear the dark blue coat she loved. The one that gripped his muscular shoulders like a second skin.

"I assume we're collecting Mr Daventry on the way."

"Erm. No. He's been detained. We're to continue without him."

Detained? Mr Daventry had assured Aaron he would be working with them on the case. "Oh well. I'm sure he'll join us at some point."

"While we're out, we'll take Gibbs and visit my lodgings above the Old Swan. I need to discover the identity of the man who came looking for me. It could be related to the case."

She smiled. "I can be ready to leave in five minutes."

He arched a brow in surprise. "I was of the impression most women require at least an hour to ready themselves for an outing."

"I'm not most women, Mr Flynn."

His gaze swept over her. "No, Miss Chance. You're unlike any woman I have ever met."

Lady Gambit

Bethlem Royal Hospital
St George's Fields

"I'm afraid you can't see Nora today." Mr Powell, the gaunt-looking Superintendent, shuffled a few papers on his desk. He had barely looked them in the eye since they'd signed the visitors' book and taken a seat in his cold office. "We had an incident here late last night."

Before Mr Flynn could say a word, Delphine sat forward. "What sort of incident?" She got the sense this man kept many secrets. Heaven knows what went on in such an eerie place after sunset. "I pray this isn't a ploy to prevent us from questioning Miss Adkins."

Mr Powell rocked nervously in the chair. His eyes were dull and droopy, and he looked like he'd barely slept a wink. "Nora tripped and hit her head. The gash required stitches. She was sent to the infirmary."

"Tripped?" Mr Flynn said with obvious suspicion. "On what? There's nothing in her cell but a bed." He stood abruptly. "I want to see her. I want access to the infirmary."

Mr Powell gestured for him to sit. "You can't see—"

"Do I need to remind you this is a criminal investigation?" Mr Flynn braced his knuckles on the desk and glared at the Superintendent. "You better hope I find her alive and well. If one of your men hurt her, there'll be the devil to pay."

His masterful tone had Mr Powell squirming. "You can't see Nora Adkins because … because she's not here. She absconded last night and is probably in Dover by now."

Mr Flynn jerked in shock. "Absconded?" It took him a moment to absorb the information, then he slapped his hand on the desk and growled, "You're lying. The woman has been a prisoner here for years. Why would she wait until now to escape? A mere week since I paid her a visit and demanded to know who is funding her keep."

Was it more than a coincidence?

Was Nora in fear of her life, too?

"Nora hit Dr Collins with a bottle of castor oil and stole his keys." In his eagerness to cast the blame elsewhere, Mr Powell's frustration turned to anger. "Perhaps you persuaded her to take matters into her own hands. You gave her the idea it was easier to overpower the doctor than a guard."

Mr Flynn's laugh said the notion was absurd.

"These baseless accusations are not helping matters, Mr Powell." Although she wasn't a skilled enquiry agent, it was clear they needed two things before they left Bethlem Hospital. "The Home Secretary has sanctioned this investigation. Your failure to help with our enquiries has been duly noted."

Mr Powell's contemptuous glare said he believed all women were mad. "Maybe you should leave the men to their work and wait outside, madam."

A growl rumbled in Mr Flynn's throat, but she raised a calming hand and smiled. "Might I deal with the matter, sir?" She would make this fool pay for his disparaging tone.

Looking a little intrigued, Mr Flynn nodded.

The tension in the room was palpable.

Aaron said the key to unnerving an opponent was to

act like you've already won. He employed the same tactic in any conflict situation. She had let her emotions overwhelm her. Let guilt and fear affect her ability to help Mr Flynn with the case. It was time she acted like the sister of four dangerous rogues and not like a naive debutante.

She looked Mr Powell keenly in the eye. "We're not leaving here without Nora Adkins' file. If you don't have it, I shall visit Whitehall and explain that your incompetence is hindering our investigation."

Mr Powell resisted. "We lost the file during the move from Moorfields, but you're welcome to rummage through the crates in the basement."

All men have a vice.
Remember that, Delphine.
You may use it to your advantage.

What was Mr Powell's vice? He wasn't a gambling man, or he would be quivering in his boots at the mention of her name. Gluttony might be his weakness. The whiff of brandy on his breath and the broken capillaries on his cheeks said he drank liquor to excess. When inebriated, men often had no memory of their wild antics.

"I want the file, Mr Powell. And I want to interview the doctor. If you prefer, I can turn this office upside down. Or I might share a story with my friend at *The Morning Herald*. The public would be keen to hear how men in positions of authority accost their patients while in a drunken stupor. I'd wager five pounds there's liquor in your desk."

The man's face turned claret red. He yanked his handkerchief from his pocket and wiped his brow. "This is tantamount to blackmail."

"Yes, I do believe it is." She lifted her chin, feeling quite pleased with herself. "The file, Mr Powell. And we want to interview Dr Collins."

The chair scraped the tiled floor as the Superintendent stood abruptly. "I'll summon Dr Collins and have all paperwork relating to Nora Adkins brought to my office." He rounded the desk, pausing to threaten them in an effort to preserve his dignity. "Then you're to leave my hospital. Do you hear me? I'll not tolerate your interference any longer." He stormed from the room, slamming the door behind him.

Mr Flynn chuckled. "Remind me never to cross you, Miss Chance. I'd hate to read what your friend at *The Morning Herald* might say about me."

She laughed, too, though a warm feeling filled her chest whenever he smiled. "I wouldn't dare put your name in print. I'd not risk the ladies in London reading about your heroic deeds."

"You don't think I deserve some credit?" he teased.

"My motives are entirely selfish. With a host of beauties rushing to form a queue behind Miss Montague, what hope would I have of kissing you again?"

The roguish look in his eyes marked a sudden change in him.

"Every hope." His velvet voice stirred the hairs on her nape. He reached for her, his firm fingers sliding slowly over hers, alluding to something illicit. "I could find you in a crowd of a thousand women. There wouldn't be a queue. There'd be you. Only you."

A coil of desire tightened in her belly. He'd carried her to bed last night, touched her in places no other man had.

Lady Gambit

Had he taken liberties? If only she could remember every tantalising detail. "As honesty seems to be the theme of the moment, I believe you have something to confess."

He did not hesitate to answer. "What do you want me to say? That it's you I think about in bed at night? You're on my mind when I rise each morning. I've imagined stripping you out of those clothes too many times to count." The intimate nature of his comments had her sex pulsing. "Tell me, Miss Chance. Do you dream about me?"

She liked this playful, passionate side to his character. It encouraged her to be bold. "I dream of more magical kisses. I've imagined you carrying me to bed, your large hands slipping over every soft curve. You didn't tuck me in but climbed in beside me."

For once, neither of us slept alone.

He hissed a breath. "We play a dangerous game."

"Is it a game?" she said, "or just two lonely people seeking comfort?" Aaron would beat him to within an inch of his life if he ruined her. It was only right they discuss the threat. "Either way, I'll not have you risking your life for one night of pleasure. Besides, I'm told such feelings are fleeting."

Mischief danced in his dark eyes. "I have every reason to believe one night would not be enough."

Judging by their fervent kisses, he was right.

"One night is all we might have. If Aaron found out, he would make you pay in ways you could not imagine."

Mr Flynn would be on his knees, begging for an end to his misery.

"I'm not afraid of your brother. But I'll not take a gift meant for your husband." His voice was firm now, resolute. "Nor would I do the unthinkable and ask you to marry a man you don't love just to ease a physical ache. A loveless marriage damages more than the two people involved."

No, she suspected these cravings weren't love.

Though she was hardly experienced enough to judge.

But what was this force of nature, the magnetic pull that made them act so recklessly? If it was lust, perhaps the feelings would fade. How were they to know? How might they find out?

"You're a man who plans for the future." His desire for financial independence was the driving force behind his success. "I live for the moment. I never expected to like you, Mr Flynn. I never—"

"Dorian. You should call me by my given name when we're alone."

She smiled. "Dorian." Her insides melted as the word slipped from her lips. "I liked you the moment we met." She'd felt an instant attraction. It hit her like a bolt from the heavens whenever their eyes met. "Still, it's unfair to draw you into an affair when there is so much at stake."

His long exhale carried the sound of regret. "I like you, Miss Chance, more than I'd care to admit, but—"

"Delphine. We're friends, are we not?"

"Delphine." Each syllable fell like a soft moan of pleasure. "If I were a different man, I would visit your bedchamber tonight and say to hell with the consequences. But that would make me as selfish as my father, and that's one thing I could never endure."

It occurred to her that Mr Flynn would always be alone.

He had not sought a companion in five years.

He would not marry for anything but love.

It was evident he had never suffered this dilemma.

Sensible adults would show restraint ... but what if this was the beginning of something special? What if their happiness depended upon one reckless decision? If she had one wish, she would rather glimpse her future than know the secrets of the past.

"You make a habit of comparing yourself to your father when you're nothing like him. I don't know what happened between your parents, but you're not—"

"My father lusted after his wife's maid. He bought her a cottage and visited her until he grew bored." His tone was like a Baltic wind, bitter and biting. The deep creases on his brow said this was a tragedy, a tale without hope. "He sired a son out of wedlock, a son he didn't give a damn about until the boy came of age and proved useful."

He spoke as if the boy were a stranger.

Perhaps that's how one dealt with pain.

They were still holding hands, and so she gave his a gentle squeeze. "He wants you to marry Miss Montague, but you refuse. He tries to buy your loyalty, which is why you work so hard, why Mile End is your sanctuary."

It would have been so easy to accept his father's gifts. The fact Mr Flynn had chosen the hard path was a testament to his moral character. Indeed, it only made her admire him all the more.

"It won't be my sanctuary for much longer. I limit my visits to Mile End because I refuse to have that man in my house. It takes skill to evade his spies. It won't take long for him to learn I own a house south of the river."

A pang of guilt hit her squarely in the chest. He'd not wanted this case, he'd not wanted houseguests either, but Mr Daventry had left him with little choice.

"Then we will leave Mile End and find somewhere else to hide." He had already done more than anyone could ask of him. "I shall send a note to Aaron at once and have him make the arrangements."

"No."

"No? But you—"

"I made a promise I intend to keep." He met her gaze. The same tenacity that had earned him his independence shone in his dark eyes. "A man is nothing without the strength of his word."

And yet, there had to be another reason he wanted her to stay at Mile End. He could have suggested joining them at another location, tried to find a different solution.

"I'm not convinced that's why you want me to stay." Her bold statement was met with silence. "If we're friends, Dorian, you must trust me with the truth."

He shifted in the chair. There was a short pause before he found the courage to say, "I like having you there. I like knowing you've touched my things. I told myself I craved peace and solitude. The truth is there's something beautiful about the chaos."

Tears gathered behind her eyes. She had taken so much for granted. The days spent cramped in Mrs Maloney's small bookshop were the happiest of her life. There was always someone to talk to, someone to laugh with, cry with. Someone to love.

She thought about their family meetings around the table at Fortune's Den, the arguments, the skylarking, the laughter. The scene was so opposed to the solemn image of Mr Flynn dining alone.

"Strong bonds are formed during hard times." She had found love and kinship amid her family's suffering. Yes, there were rules. Yes, Aaron kept secrets, but she should have had the faith to challenge him. He would have listened if she'd fought harder. "What is the definition of family?"

He shrugged. "How should I know? I was only allowed home from school if my father agreed to visit. My mother blamed me for his inconstancy. I was the insufferable wretch who kept him away."

She brought his hand to her lips and pressed a lingering kiss to his broad palm. "Family is not defined by blood. Family is about friendship and trust and loyalty."

"One loyal friend is worth ten thousand relatives."

She smiled. "You quote Euripides. The ancient philosophers were so wise. How is it, hundreds of years later, we're still learning the same lessons?"

"Ignorance is the curse of humanity."

Upon hearing the harried clip of footsteps in the corridor outside, she released his hand but had one more thing to say before they were interrupted.

"Whatever happens between us, know that I will always be someone you can count on. There will always be a place beside my hearth for you." Their lives were bound together now. "Should you ever crave company and a little chaos in your life, you can always depend on me."

Chapter Ten

Dr Casper Collins, an ageing man with bad breath and flabby jowls, stood beside the rickety bed in his office, a poultice pressed to the raised lump on his head. "Nora Adkins is the devil incarnate."

"Oh? Why do you say that?" Dorian recalled the woman who had pranced about in her cell spouting gibberish. Had Nora lost all grasp of reality, or was she trying to convey a covert message?

"A mere mortal cannot move that fast." The doctor would rather blame the supernatural than his lack of foresight. "I left her lying there, blood seeping from the wound, while I went to fetch a bandage. I didn't know she was behind me until she thumped me with the bottle."

"Was she not strapped to the bed?" Dorian stepped past the doctor to examine the unbuckled leather straps. As always, his gaze drifted to Miss Chance, who was attempting to read a note on the doctor's desk. "Did a guard or porter not wait in the room? Is Nora Adkins not considered a dangerous patient?"

The doctor's cheeks reddened. "It was late. The porters were dealing with a tussle between two patients in the women's gallery. Nora was injured. She could barely walk, let alone attack a man in a wild frenzy."

Miss Chance silently urged him to keep the doctor talking, and then she turned the note to face her and scanned the script.

"The Superintendent said she fell. Would that be your medical opinion?"

The doctor nodded. "She hit her forehead while locked in her cell. I can think of no other explanation."

Dorian could. An aggressive guard sought to punish Nora, and that's why she walloped the doctor and ran. "Might a member of staff have attacked her? Someone with a key to her room?" Someone keen to silence a witness.

The man's cheeks ballooned at the ridiculous suggestion. "Any rumours of mistreatment are baseless. Yes, we restrain some patients for their own safety, but to my knowledge, we do so with the utmost care."

"Did Nora say anything while you were tending to her wound?" Miss Chance said, stepping away from the desk so as not to arouse suspicion.

"Just the same gibberish she has been spouting for a week."

"What exactly did she say?"

The doctor wiggled his forehead and winced. "Forgive me. It's hard to think with this throbbing pain. Erm … she said something about Lucifer and a red eye on a stick making people dizzy."

"Anything else?" Miss Chance was determined to

press the doctor for information. "Think. It may be important. Nora may be a danger to herself and the public. We must locate her without delay."

The doctor pursed his lips. "She said something about finding the girl before it was too late. Then she stole my keys and locked me in this room."

Finding the girl?

Had Nora escaped to find Caterina?

How would she know where to look?

"I'll need to see her room," Dorian said firmly.

The doctor obliged and accompanied them to the dank cell at the end of the long gallery. All was quiet. They passed people shuffling along the capacious corridor, looking befuddled about where to place their feet. They met the blank stares of those behind locked doors, their solemn faces pressed to the bars.

"When someone absconds, it unsettles the other patients," the doctor explained, opening the door to Nora's cell. "It's like the lull before the storm. It will be hell in here tonight."

Miss Chance put her hand to her mouth as she crossed the threshold. The pungent stench of filth and bodily odours were often worse in the height of summer. "It's hard to believe Miss Adkins spent sixteen years in this room." Creases formed on her brow as she scanned the small space. "Most patients are released within months."

The place was cold, dank and dreary.

There was nothing in the room but a bed.

"We consider Miss Adkins an incurable case," the doctor said, unperturbed by the pitiful conditions. "I believe they held her for a month at the old site in Moorfields before transferring her here."

"Has she received any visitors?" Dorian hoped there was a record in the files. One name would be enough. One name might be the only clue they needed.

"Not to my knowledge."

"Then who pays to keep her here?"

The man gave a nonchalant shrug. "A family member. They pay a lump sum to the board per annum. That's what my predecessor said."

Something strange was afoot.

Nora Adkins had the air of a person raised in the rookeries. Someone of modest means could not afford to keep a relative at Bethlem. Not for sixteen years.

Aware the doctor had no more information to impart, and keen to rifle through the files, Dorian asked him to escort them back to the office.

The Superintendent was waiting for them outside the apothecary shop in the hall. He marched towards them and handed Dorian a pile of papers bound with tatty string. "That's all I have on Nora Adkins. Approach the board if you have plans to return. I'll not have your visits unnerving the patients. Nora would still be in her cell if you'd not come to harass her."

Desperate for them to leave, Powell gestured to the burly porter tapping his foot by the open front door.

Dorian found this weak attempt at intimidation amusing. "Your sly manner tells me you're hiding something, Powell. For your sake, I hope I'm wrong. If you're to blame for what happened here, it will be your neck for the noose."

They left Powell quaking in his boots and walked to St George's Road, where Gibbs had parked the carriage. Daventry's man was a blunt fellow who made it clear he was a colleague, not their servant.

"Mr Daventry arrived with a note." Gibbs reached down from atop his box and handed Dorian the missive. "We've a detour to make before we visit the Old Swan. I'm to take you to Nelson Square. It's half a mile as the crow flies. The details are in the letter."

While Miss Chance watched him intently, Dorian broke the seal and scanned the missive. "It appears your brother blackened Meldrum's eye when questioning him this morning. Daventry believes the lord is hiding at his sister's house in Nelson Square while the lady is taking the waters in Bath."

Miss Chance was not surprised to hear of her brother's violent outburst. "Is there any mention of a confession?" Her sudden laugh said she knew the answer. "Strike that from the record. Had Lord Meldrum given my brother cause to believe he was responsible for the shooting, he'd be preparing for a dawn appointment."

He glanced at the paper in his hand, a visceral loathing taking command as he read the last few lines. "Meldrum denied any involvement but has made you an offer of marriage. He will make you mistress of Farnworth Park if Aaron agrees to clear his debts."

The lady's cheeks ballooned. "As if I would be so shallow as to accept. Surely he knows Aaron would never place money or reputation before the wishes of his kin."

"Lord Meldrum is a respected man." And one Dorian would likely throttle if he laid a hand on Delphine Chance.

Lady Gambit

"Respected enough that people would overlook your status. Your children would hold an important place in society."

She looked at him like he had two heads. "Whether I'm heir to a fortune or from lowly beginnings, I will marry for love. Shame on you for suggesting otherwise."

He stepped closer and lowered his voice. "All the more reason we should keep a tight rein on our emotions. I would hate for you to regret giving me the gift meant for a man you adore." His words lacked conviction. Having her had quickly become the only thing he coveted.

"You're the man I admire most," she said, offering every temptation. "Is that not a promising beginning?"

Gibbs coughed to gain their attention. "Can you have this discussion in the carriage? I'm paid to ferry you to Nelson Square, not listen to a lovers' quarrel."

"We're colleagues, not lovers," Dorian snapped.

"And I'm the Sultan of the Ottoman Empire. Move your arses."

Dorian shot the man a stern look and opened the carriage door. He knew Gibbs was as coarse as they came but admired his honesty.

"When we question Lord Meldrum, we should focus on the facts," Miss Chance said once they'd settled inside the conveyance. "We will use other methods to frighten the lord into confessing his sins."

"What facts?" Dorian held the overhead strap as the vehicle picked up speed. "We know nothing about Meldrum except that he's destined for the Marshalsea." Although noblemen always found a way to save their rotten necks.

The aristocracy was a mischief of rats.

They gathered in cities, greed making them fat.

"We know he's on Bethlem's Board of Governors. I saw a letter on the physician's desk." She sounded proud of her efforts as she fixed her intelligent gaze upon him. "And we know he visited the hospital last night when Nora was reported missing."

"We do?"

"We do." She reached into her reticule and removed a small scrap of paper. "The physician was warned not to mention Lord Meldrum's secret visit." She touched his hand when giving him the note. Her coy grin said it was deliberate. "We might use it as leverage."

He scanned the barely legible script. "I'm impressed. You saw the importance of biding time." He wasn't sure if it was admiration causing his heart to gallop or the thought of how he might reward her for her efforts. "A good investigator knows not to question a witness until they have gathered more facts."

"As Aaron is dealing with Lord Meldrum, I planned to give him the note, but perhaps there's a reason fate left it for me to find. Just like there's a reason we've been forced to work together."

"I don't doubt there's an invisible force at play."

This ineffable bond they shared transcended the ordinary.

Her mouth curled into a smile that could light the night sky. "You see how much easier it is when we're both open and honest. Let's make a pact not to keep secrets."

He laughed. "Very well, though don't ask me what I'm thinking unless you're prepared to hear the answer."

Lady Gambit

The carriage rolled to a stop in Nelson Square. To avoid warning Meldrum of their arrival, Gibbs parked on the east side of the square, though he still had a clear view of the impressive townhouse.

"I'll move the carriage once you're inside," Gibbs said as they alighted. "After I've made sure we're not being followed."

Miss Chance placed a calming hand on her chest. "If only we'd been this careful the day my brother was shot."

"It takes one mistake to change the course of fate," Gibbs said. He had been spending too much time with Lucius Daventry because there was something of a wise scholar in his tone. "It might be years before you understand why the gods moved the playing pieces."

Dorian suspected the gods had a small part to play. Daventry had forced him to take the case, to have Miss Chance as a guest at his house and work alongside her. Daventry had left them alone to explore their growing desires. Was it a coincidence Destiny and Daventry began and ended with the same letter and had the same number of syllables?

He was still thinking about the dramatic turn of events when the young butler greeted them at Meldrum's door. As agreed, Miss Chance introduced herself as she was more likely to gain entrance.

"I shall enquire if his lordship can receive you."

"I'm quite certain Lord Meldrum will want to see me," she said with a winsome smile. "Please explain that I am here with my chaperone to discuss his recent proposal."

The butler looked down his nose at Dorian and

demanded to know his name. Then he bowed and said, "Please wait here."

Less than a minute later, they were ushered into the opulent drawing room, where Meldrum sat cradling a glass of brandy and nursing a bruised eye.

He rose, albeit awkwardly, his good eye coming to rest on the enchanting woman who had no plans to marry him. "Miss Chance. What a pleasure." Meldrum was trying to be charming, but the thread of fear in his voice was unmistakable. "I must admit, I am somewhat surprised to see you here. Indeed, I must ask how you knew where to find me?"

Miss Chance gave a charming smile. "I overheard Aaron cursing you to the devil, my lord. He told my brother Aramis that if he wished to question you further, he might find you at your sister's abode."

Meldrum visibly shivered. He was a short man of thirty, with a mop of golden hair and a cherub-like face. He was dressed impeccably in a dark green coat and beige trousers. Yet Dorian imagined him creeping into Miss Chance's bedchamber at night, wearing a white nightshirt and a wicked grin.

"Does your brother know you're here?" Meldrum's bottom lip quivered.

That's when he dared to look Dorian in the eye.

They knew each other, of course.

Meldrum was a coward who'd hidden behind the other boys at school until Dorian learned the importance of the term *divide and conquer* and spent a week singling the bullies out. Meldrum had pissed the bed the night Dorian stuffed dirty stockings in his mouth and warned him not to join the fight again.

"Do you honestly believe he would permit me to come here alone? I asked Mr Flynn to accompany me." She glanced at him over her shoulder, her eyes softening momentarily. "Mr Flynn is exceptionally skilled at locating missing persons. I have hired him to find my parents."

Meldrum kept his tone even when he said, "I'm told you'll soon be master of Helmsley Hall, Flynn. Your father was boasting at the club and said we'd read the announcement soon."

Helmsley Hall was the gift the Marquess of Bexley had bestowed upon his illegitimate daughter, Miss Montague.

"You're mistaken. My father does not determine who I marry." He could feel Miss Chance's intense gaze boring into him. "When the time comes, I shall choose my own bride, just as I've chosen my own profession."

Meldrum snorted. "You'd rather live above the Old Swan than at Helmsley? I know men who would give their right arm to marry a woman as divine as Miss Montague."

"What I choose to do is not your concern. I'm here in a professional capacity. As Miss Chance said, I've been employed to find her parents, and hired by the magistrate at Bow Street to catch the blackguard who shot Theodore Chance."

Meldrum stepped back, his confidence faltering. "If you've come to blacken my other eye, be assured I had nothing to do with that blasted shooting. Only a fool would maim one brother when there are three more waiting in the wings."

The door suddenly burst open. A gentleman in his late thirties with a thick moustache and side-whiskers strode into the room. He took one look at them and came to a crashing halt.

"Don't mind Bertie." Meldrum gestured to his dark-haired friend.

Bertie raised his hands in mock surrender. "I do beg your pardon. I didn't know you had guests. I shall leave you in peace."

Bertie made to retreat, but Meldrum wouldn't hear of it. "Stay. If Flynn means to accuse me of attempted murder, I want a witness."

"We're here to discuss your marriage proposal, not to accuse you of a crime," Miss Chance said as per the plan, though the thought of her marrying any man turned Dorian's stomach. "Mr Flynn will want to ask you a few questions. My brother was shot during an attempted abduction. He needs you to prove that your desire to settle your debts did not lead you to do something foolish."

With Meldrum drowning in a mire of debt, he had no option but to invite them to sit. "I'm innocent of any crime. I have nothing to hide."

Bertie—introduced to them as Gerald Bertram, an old friend Meldrum met on his Grand Tour—took the chair by the hearth. Keen to woo the woman who might save him from the Marshalsea, Meldrum cupped Miss Chance's elbow and escorted her to the plush sofa. Dorian sat in the adjacent chair and was forced to watch Meldrum fawn over Miss Chance.

Meldrum turned to face the lady, his knee brushing hers. "Your brother said he would rather tie a noose around his neck than call me kin. What makes you think you can persuade him otherwise?"

Miss Chance's smile radiated confidence. "My brother cares about my welfare. If he thinks I am happy, he will agree to the match. But before we continue, I must know you did not plan to have me abducted to force my brother's hand."

Meldrum shrugged. "What can I do but give you my word?"

"You can help to find those responsible."

The lord stared blankly. "Isn't that Flynn's job?"

"If you want to win the lady's hand, you must show willing," Bertie said with a weak chuckle. "You can ask at your club. You can pester the *ton*'s best gossips. It's the obvious place to start."

Dorian might have agreed but could think of nothing but Meldrum's pasty white paws mauling Miss Chance.

"The lady knows you're marrying her out of desperation," Bertie said. "A romantic gesture may soften the blow."

Meldrum snorted. "I think a title is compensation enough. She can have the run of Farnworth Park. I'll not trouble her there."

And Aaron Chance would be forever keeping the bailiffs at bay.

Bertie sighed. "Forgive my friend. He's a dolt who's forgotten that all men are equal in the Marshalsea. Fear not, Miss Chance. A strong woman might be just the thing to help put his priorities in order."

Meldrum's cheeks flamed. "What the blazes, Bertie! You're supposed to be on my side."

"Trust me, I am." Bertie laughed. "I am."

"You're aware I have no memory of my parents?" Miss

Chance looked at her clasped hands resting in her lap. "They may be criminals. Aaron took me in while I was living on the streets. Why would you want to court scandal by marrying someone the *ton* considers inferior?"

The devil covered her clasped hand with his own. "I knew you were beautiful from the rare glimpses I've seen. Sitting with you now, I find there's something quite compelling about your countenance."

The muscles in Dorian's abdomen tightened.

It took every effort to remain in the chair.

He pursed his lips before he swore and ruined the investigation.

"You flatter me, my lord. But I cannot consider your suit until Mr Flynn has vouched for your innocence. He can only do that if you answer his questions."

Glad of the distraction and that Meldrum was prompted to release Miss Chance, Dorian said, "What do you know about Nora Adkins?"

"Who?"

"She's a patient at Bethlem Royal Hospital. You're on the Board of Governors. You visited the hospital late last night when Nora Adkins absconded."

Meldrum paled. He tried to hide his shock with a frown. "What has that madwoman escaping got to do with the attack on Miss Chance and her brother?"

Dorian shrugged. "Nothing. Everything. Please answer the question, my lord. Have you had any dealings with a patient named Nora Adkins?"

The lord mumbled his frustration. "I'm not permitted to discuss a patient with anyone outside the hospital. We're bound by—"

Lady Gambit

"Cursed saints! Tell them what they need to know." Bertie gave an exasperated sigh. "Flynn is leading a criminal investigation. He's well within his rights to demand the basic information." He paused before blurting, "Meldrum is being blackmailed. He will show you the letters."

Meldrum shot to his feet. "You damned fool! Why the devil did you tell them? I'll be the laughing stock of the club. Flynn will use this to ruin me."

The lord was doing an excellent job of that himself.

"Because you need professional help but are too stubborn to ask." Bertie faced Dorian, a pleading look in his eyes. "Meldrum inherited the problem from his father. He's had no choice but to comply with the demands. Heaven forbid the public learn that they've kept a sane woman locked in a cell for years. Let alone a peer is responsible."

Miss Chance failed to stifle a gasp. "How dreadful."

"I assure you," Dorian began, wondering how Meldrum's father knew Nora Adkins and what it had to do with Miss Chance, "you may speak in the strictest confidence. I shall use any information you have to find the culprit."

Protecting Miss Chance was all that mattered.

If he had to protect this fop in the process, so be it.

After a brief debate, Meldrum left to fetch the letters.

Bertie wasted no time and was quick to spill the beans. "He's terrified this Nora woman knows he's the one keeping her in Bethlem. That's the real reason he relocated to Nelson Square. He's scared out of his wits."

"He *was* keeping Nora at Bethlem," Dorian corrected. "She is currently at large in the city. There is one consolation. If Nora Adkins is mad, the public will help us find her." Yet the woman's shrewd actions said she might be entirely sane.

"The Superintendent sent Meldrum a note last night." Bertie kept his voice low as he glanced at the door. "They've been paying him to turn a blind eye for years, but that's beside the point. Find the blackmailer. He's the one who wants the woman kept locked in a cell. Find him, and we'll all sleep a little easier at night."

Meldrum returned. His hands shook as he gave Dorian the letters. "The first one is dated August 1814. My father was on the Board of Governors at Bethlem. It's around the time they were moving to new premises in St George's Fields."

The paper was tatty and foxed, and the ink had faded. The blackmailer wrote in large, bold strokes. He knew about the lord's mounting debts and his affair with his wife's cousin. He knew the lord had stolen money from a benefactor to pay his debts, money meant for the hospital's relocation.

"My father found Nora Adkins with her hands and feet bound in a disused property in St Giles," Meldrum said, gesturing to the letters. "He fed her laudanum and invented a story to have her committed. When he died, more letters arrived, urging me to keep the pact or face ruin."

Dorian flipped through the missives. "And you've been accepting money to keep Nora at Bethlem ever since?"

"A tea chest arrives every January filled with a hundred sovereigns." Meldrum's voice brimmed with shame. "Just like the agreement the blackmailer had with my father, the money is used for the patient's keep."

"Have you ever spoken to Nora Adkins?" Miss Chance said.

He turned to her and smiled as if the sight of her lightened his mood. "Once, in a futile attempt to discover the blackmailer's identity."

"Did she say anything that might help Mr Flynn discover her whereabouts?"

"One thing. She said all that mattered was finding Caterina."

Chapter Eleven

The Old Swan
Long Lane, Smithfield

The old timber tavern had stood in Long Lane for two hundred years. It was an area popular with cloth merchants, and being a stone's throw from Smithfield Market, it was a bustling hive of activity. Hawkers walked the street selling their wares. Grocers stood on the pavement arranging produce in carts outside their shop windows. Children and dogs darted about, getting under people's feet.

Delphine looked at Mr Flynn as the carriage stopped outside the quaint tavern. He'd hardly said a word since Lord Meldrum grasped her hand and renewed his desire to make her his wife.

"How long have you lived here?" she said, breaking the silence.

Brief seconds passed before he answered. "Seven years. I took lodgings above the tavern when working at

Bow Street." His eyes remained downcast, his mouth a thin, pensive line. "My father offered me a townhouse in Mayfair and a sizeable allowance if I agreed to stop working. He said he'd not paid for my schooling to watch me wrestling with ruffians."

She studied him, a new hunger taking command of her now. The need to learn everything about him, every secret, every hope and aspiration, was another craving she could not sate.

"You never mention your mother."

His eyes rose to meet hers.

The pain she saw there cut to the bone.

"She died when I was fifteen. I'd not seen her for three years." The cold, distant tone of his voice spoke of indifference. "When my father tired of her, she married a merchant. I wasn't welcome in the house, and she severed all ties."

His mother had abandoned him?

Tears gathered behind her eyes. Questions bombarded her mind. An inner voice warned her to change the subject, but they'd agreed to speak openly, and bad feelings festered.

"So you stayed with your father when you came home from school?" Had something awful happened? Was that the reason for his growing animosity towards the man who'd sired him?

His snort dripped with mockery. "The Earl and Countess of Retford would not permit a bastard to live in their mansion house. Especially when the lady is barren and has failed to give her husband an heir."

Her heart constricted before the next question left her lips. "Where did you go during the holidays?"

His eyes remained locked with hers. Had he seen her throat tighten? Did he know she could feel his pain? "Where does a boy go when he has no home?"

Nowhere.

A tear slipped down her cheek. She imagined he would rather live in a gaming hell with people who loved him than have the freedom to roam the world alone.

He leaned forward and dashed away her errant tear, though he continued stroking her cheek once it was dry. "There's no need to cry for me, Delphine. What hurts us makes us stronger. I'm a better man for their neglect."

"You're an exceptional man."

"You're the first person to say so." His gaze dipped to her lips. "God granted me a boon the day he forced me to take your case."

She wanted to kiss him, to throw herself into his arms and hold him tightly. What if she'd not met him that day? What if she'd had a change of heart? It hurt to think of him wandering the empty corridors at Mile End. It hurt to think of them going their separate ways once the case was solved.

"We have Mr Daventry to thank. He can be quite a hard taskmaster. Aaron would not have permitted me to remain at Mile End had the gentleman not been so insistent."

A smile played on his lips. "Daventry excels at manipulation." He glanced at the bundle of papers on the seat beside him. "Now we need to discover who is manipulating Lord Meldrum."

Her skin crawled at the memory of Lord Meldrum's clammy hand clasping hers. She would rather spend her days alone in silent prayer than marry the ignoble fellow. Once he owned her, she would be nothing more than a pawn in his game. "We're going around in circles. For every question we answer, another is revealed."

"That's the nature of enquiry work. Once all other possibilities are exhausted, we will be left with the truth."

She didn't want to think about that day.

It would come soon enough. Dorian Flynn was too clever, too committed to neglect his duties. Until then, she must make every second count.

She peered at the Old Swan's facade. "I would like to visit your room, if I may. I'm curious to see how it differs from Mile End." And the desire to touch his private things was doubtless part of this growing addiction.

"Do you think that's wise?" The gleam of something forbidden in his eyes stole her breath. "The room is small and quite cramped. There's barely space for one. We'll be bumping into each other."

An erotic image entered her mind. Him kissing her against the door, his mouth hot and insistent. Her breasts crushed against his chest, his large hands gripping her buttocks. She might have pictured him tearing off his coat, his breath coming in ragged pants, but Mr Gibbs broke her reverie by thumping on the carriage roof in a fit of impatience.

"I'm paid to work," he called when Mr Flynn lowered the window. "Not sit like a stuffed bear while you whisper sweet nothings in the lady's ear. Get the information you need and let's be on our way."

"Oh, he's so rude," she said, biting back a grin.

Mr Flynn smiled as he gathered the papers and opened the carriage door. "Gibbs has a point. You're a delightful distraction, Miss Chance."

"So are you, sir. This mutual appreciation makes it hard to concentrate." She accepted his proffered hand and almost lost her footing when she struggled to tear her gaze from his fingers.

"What is it?"

She gave a coy shrug. "Every time you touch me, something magical happens. It's quite baffling."

"It's not baffling at all." He made sure her feet were firmly on the pavement before releasing her. "Our need for each other is like a feral beast. Now it's been awakened, it won't rest until it's sated."

Sparks of desire ignited a fire in her belly. "Perhaps we should do something about it before it becomes too difficult to focus on the case."

"I thought we agreed there was nothing to be done." He noticed Gibbs glaring at them and lowered his voice. "We'll have this conversation once we're alone. I need to fetch a few things from upstairs. We can talk then."

Something in his eyes said they would do more than talk.

He turned to Gibbs. "We'll be an hour at most. You might question the shopkeepers. Attempt to get a description of the man who lay in wait for me last week. He may have pestered them for information."

Gibbs had other ideas. "I'll search the tavern and wait inside. I've orders to protect Miss Chance. There's no telling who's lurking there."

Mr Flynn tutted. "I can protect Miss Chance."

"I don't see how. Your eyes never leave her lips."

Mr Gibbs marched into the premises but stopped to hold the door open for her. That's when someone called Mr Flynn's given name. When he froze in the doorway, dread marring his rugged features.

"Dorian!" came the stern voice again.

A tall, broad man stood on the pavement, the breeze ruffling his swathe of grey hair. From the impeccable cut of his coat and the elegant equipage parked in the lane, this overbearing fellow was the Earl of Retford.

Mr Flynn did not turn around or attempt to introduce her. He touched her waist lightly and whispered, "Wait for me inside the tavern. Tell the landlord you're my guest. Go now. I shall join you in a moment."

Before she could offer comforting words or place a calming hand on his chest, he ushered her over the threshold and closed the tavern door.

Noticing she looked lost, and unlike his usual clientele, the landlord rounded the counter. "Can I help you, miss? If you're looking for Mrs Pinkerton's shop, it's at the end of the lane. Folk say she has the prettiest ribbons this side of the Thames."

She glanced out the leaded window to where the earl stood, his hands braced on his hips. "I'm here with Mr Flynn. He asked me to wait inside."

The landlord followed her gaze. "Ah! I see. The earl came looking for him earlier. Sent his groom in again twenty minutes ago. Happen he's determined to talk to Mr Flynn today." He gestured to the circular table near the window. "That's his usual seat. Why don't you wait there? I'll fetch you a small mug of ale."

"Thank you." She took a seat, removed her bonnet and placed it on the table.

She saw Mr Gibbs, busy checking every nook and cranny. He studied the men huddled around a table, taking turns to flick a coin into a narrow pot.

Nerves had her wringing her hands. It didn't help that the window was open or that sitting at Mr Flynn's table gave her a perfect view of the street. She could hear every cross word spoken, see the lines of frustration etched on the earl's brow.

"Who is she?" The earl jabbed his finger at the tavern door.

"A client," Mr Flynn said bluntly. He pulled back his shoulders and straightened to his full height, a defence against a titan. "I'm investigating a case of attempted murder."

The earl scoffed. "It's obvious she's more than a client. It's bad enough you're peddling your services like a common hawker. If you must bring these street girls home, for God's sake, do so after dark."

"Or I could buy her a cottage and visit her there."

The earl's face twisted into an ugly mask of outrage. "Yes, if you must, but don't fornicate in the street like an animal."

"Fornicate?" Mr Flynn hardened his tone. "I handed the lady down from a carriage. Since when is that considered disreputable?"

"Lady, begad? Only a harlot accompanies a man into a tavern."

Lady Gambit

The words sliced through her with sabre-sharp precision. She put her hand to her mouth to stifle a sob. The truth was hard to hear, but she was not ashamed of her friendship with Mr Flynn. Kissing him felt like the most natural thing in the world.

Mr Flynn was not ashamed, either. He gritted his teeth. "Call her that again and it's the last word you will ever speak to me. Don't give me a reason to sever all ties."

The earl's eyes burned with indignation. "Have you taken leave of your senses? You could have the world at your feet if only you weren't so stubborn."

Mr Gibbs chose that inopportune moment to bring her a mug of ale. He plonked it down on the table and pulled out a chair. "Don't let that devil's words upset you. Take a swig of ale. It's better than most I've tasted."

Her hands shook as she reached for the stoneware mug. "It's not personal. How could it be? The earl doesn't know me." Yet she wished she was a society lady, someone special enough to appease the earl. Someone accomplished in art and music. Someone who walked like they were floating on air.

"Happen it wouldn't matter if he did," Mr Gibbs said bluntly.

"Thank you for your confidence, Mr Gibbs."

"I don't mean you ain't good enough for the likes of them. You're too good if you ask me. I mean nothing pleases a nabob. Their kind are never satisfied. Vanity. That's the ingredient that spoils the soup."

In the silence that followed, she heard the earl shout, "Do you know how embarrassing this debacle is?"

"As embarrassing as being the only boy at school on

Christmas Day?" Mr Flynn countered. "You lost the right to play God with my life when you left me alone for the sake of appearances."

"I thought you were with your mother."

"The school wrote to you on many occasions."

Like a guilty man in the dock, the earl muttered and mumbled as he attempted to defend the accusation. "What has the past got to do with anything? People make mistakes. I mean to rectify the situation by—"

"Trying to force me to marry for money and status."

"Mr Flynn?" A woman dressed in the first stare of fashion entered the fray. She appeared like a golden-haired angel from heaven—all sweetness and light as she gripped her pretty parasol and fluttered her lashes.

Mr Flynn inclined his head and modified his tone. "Miss Montague. Forgive me. I did not see you standing there."

"I did not mean to creep up on you, sir. I confess, I was to remain in the carriage until your father gave the signal." She glanced at the Old Swan's facade, a little knot of confusion forming between her perfectly arched brows. "Is this where you live?"

"Yes," he said, though Delphine sensed his inner torment. A desire to prove he didn't need his father's help or his money. A desperation to keep his private affairs a secret.

"How bohemian." Admiration swam in the beauty's blue eyes. "I came to invite you to dine with us tonight. My father has business in town and is here for a week. You know the address. Berkeley Square at seven? I believe we have a great deal to discuss."

Lady Gambit

Miss Montague was a delightful picture of perfection.

The Earl of Retford thought so, too.

The lady presented her gloved hand. "Will I see you tonight, Mr Flynn?"

He clasped her fingers and pressed a light kiss to her knuckles, but one of the sotted fools jeered as his coin fell into the pot, and Delphine missed Mr Flynn's reply.

Dread filled her chest.

She was going to lose him.

This time, her memory would be her tormentor. Every look, every tender touch and unforgettable kiss would become the bane of her existence.

"Is there a rear exit, Mr Gibbs?" Unable to bear the sight of the graceful Miss Montague a second longer, Delphine downed her ale and stood. "Excuse me. I find I'm in desperate need of air."

Run! Run, my darling. Save yourself.

The desire to flee had her tearing through the taproom. The landlord called to her. Mr Gibbs stomped behind, but she knew running was the only way to numb the pain.

Why had she not heeded Aaron's advice?

Why did the thought of losing Mr Flynn hurt like the cut of a knife?

Too many questions bombarded her mind. A mind that was dark and fathomless. A useless mind unable to provide any answers.

She reached a wooden door in a narrow corridor, but it was locked. Feeling trapped, she gripped the handle and rattled with all her might.

Aaron would fix everything.

He would keep her hidden at Fortune's Den. Mr Flynn

would marry Miss Montague and learn to be happy. And things would return to how they were before she had made a dreadful mistake.

Nothing will ever be the same again.

A woman's harried voice entered her head.

You'll live, and you'll be happy.

I promise you that, my darling.

When I tell you to run, run. Your life depends upon it.

"Who are you?" she cried as a tidal wave of grief swept her legs from underneath her. She collapsed to the cold stone floor. "Do not forsake me. I need you."

"I'm here." Mr Flynn's rich masculine voice cut through the chaos. He thrust the papers at Mr Gibbs and instructed him to keep them safe. Then he scooped her into his muscular arms. "Hold on to me tightly. Rest your head against my shoulder."

He held her close as he marched through the taproom and up the stairs to a room on the first-floor landing.

The musky scent of his cologne enveloped her. It calmed her restless spirit, much like the night after their first meeting, when she slept with his handkerchief beneath her pillow. She sagged against him and closed her eyes, feeling safe for the first time in days.

Would this be the last time he'd hold her?

Would Miss Montague charm him tonight?

Would he realise he had the world at his feet?

Tears gathered behind her eyes, an impending storm as desolate as her memory. But then another voice echoed in her head. One she knew and loved dearly.

You're Delphine Chance.

Never forget it.

Lady Gambit

She opened her eyes and met Mr Flynn's concerned gaze. "Thank you for rescuing me. I'm fine. You can put me down, Mr Flynn."

He was standing in a small bedchamber, much like the one above Mrs Maloney's bookshop. It was clean and tidy and smelled of him.

"What the devil happened?" He lowered her gently to her feet. His hands slid over her body to ensure she kept her balance. "Did you remember something, something about your parents?"

She held his forearm, the desire to touch him like the sweetest torture.

"It's nothing. Sometimes, the weight of my problems overwhelms me." She tried to push thoughts of Miss Montague aside. "Pay it no mind. We should question the shopkeepers and return to Mile End. If we stand any chance of finding Nora Adkins, we must search her file for clues."

His brows knitted together. "You were eager to see my room. Now you mean to leave without taking a peek. Why?"

The knot in her stomach tightened. Her insecurities were not his fault, and so she pasted a smile. "You're a private man. I wasn't sure you'd want me examining your personal possessions."

He released her. "I have no secrets from you."

The intimacy of the moment fed her infatuation with him. "I keep one or two from you," she said with a coy grin.

"Yet we made a pact to speak honestly."

To be honest meant telling him she was jealous. That

she was likely a thief, a nobody who could never compete. That losing him would be a pain she could never bear.

To protect her heart she should lie, but then she pictured the young boy waiting at the window for no one to come. The man who'd chosen a solitary existence because it hurt less than feeling unloved.

"You do not need Aristotle's wisdom to know you're the only man I have ever wanted. The only man who has ever made my heart sing."

He arched a brow. "How can one judge with limited experience?"

"I have four brothers. I know what I admire in a man. I know what I feel when I'm in your company." Though she struggled to put it into words.

She moved to inspect his room, forcing herself to focus on one object at a time, though her greedy gaze darted about like a March hare. She noticed his shaving implements and soap arranged on the washstand. The white shirt folded neatly on the bed. The unlit fire in the grate. One clean glass turned upside down on the dresser, along with one clean plate.

He inhaled sharply when she touched the forest green coverlet on his bed.

"Everything is so neat."

"I pay the landlord's wife to tidy the room daily."

She would take the role without pay, though would spend most of the time lying on his bed, her face buried in his pillow. "Let me know if the position becomes vacant."

The book on his nightstand conjured an image of him sitting alone in the candlelight, trying to fill the empty hours. The silver flask probably contained brandy, a means

Lady Gambit

to warm his bones and help a troubled man fall asleep. It didn't bear his initials. It wasn't bought as a gift.

"Reading calms the mind and soothes the soul," she said, resisting the need to open the nightstand drawer. "I spend a lot of time on my own, lost in the pages of a book."

"It's one of the many things we have in common." His hand came to rest on her arm, and he drew her around to face him. Warm brown eyes studied hers. "Are you going to tell me why you ran?"

She shrugged like it didn't matter. The earl thought she was a harlot, but that's not what upset her most. "I panicked. I was afraid and heard the familiar voice telling me to run. All I could think about was putting some distance between us."

"Between us? Why would you run from me?" It took him seconds to come to a logical conclusion. "You left your bonnet on the table downstairs. That means you sat by the window and heard my father's vile diatribe."

Shame's heat rose to her cheeks. "I am a harlot. We've spent the day alone, but my brother thinks Mr Daventry is our chaperone. I've kissed you twice and—"

"It was more than a kiss. We devoured each other's mouths until we could hardly breathe. If you were a harlot, I would be inside you at every given opportunity."

"You would?" A delicious shudder ran through her, but then she recalled Miss Montague's tempting offer, and jealousy twisted in her gut. "A better opportunity awaits you elsewhere. Miss Montague is a good match for you." Oh, how it hurt to say those words. "Bitterness has made you blind to what is obvious to most."

He jerked in response, though his hand never left her arm. "I don't want to strip Miss Montague slowly out of her clothes. I have no desire to settle between her thighs or bury my face in her hair. I don't want to lie naked with her in bed, drinking wine, making love."

She swallowed past the growing lump in her throat. He painted magical scenes. Dangerous scenes. "Lust has you in its powerful grip. I know because I'm at its mercy, too. I would give myself to you in a heartbeat. But when you dine with Miss Montague tonight, I want you to imagine it might be the same if you kissed her."

"I'm not dining with Miss Montague tonight."

"But I thought—"

"You thought what? That I'd kiss one woman and entertain another. Allow me to remind you what I said when we met. I'm not in the habit of kissing anyone. I cannot explain what's happening between us, though I suspect it's a damned sight more complicated than lust."

They stared at each other.

The unexplainable thing thrummed in the space between them.

"Dorian, everything about my life is confusing. Everything except how I feel about my brothers and how desperately I want you."

He inhaled sharply. "Then forgive me if I take liberties, but I cannot fight these feelings anymore." He tucked her hair behind her ear and cupped her cheek. "I refuse to fight them anymore." His mouth found hers, the kiss unlike the others they had shared.

It was soft and slow and sensual.

An act of surrender.

Their breath mingled as they dared to kiss open-mouthed. Tingles scattered over her skin. The intense passion that always consumed them simmered in her blood. Whatever happened between them, she wished for one thing.

If she must dream at night, she didn't want to picture a faceless man or feel the panic of drowning beneath the weight of her burden.

She hoped to dream of this perfect moment. To remember the taste of Dorian's lips and the warmth of his touch. To remember how beautiful it felt to know that someone truly wanted her.

Chapter Twelve

Dorian prided himself on being a professional man. A stickler for rules. Too sensible to fall for a woman's charms. Too focused to let romantic notions affect his long-term goals. Yet he lost sight of everything when he kissed Delphine.

He should be questioning the landlord, discovering if anyone else had come looking for him in the last few days. But her mouth was so warm and wet he forgot about the case, about his father's selfish schemes, about what this meant and where it would end.

It was all so confounding.

He would fight a heathen army for her and die with her name on his lips. If Meldrum touched her again, he would string him up from the nearest bough. To hell with the consequences.

But he was too damned weak to drag his mouth from hers.

Too feeble to find the strength to say no.

How could he when she had found the secret door to

his heart? Why would he refuse when she was the one person who gave his life meaning?

She broke contact first, her breath coming in ragged pants. She looked up at him, arousal swimming in her bewitching brown eyes. "I love my brothers," she uttered, "but these moments with you are amongst the happiest of my life."

She enriched his life in ways he couldn't explain. "It's hard to believe we've only known each other mere weeks." He'd spent a lifetime becoming a man who would make any father proud. Now he would ruin an innocent because he was too damn selfish to let her go.

Yet he couldn't help but feel this was part of a larger plan.

Indeed, there was only one way to appease his conscience and satisfy his desires. A way that would bring Armageddon down upon them both.

Marriage.

His father would disown him. He would seek ways to end the marriage, devious ways that would leave Dorian free to wed Miss Montague. Before that, Aaron Chance would beat him to a pulp. During a private conversation, he had stared Dorian in the eye and warned him what would happen if he dared to touch Delphine.

"I feel like I've known you forever." She pushed a lock of hair from his brow, and he was lost in the tenderness of her touch. "Which why I sense something is troubling you. Is it the case? Is it your father? Is it something I have done?"

"It's not you," he was quick to reassure her. He kissed her once on the lips. How could it be her? She had quickly become the only thing that mattered. "It's what our families will do if they learn of our secret liaisons."

Though she smiled, a glimmer of fear crept into her expression. "I know my brothers make vile threats, but I will find a way to appease them."

"My father will unleash the devil's wrath on those you love." He had to let her know what they risked to spend these precious moments together. "He will do everything possible to ruin your family."

Her mocking chuckle said she was confident Aaron Chance would save the day. "It won't come to that. Too many men are in my brother's debt. It gives him a power beyond compare. But let's not think about it until we've solved the case. We can address the problem then."

Solved the case?

He almost scoffed.

Nora Adkins was at large, no doubt running from the fiend who'd tried to kill her to hide the truth. How could they unlock the secrets of Delphine's past when she had no memory? Who were her parents? Who was blackmailing Lord Meldrum? And did the devious Mrs Haggert have a part to play?

They had files to read.

People to interview.

But in this moment, nothing mattered more than kissing her, touching her, indulging in every erotic pleasure. He was a man, not a blasted saint. A man who'd caught a glimpse of the one thing he'd longed for his whole damn life.

She laid a hand on his chest. The same irresistible impulses drove her, too. "I've never felt like this about anyone. I'm tired of feeling trapped by rules and obligations. For once, I want to make my own choices, and I choose you, Dorian."

She came up on her toes, brushed her mouth over his and coaxed his lips apart. He moved with her, bewitched by their softness, every muscle tightening when her tongue slid sensually over his.

Merciful Lord!

She tasted divine.

He would die if he didn't have her.

Seeing Miss Montague confirmed he had room in his life for no one but Delphine. With her, every mundane task would become an erotic exploration. A visit to the stables would lead to a roll in the hay. Passing in the corridor would become a rampant romp in an alcove. A moonlit night would be an excuse to make love under the stars.

"Do you understand what will happen if we don't stop kissing?" His cock was a solid rod in his trousers. He needed her beneath him in bed so he might ease the damnable ache.

She looked up at him, all swollen lips and shy smiles. "I know we'll make love, but I don't know where to begin."

He brushed the backs of his fingers across her cheek. "You're doing a remarkable job so far. I've never been so aroused. Perhaps you'd like to feel the evidence for yourself."

She bit her bottom lip and nodded.

He captured her hand, smoothing her fingers slowly down his abdomen to the hard ridge demanding her attention. "That's what you do to me." His heart was racing, his blood pumping too fast. "I feel like I've been waiting a lifetime for you to touch me."

He'd waited forever to feel a connection like theirs.

Her little gasp mirrored the spark of intrigue in her eyes. "Is it painful?" She stroked him from root to tip. Sweet mercy! Those dainty fingers had a power of their own. "I heard Aramis telling his wife the ache is pure torture."

He grinned. "The torture is longing to be inside you, though fearing it might not happen. It's knowing how badly I need your touch."

A teasing smile stole over her lips. "Unfasten your trousers."

That wasn't the reply he'd been expecting.

He held her gaze while unbuttoning the placket.

Hers dipped the moment his cock sprang free, her eyes widening in alarm. "I should have known everything about you would be large. Thank heavens I know there's pleasure to be had between a couple in bed." She flexed her fingers. "May I touch you?"

"I might die if you don't."

The feel of her warm hand on his skin was beyond divine. Her fingers circled his shaft, exploring how easily they glided back and forth. The sweet agony in those strokes had him tilting his head back and hissing a breath.

"Tighten your grip."

She firmed her fingers. "Like that?"

"Just like that."

"The wait is pure torture for me, too, Dorian." The sultry sound of her voice had arousal pumping through his veins. "Only you can fill the emptiness. I fear having you will make me want you all the more."

"You're sure about this?" His cock wept in anticipation. He was seconds away from laying her down on the bed and taking her fully clothed. "We can be intimate without me taking your virtue."

He meant every word.

He would honour her decision.

"What about Mr Gibbs?"

"Gibbs can find his own pleasure." He chuckled. "He's gone to warn Aaron that Nora Adkins is on the loose. We have until he returns to indulge our whims."

Her smile said she welcomed his attentions. Her hand moved from his cock to his coat, and she was suddenly pushing the garment off his shoulders. "Then we should not delay."

She stepped back—though he felt colder for it—and unbuttoned her pelisse with haste. He gaped in awe as she undid the pearl buttons and shimmied out of her dress. While she removed her petticoat and corset, he stared at the luscious curve of her breasts.

"Are you not undressing?"

"In a moment." While he noticed the shadow of rosy nipples beneath her chemise, he felt the heat of her gaze caressing his manhood. "I'm merely enjoying the show."

She smoothed her hands over her hips, drawing his gaze from her moist red lips to her slender waist. "Should I keep this on?" she said, her tone turning coy.

"No, love. Show me everything. We've nothing to hide from each other." Though his voice carried the sheer strength and confidence of his masculinity, the old weakness surfaced.

He had plenty to hide.

Her apprehension pushed to the fore, her little shrug drawing his attention back to her breasts. "Is it normal to be nervous?"

"I'm nervous, too. You're all I've thought about for days." Though he'd won the fight with his conscience, and her beauty held him spellbound, his scarred skin would repulse her.

"I want *you* to undress me," she said, pulling the pins from her hair and shaking out the wealth of ebony curls.

God, she stole his breath.

"It would be my pleasure." His hands were on her in seconds, gathering the hem. If there'd been time, he'd have kissed his way up her thighs, tongued her womanhood, left a scorching trail to her breasts.

"You're right. It's a little cold." She used her arms to cover her modesty as he dropped her chemise on the floor.

"I'll soon warm you." He reached for her hands, interlocking their fingers as he spread her arms wide so he could look at every delicious inch of her. His cock swelled. Every muscle in his abdomen tightened. "You're so beautiful." So beautiful his lungs ached for air.

"So are you." She tugged her hands free and began unbuttoning his waistcoat. The minx stroked his cock before unknotting his cravat. "Is it wrong to hope Gibbs encounters a herd of cattle blocking the road? I don't want this day to end."

He traced his fingers slowly down the curve of her

back. "We're at the mercy of our passions. This might be the first time we make love, but it won't be the last."

Staring at the open neck of his shirt, she said, "Is it always like this between lovers?" She drew her fingers gently down his throat to the dusting of dark hair on his chest.

"Like what?" He couldn't take his eyes off her.

"Magical."

"Only with you."

His reply must have given her the courage to be bold. "I need you out of these clothes, Dorian." She was pulling the fine lawn shirt over his head, unaware of the ugly marks on his back. "Finding missing people must be physically demanding."

"More frustrating than demanding."

"Your body is pure muscle." She slid her arms around his waist, her fingers fluttering over his back while her naked breasts brushed against his chest.

It was the sweetest torture.

His blood burned. He'd never been so hard. But he was waiting for the heat of passion in her eyes to dim, waiting for her to feel the subtle roughness of his skin, the physical record of painful experiences.

"Every man has a vice," she whispered. "What's yours?"

"You." He was addicted to her taste. He craved her touch. Though he knew taking her virginity was wrong, he'd rather perish in hell than deny himself the pleasure.

"Then indulge yourself." Her voice carried the hum of arousal. But then a frown marred her brow, and her fingers found the marks that had turned him from a boy into a man overnight.

She moved to study his back.

Then he heard the sound he dreaded.

He heard her gasp of pity.

Every part of her body ached to join with him. The hunger writhing in her veins was like a compulsion she had to feed. But the flames of desire cooled the moment she stepped around him and saw the scars on his back.

She couldn't prevent a gasp from escaping.

Tears sprang to her eyes as she counted the scars. There were four. One long one cutting across his upper back—the skin dark and thick where it had healed. Three smaller ones on his lower back, dissecting the furrow of his spine.

"It's not pretty," he said, the words coated with shame.

"They look like whip marks." A vision of him crying in pain burst into her mind and she fought the need to sob aloud.

"I was forced to defend myself at school. It was the punishment for disobeying the rules." His tone carried the same air of detachment she heard whenever Aaron spoke of the past. "The aristocratic fathers of entitled brats couldn't permit a bastard to beat their sons."

"Does your father know what happened?"

"I have no idea. One of my tutors bandaged the

wounds. He took pity on me and kept me company whenever I was left alone at school. Mr Brown was my saviour. The man who taught me the importance of making my own way in the world."

She didn't think Mr Brown should take all the credit. Dorian Flynn was a remarkable man in his own right. His back told a story of healing, of the resilience he'd needed to survive. But it was the tale of the vulnerable boy that brought a lump to her throat.

"Do you want to talk about what happened?" Giving him the opportunity to air his grievances was the least she could do. "Or we can continue undressing if you prefer."

"Nothing will prevent me from having you, Delphine. Certainly not a distant memory from the past."

"Then I shall continue. Tell me if you want me to stop."

He laughed. "Who is being ravished here?"

"Isn't it obvious? I'm seducing you." She smoothed her hands over his back and pressed a series of slow, shivery kisses down his spine. "Men like to think they're in control, but I've been seducing you since I laid eyes on you in Miss Darrow's yard."

"Then it's time to switch roles." He faced her, claiming her mouth in fierce possession, his tongue diving in long, deep strokes until she was damp between her thighs.

There was no sign of the vulnerable man, just a powerful specimen of masculinity who could arouse her to the point of madness in seconds.

Before she knew what was happening, he'd stripped off his boots and trousers and carried her to bed.

"Do you know what I mean to do now, Delphine?"

Tingles danced over her skin when he whispered her name. She watched as he kissed his way up her thigh, his dark eyes almost predatory. "You look like you're going to eat me."

"That's exactly what I mean to do." He buried his head between her legs. "Eat you, lick you, wring every last whimper from your lips."

She was so drunk with desire, she let him kiss her most intimate place. She let him suck her, let him ease his long fingers into her and pump slowly until her world shattered, and she cried out.

"Dorian!"

He rose above her, his toned body swamping hers. "We don't need to continue. It's not too late to stop."

She wasn't sure if he was joking. She was certainly in no mind to dress and go about her day. Taking this man into her body was the only thought on her mind. "Why would I want to stop? I need you." She ran her hands over the corded muscles in his arms. "Don't wait."

He bent his head and kissed her, his tongue penetrating her mouth with consummate skill. Then he was nudging her legs wider, pressing her down into the mattress, whispering how he was going to make her come hard again.

"Soon, you'll be hugging every inch of me, love."

She did not know what to expect. No one had told her how it would feel to make love to a man. But when Dorian eased into her body, the sudden wave of emotion took her by surprise.

"Are you all right?"

"Yes." She looked up at him, sucking in a breath as he stretched her, claimed her, owned her. Indeed, she couldn't shake the thought that she belonged to him now. "Don't worry. It doesn't hurt."

Why would it hurt?

He chased all her pain away.

Perhaps that's why she rolled her hips, clung to him, encouraged him to fill the emptiness again and again and again. Why they were sweat-soaked and panting yet still couldn't stop.

Even when they lay drowsy and sated in the warmth of his bed, her hand on his chest, his on her hip, one thought brought clarity.

She didn't care if her past remained a blur. She wanted to remember nothing other than how glorious it felt to make love to Dorian Flynn.

Chapter Thirteen

"How are you feeling this morning?" Delphine touched Theo's brow and the back of his neck, thankful he was not burning with a fever.

"Strong enough to be out of this godforsaken bed." He winced as he straightened and leaned back against the plump pillows. "But now that Nora woman is on the loose, Aaron insists I remain at Mile End."

Aaron had arrived to take supper with them last night. He'd questioned Dorian about the case, demanding a detailed account of his progress. Dorian made no mention of them progressing from kissing to making love but invited Aaron to sit with them in his study, and together they examined Nora Adkins' file.

"Aaron feels better knowing you're here with me," she said, trying to heal her brother's wounded pride. Theo may be injured, but he would find the strength to tackle an intruder. "Mr Flynn has supplied you with weapons in case anyone attempts to enter the house." She gestured to the duelling pistols in the open walnut box on the dresser. Making Theo feel useful was crucial to his swift recovery.

"I trust Flynn is behaving like a gentleman." Theo's intense gaze showed no sign of weakness. "I pray he's not as *familiar* as he was in Miss Darrow's yard."

She kept an impassive expression, though every cell in her body tingled at the memory of Dorian buried deep inside her. "Mr Flynn is the son of an earl and every bit a gentleman."

"My father was an earl's son and a reprobate whose family disowned him. The scoundrel forced his own child to fight in the pits to line his pockets. So forgive me if I have concerns about the ill-begotten Mr Flynn."

She sat on the bed and touched his arm affectionately. "Mr Flynn is not the enemy. He saved your life. You're lucky he came to the rescue after the dreadful way you behaved in Miss Darrow's yard."

Theo tutted, his mouth twisting into a cynical line. "I owe the man a debt, but that doesn't mean I won't throttle him if he touches you."

If only you knew how badly I need his touch.
Or knew how my heart aches for him.

"You owe Miss Darrow an apology." The modiste nursed Theo like he was her own brother. She was in no rush to return home and must have lost clients in the process. It didn't seem to matter. One might think she had a reason to hide at Mile End, too. "She's seen to your every comfort and has barely left your bedside."

"I'll not apologise to a woman who lied to me."

"I hope you've thanked her for her efforts."

"Of course. I'm not completely heartless."

The remark brought instant relief. She'd come hoping to find the playful rogue who could make women jump through hoops, only to find the light in Theo's blue eyes had dimmed.

"Do you want to hear about the progress we've made?" she said, quickly changing the subject as she was leaving for Covent Garden in an hour.

"Our daily discussions are the only thing keeping me sane."

She told him what Mr Flynn had found in Nora's file last night. "Mr Powell lied. There was a record of Nora's admission papers. They state Meldrum found her on London Bridge, not in a building in St Giles. She was committed to Bethlem for harassing passersby and threatening to jump into the Thames."

"Meldrum did say his father had concocted a story."

"Yes, but it gives us a reason to question Mr Powell again." Dorian was convinced the Superintendent had something to hide. "Lord Meldrum signed her committal papers, as did Mr Powell. Both agreed she was suffering from delusional insanity. Nora has not had her case reviewed for more than a decade. When one considers the injustice of it all, it would drive me a little mad."

Theo narrowed his gaze. "You seem different today."

"I do?" She felt the first flare of a blush creeping up her neck. She was in love. Her heart ached whenever she thought about Dorian Flynn. The minutes spent apart felt like hours, the hours like a lifetime. "I'm excited at the prospect of discovering the truth, that's all."

He appeared unconvinced. "You look radiant. Like you're glowing from the inside. Despite the stress of the case, you look happy." His brows dipped into a frown. "Is it Flynn? Men can be charming when they want something."

Charming? Dorian Flynn was irresistible.

"It has nothing to do with men, Theo. For the first time in my life, I feel alive." It was not a lie. "I feel useful, and get to do something more interesting than choosing a new bonnet."

He fell silent, his shoulders sagging. "I didn't know about Mrs Haggert. Had Aaron confided in me, I would have persuaded him to tell you." He reached for her hand and gave it a gentle squeeze. "I know he lied, lied to us all, but all he wanted was to keep you safe."

She didn't blame Aaron.

She would never punish him for caring about her.

"I know," she said wistfully. "I love Aaron dearly. But once we uncover the truth, I cannot go back to hiding in the shadows."

A life without purpose was no life at all.

"No," he agreed. "It must be frightening … getting closer to knowing who you are after being in the dark all these years. I pray you're not disappointed."

Her stomach roiled at the prospect of what she might find. "What could be worse than being left on the streets and spending a year in Mrs Haggert's hen house?"

His expression turned as grave as her thoughts. "Just promise me you'll remember you have a home. Whatever happens, you will always be part of this family. To me, you will always be Delphine Chance." He swallowed hard. "I don't want to lose you."

She blinked back tears and gripped his hand. "You will always be my brother, Theo. Someone dear to my heart. Someone I cherish and adore."

"I couldn't love you more if we shared the same blood."

In the still seconds that followed, affection flowed between them.

She stood before she wept again and became a bumbling wreck. "Well, there's no rest for the wicked. No doubt Miss Darrow is waiting outside with your breakfast tray. Be kind to her. We know nothing about her background, and I'm sure she thought she was doing a good deed when she allowed me to meet Mr Flynn."

Theo pursed his lips and nodded. "What are your plans for today? Return to Bethlem and interview Powell?"

"Yes. If Mrs Haggert can be believed, and I am Caterina, then Nora Adkins knew me. We need to know who blackmailed Lord Meldrum to keep her locked away all these years." It might be the only hope they had of finding Nora.

"You're sure the letters Meldrum showed you are genuine and he's not involved?" Theo's disdain was evident. He often referred to the lord as an obnoxious prig. "Perhaps his father wrote them in case the truth came to light."

"Anything is possible." And Lord Meldrum did seem overly keen to marry her when he had plenty of other options. "That's why I have an appointment with Monsieur

Chabert this morning. The mesmerist helps people unlock hidden parts of their memory."

Nerves pulsed in her throat. It was Dorian's idea. Despite her distrust of mesmerism, he had called in a debt to secure a meeting.

Theo jerked as if he might leap out of bed. "What the blazes? Flynn is not to leave you alone with the fellow. I've heard all kinds of horror stories, tales too lurid to repeat."

"Mr Flynn assures me he won't leave my side."

"Daventry better be there," he said, a little panicked. "Other than Aaron, he's the shrewdest man I know."

"He will be." She offered a confident smile, not one filled with doubt. Mr Daventry was to meet them outside Monsieur Chabert's abode at eleven o'clock. The question was, would he show? "You can trust Mr Flynn. He would not see me harmed just to solve the case."

"Flynn has his own agenda. All men do."

She ignored the comment. He didn't know Dorian the way she did, and her brothers were suspicious by nature. "There's no need for concern. I'll put your mind at ease the moment I return home."

"Home? How strange you should call it that."

"It was a mere slip of the tongue," she lied.

Home was Mrs Maloney's bookshop or the opulent Fortune's Den.

Home had quickly become a beautiful manor known as Mile End.

Home was anywhere belonging to Dorian Flynn.

Chabert's Physiology of Mental Disorders
Seymore Court, Covent Garden

The peel of St Martin's bells echoed in the distance, marking the strike of the eleventh hour. There was no sign of Mr Daventry, whose office was a short walk away. No sign of his agent striding briskly towards them carrying a note.

"We should proceed without him." Delphine scanned the length of Chandos Street, trying to distinguish the gentleman's top hat amongst a sea of heads. "Perhaps Mr Daventry arrived earlier and is waiting inside."

Dorian's hand came to rest gently on her back like it had yesterday when he held her naked body in his arms and kissed her tenderly. "Or perhaps Daventry knows how much we value these precious moments alone."

Desire unfurled in her belly. "I lay awake last night, wishing we were still in your quaint little room above the Old Swan." Wishing they were making love.

Heat flared in his hypnotic brown eyes. "We may have cause to return there again this afternoon. The description of the man who came looking for me is somewhat vague."

According to the landlord, the mysterious visitor had a West Country accent. The silversmith next door thought he hailed from West Sussex. Both agreed he had a forgettable face. Both said the man refused to discuss the private nature of his business.

"Then we should not delay." Excitement gave way to trepidation when she glanced at the entrance to Seymore Court. The narrow alleyway led to Monsieur Chabert's premises. The place where her darkest memories might be revealed. "Although before we visit the Old Swan, we must gain the answers we need from Mr Powell."

Dorian gritted his teeth and cursed Mr Powell to Hades. "Damn the devil. He's been playing us for fools. If we don't get the truth from him today, I'm taking him into custody for hindering the investigation."

Judging by the anxious look on Mr Powell's face when she suggested he had a problem with liquor, he would comply.

Not wanting to be late for the appointment, she approached the alley. All four doors in the dim passage were painted black. The tall brick buildings loomed over her like silent soldiers, forever watchful, the weight of the chilling things they'd witnessed hidden behind the stone facade.

A shiver crawled over Delphine's shoulders when Dorian stopped walking and gestured to a door. There was no shiny plate outside alluding to Monsieur Chabert's business. No wooden plaque bearing the mesmerist's name or profession. Whatever occurred behind the door of Number 20, Seymore Court was a guarded secret.

"Are you certain this is the right place?" She hugged Dorian's arm tightly, her thoughts like frenzied whispers telling her not to proceed.

Theo's warning echoed in her mind. What horrors had

occurred here? People said mesmerism was akin to witchcraft. Would she lose something more precious than her memory? Would her attachment to Dorian fade like a morning dream?

Dorian faced her, though his fetching countenance did little to settle her nerves. "I've had dealings with Chabert before. He's skilled in the complex workings of the mind." He glanced at the entrance to the alley, making sure they were alone before kissing her tenderly on the lips. "He will help you understand why you cannot remember anything about the first ten years of your life. Though it could take months to unravel every thread."

She swallowed past a lump in her throat. One's memory was a delicate instrument. "In unlocking the door to the past, I may forget other things. What if these last few weeks become a blur? What if I forget about you?"

What if they were gambling with their future?

She had expected another kiss to reassure her but noted an element of fear in his eyes. "I'm sure that won't be the case, but we will seek Chabert's advice before we proceed."

He turned to the ominous black door and knocked three times in quick succession. He counted to five and knocked again.

"Anyone would think we're meeting the Crown's best spymaster." She tried to sound jovial, but the mysterious ritual played havoc with her nerves. It didn't help that Dorian had consulted the Frenchman as a last resort. "Why the secrecy?"

"People are distrusting of things they don't understand. Chabert was attacked in the street by a client's husband."

Lady Gambit

Dorian paused upon hearing the clip of footsteps in the hall beyond the door and looked at her. "Chabert is a quirky fellow. His methods may seem unusual, but we can trust him. If there's a way to unlock your mind, he will know."

The scrape of metal and the jangle of keys preceded the door creaking open mere inches. Large brown eyes peered at her through the tiny gap. "Can I help you, madame?"

Dorian stepped closer. "It's me, Chabert."

Recognition dawned. "Of course. Forgive me. I sat on my spectacles this morning and broke one lens." He opened the door and scanned the deserted alley before beckoning them inside. "Come into the sitting room. It is more comfortable there."

Monsieur Chabert was a short, slender man with wavy black hair. Though he looked to be around forty, he had an innocent, boyish face. They followed him along the sparse hallway. He moved slowly, almost gliding in an effort to remain silent as he led them into his unusual sitting room.

Red velvet curtains and dark oak furniture added an element of warmth to the gloomy space. The console table was littered with strange objects—a picture of an eye, a musical box shaped like an egg, a wooden tower with a hundred steps circling the structure. Her gaze drifted to the painted mural filling one wall. A Japanese woman stood on a footbridge over a river, staring at a path that disappeared into a forbidden forest.

Once the introductions were made, the Frenchman said, "May I fetch refreshment?" He motioned to the plush sofa and invited them to sit. "People, they say it is a warm summer's day, but they have never lived in Toulouse."

They laughed before declining his kind offer.

She could barely breathe, let alone drink.

"You should have a dram of something to settle the blood, madame." He used his thumb and forefinger to indicate a small measure, though it was the subtle insistence in his voice that made it impossible to refuse. "I sense your hesitance, but you must have faith in the process for it to succeed."

She inhaled slowly to calm her thundering pulse. "I shall do whatever you advise, monsieur, but there are questions I must ask before we begin."

He anticipated her first question, saying, "There is nothing of the supernatural in my methods." He moved to the drinks table, his steps as seamless as a ghost's. "Imagine the mind. It is like a warren of corridors with an endless series of doors. Some are open. Some are closed, but they open with ease. Some are locked, barred to all intruders. Even to you."

Seated beside her on the sofa, Dorian touched her arm gently. "We tend to suppress what is too painful to process."

"Or we label it as something it is not. Jealousy is just a mask for fear." Monsieur Chabert returned to the sitting area and gave her a small glass of sherry. "Often a memory can be distressing, but the emotion we attach to it is the key to opening the door."

The Frenchman encouraged her to toss back the drink. It wasn't sherry—she realised once it was too late—but perhaps some other fortified wine that tasted far too bitter. Every muscle tensed as it slid serpent-like down her throat.

"The drink, it will relax you so I might access your memory."

"It's not sherry," she gasped.

"I did not say it was."

Then what in God's name was it?

Amid the rising panic, nausea roiled in her stomach. She clutched her throat. There was no time to prepare. She had reached the point of no return. She was trapped, about to plunge into the darkness, into a mysterious maze of fog only this stranger could help her navigate.

"I'm here. You're safe." Dorian knelt before her, clasping her face in his warm hands, reassuring her all was well. "I'll not leave your side, not for a second."

If only that were true.

Indeed, she hoped it took forever to solve the case.

Blinking to clear her vision, she looked for Monsieur Chabert. "Promise me I won't forget him. Promise me I will feel the same when I wake from this strange stupor." She would forsake every lost memory to keep her love for Dorian alive.

The Frenchman gave a curious hum. "Ah, you are lovers, *non*? Be assured, madame, I do not meddle with the heart, only the complex tunnels of the mind."

Dorian was more than her lover.

He was her friend, her confidant; he was everything.

"I cannot forget him," she reiterated.

"Of course. And if your heart is true, nothing will change."

Monsieur Chabert instructed Dorian to help her from the sofa to the wooden chair facing the richly painted mural. "Stand behind and keep your hands resting on her shoulders. You will be a constant reminder of the present. The reason she will return."

The fellow swept across the room and closed the heavy red curtains. Darkness descended. Though the feel of Dorian's strong hands on her shoulders brought an instant wave of comfort.

While Monsieur Chabert busied himself with lighting the many candles dotted about the room, Dorian bowed his head and whispered, "Don't be ashamed to say what comes into your mind." His thumbs caressed her neck in lazy strokes that had her closing her eyes and rocking gently to the soothing rhythm. "We keep no secrets from each other."

She had a secret.

A secret love that grew stronger by the day.

Indeed, as her mind turned woozy, and she felt herself slip back from reality, she feared she might make a confession.

The Frenchman appeared before her, and she became fixated with the swirling pattern on his waistcoat. "Look into my eyes, madame." He spoke softly, like a melody one could not get out of their head. He tilted her chin so their gazes locked. "Hold this tower and place your finger gently on the bottom step." He cupped her hands around the stone form. "Close your eyes and listen only to my voice. When I tell you, you will begin counting the steps. Each one leads to a door in your memory."

She did as he asked.

In a deep, soporific tone, he began describing the cylindrical tower, telling a story of how it was built and how the staircase curved round and round. Every word bewitched her, the spell like a persistent hand drawing her down into a peaceful abyss.

Upon hearing his instruction, she started counting, letting her finger climb each tiny stone step. She lost count when she reached twelve, though she was not awake or asleep but somewhere in between. That's when Monsieur Chabert lifted her eyelids and peered at her pupils.

A lengthy silence ensued before he asked his first question.

"You open a door. Inside, you see your ten-year-old self waking in the entrance to a baker's shop. Picture it for me, the sounds and smells of the city. Do you remember why you chose to rest your weary head there?"

It took a little more prompting before an image formed in her mind's eye. She recalled being cold but thankful it was summer and not the dead of winter. She remembered being terrified. Helpless. Alone.

"B-because the step was deep and hidden in shadow," she said but then realised someone else had made the suggestion. Someone had guided her to that specific place on that particular night. "I was told to stay there."

"By whom?"

She tried hard to focus but couldn't see a face. "I don't know."

"Where did you come from?"

The answer was out of reach, far beyond her grasp. More questions followed, but her mind was a blank canvas and she lacked the ability to lift the brush and paint a picture.

"Has someone tried to access her memory before?" she

heard the Frenchman ask. "There is a resistance beyond what I would usually expect."

Dorian spoke, his voice a beacon in the darkness. "Not that I'm aware. If there has been some mind manipulation, it would have occurred before she met Aaron Chance."

"I suspect one session will not be enough to gain the answers you seek. Fear prevents her from opening the doors."

Keen to keep her in this lucid state, Monsieur Chabert urged her to open her eyes and focus on the mural. He brought the picture to life by telling the story of a woman searching for a lost child missing in the woods. Again, his words were so compelling she imagined crossing the bridge and calling her own name.

"Find the girl," he said when her lids grew heavy, and she felt herself sinking deeper into the dream. He encouraged her to take steady steps along the path towards the woods. "Find Caterina. She is alone in the darkness, longing to return home."

As she moved closer, the woods became a park. Despite the gloom, she recognised the views of Westminster in the distance and knew the path around the reservoir meant she was in Green Park.

Fear slithered through every vein in her body.

The desperation to run had her in its powerful grip.

"Where are you?" Monsieur Chabert persisted.

"Green Park." She was permitted to say that. It was not breaking the rules. It would not have her dangling from the hangman's noose, limp like a cloth doll. "I must hide."

"From whom?"

She saw a figure, nothing more, but knew to keep her

lips pursed tightly. They would slice out her tongue and feed it to the crows.

Monsieur Chabert grumbled in frustration. "Someone has been tampering with her mind. I have seen this before. When under a mesmerist's spell, the person is compelled to answer. Miss Chance, she knows the truth but has been conditioned to remain silent."

Death comes to those with loose tongues.

She didn't want to die.

Not while scattering the flowers or when—

She gasped aloud then. "I'll die if I scatter the flowers. My mother will die if I don't." She knew it was important when the words left her lips but had no idea why.

Monsieur Chabert muttered something in French, which sounded much like a curse. "I must bring her out of the trance. Her mind, it is too fragile. The damage was done in her formative years. Who would do this to a child?"

Dorian rubbed her shoulders. His touch calmed her restless spirit. The love in her heart was an anchor, mooring her to the present and the reason she had come to visit Monsieur Chabert.

"Wait!" she cried because there was something else she could say. A secret no one had tried to erase from her memory. "I was told to hide in Green Park, told someone would come, and I should go without a fuss." Fragments of a memory returned. Strange flickers in her mind's eye. "I was scared and confused and hid in the wrong place. It took them longer to find me."

"Them?"

She recalled seeing them as she peered through the

verdure, the moon a haunting silhouette behind them. She remembered the stark warning, the unsettling words they repeated for days on end.

You say nothing, do you hear?

If they threaten you with the noose, button those lips.

"Who told you to hide in Green Park?" It was Dorian's voice this time. "Who came to fetch you the night you ran? Was it Davey?"

"No." She inhaled deeply as the dense clouds dispersed and a picture formed. What she saw left her rigid in the seat. "It was Mrs Haggert and a faceless man with a ruby-topped walking stick."

Chapter Fourteen

Mrs Haggert had lied.

Davey hadn't stumbled upon Delphine in Green Park. Mrs Haggert had dragged the child from her hiding place. But who was her sinister male companion? Who was the faceless man with the ruby-topped walking stick?

Nora Adkins' words flitted through Dorian's mind as he waited for Chabert to bring Delphine out of her trance. Mention of the unusual accessory proved Nora wasn't completely mad. She may have spouted nonsense, but she had described the man who kept her a prisoner in Bethlem.

Big black hat. Big shiny shoes. One ruby eye on a stick.

It had to be the man who collected Delphine from Green Park.

But what was his connection to Mrs Haggert?

Unfortunately, there was only one way to find out.

"When you open your eyes, you will remember events with renewed clarity." Chabert's words were a little firmer now, though still highly persuasive. "Memories, they will begin to appear from the shadows. But you will not be afraid. You will welcome them into your heart like long-lost relatives."

He met Dorian's gaze.

A silent caution not to force her to remember.

"On the count of five, you will become aware of Flynn's hands on your shoulders, and you will know you are safe."

The comment caused a quickening in Dorian's core. He recalled how delicate she felt in his arms, how fragile and vulnerable she was during moments of self-doubt. She was the beauty amid the chaos. A reason to make plans for the future. Just as her inner strength had helped to tear down his barricades, he would spend his life helping her to cope with her painful past.

"Three … four." Chabert paused before reaching five. He clicked his fingers as the last number left his lips. "You may feel tired," he said, lifting Delphine's chin and gazing deeply into her eyes. Whatever he saw, he seemed satisfied. "Or you may have an unusual burst of vigour. Either way, your mind will be calm, madame, your thoughts like gentle ripples on the water."

"Thank you, monsieur," she said, her voice a mere whisper.

Dorian rounded the chair, his hands slipping off her shoulders. She looked dazed and blinked like she had just woken from a peaceful slumber.

"Do you still remember me, Delphine?"

He would never forget her.

He would never forget the warmth of her smile, the flame of passion in her eyes, and the arousing cadence of her voice as she writhed beneath him, urging him to claim her virtue.

A knot of dread tightened in his throat. Now he knew why Aaron kept her within arm's reach. Love came with the fear of loss. And there was no question Dorian was in love with her.

Her eyes met his. He could drown in those hypnotic brown pools.

"You're not the kind of man a woman forgets," she said. "The space reserved in my mind for you, Dorian, is too sacred for a mere mortal to erase." The sultry edge to her voice had his blood pooling in his loins. "Making more memories will ensure you're never far from my thoughts."

The desire to slake a physical need had him whispering, "I'll give you a memory you'll never forget. I'll be the last thing you think about in bed tonight. The first thing on your mind in the morning."

The hitch in her breath said she wanted him just as badly. She glanced at Chabert, who was busy making notes at his escritoire. "There's a pretty orangery in your garden. It's the perfect place for a secret rendezvous. We might meet there tonight."

"I shall bring the champagne."

Dorian might have kissed her quickly had Chabert not crossed the room and thrust a note into his hand. "I remember talk of a fellow skilled in mind manipulation. A technique he had learned in Vienna. His name was Tobias Trigg. I mention him because he carried a silver cane with a round ruby encrusted in the handle."

Disturbed by the coincidence, Dorian stood and read

the note, shocked to find Tobias Trigg had premises in Seven Dials.

Damn Mrs Haggert. The fabulist had stared them in the eye and invented an elaborate tale. But one did not enter the hen house and cast aspersions, not without evidence. First, they needed to learn everything they could about Tobias Trigg.

"You say *was* like Mr Trigg no longer exists," Delphine said.

"Some say he is alive, but I fear he is dead, madame," Chabert replied, putting paid to Dorian's plan. "I have not seen or heard of him in years. But there may be a record of him at Bow Street. Complaints were filed against him for his irregular methods."

They didn't press the mesmerist for more details because he mentioned his next appointment and began tidying the room. While Dorian helped Delphine from the chair, Chabert dabbed cologne on his wrists and combed his hair.

"Might I ask you to straighten my cravat, madame? I must fix my spectacles. It hurts my head to squint."

"Of course."

Chabert studied her as she obliged him. "Remember, the past has no bearing on the present unless you confuse the two. Live for the beauty of the moment, and happiness shall be the reward."

After that snippet of wisdom, he peered at his pocket watch, then ushered them into the hall and over the threshold.

"Thank you again, monsieur," Delphine said.

"I bid you *adieu*! Return tomorrow if you have any

questions. Try to avoid unnecessary exertion." He gave a sly wink and shut the door.

"How strange," she said as they navigated the narrow passage.

Moments after they'd emerged onto Chandos Street, the reason for Chabert's titivating approached the alley. The vivacious brunette glanced over her shoulder before slipping into the shadowed walkway.

"I have a strange suspicion his next *client* is married," Delphine said, holding Dorian's arm as he scanned the street, searching for the armed thugs.

"Chabert has no scruples. He's sworn never to wed."

"Are you not of a similar mind regarding marriage, Mr Flynn?"

"Keep moaning into my mouth when we kiss, and I may have a change of heart." His cock stirred at the memory, hardening at the mere thought of what he would do when they were alone in the orangery.

"When you kiss me like I'm the most desirable woman in the world, how can I not express my pleasure?" Her fingers tightened over his bicep, moving in long, slow strokes as if massaging his aching manhood. "Do you really have champagne at home? I've only seen you drink brandy."

"I have a bottle of Taittinger in the cellar. A gift from a grateful client who had me scouring Hyde Park, looking for her lost Pomeranian." Lady Allscott hadn't hired him. She'd accosted him on his morning ride and prodded him with her stick.

"You find missing dogs as well as people?" Amusement danced in eyes that dazzled him. Eyes that would caress him across the dining table tonight, urging him to discard his beef and focus on dessert. Eyes he could easily wake to each morning.

Stone the crows!

He was so enthralled by her that logical thought had abandoned him. "Finding people is my speciality, but how could I not help a woman in distress?"

She feigned a sad pout. "And I thought you'd made allowances for me. I thought I'd bewitched you into becoming my hero."

"Your hero?" He'd made love to an innocent. It was hardly noble. He stepped a little closer, bent his head and lowered his voice to a whisper. "When it comes to you, I'm every bit a rogue. If we were at home alone, I'd hike those skirts up to your waist, bend you over my desk and make you sing *bel canto*."

She gulped. "Why wait until we're home to be wicked? We have a comfortable carriage. I'm still a little dizzy after being put in a trance and may need to straddle your lap."

His growl of approval did little to convey the carnal need to mate. "Do you know how hard I am for you right now?"

She glanced at his trousers and gave a throaty sigh. "I need you to strip me out of these clothes, Dorian. I need to be naked with you in bed. Let us return to the Old Swan. If only for an hour."

Lord have mercy!

He was going to spill his seed there and then.

"What perfect timing." Daventry appeared, dressed head to toe in black. He doffed his hat to Delphine. "I hoped to catch you. I'm curious to know what you learned from the mesmerist."

It was rotten timing.

Dorian's blood burned in his veins. His cock had command of his thoughts and senses, a devil urging him to bury himself inside the woman he loved and pump hard until he reached completion.

"I see you're still somewhat dazed, Miss Chance," Daventry said, surely noting her flushed cheeks and ragged breath. "I've news to impart but will wait until your heart settles."

"Yes. Delving into one's hidden thoughts is daunting." She glanced back at the alley as if she'd forgotten where she was. "We were just on our way to see you."

That would have been the most logical course of action had the primal urge to make love not become a distraction. But their need amounted to more than physical desire. She had entered his life in a stunning vision of gold silk, but her courage, kind nature, and passionate heart held him spellbound.

Seeking a distraction, Dorian said, "I'm surprised you didn't keep our appointment. We expected to see you here at eleven."

"Chabert's process requires the participant to relax," Daventry explained. "My presence may have prevented Miss Chance from falling into a trance. And I had important business across town."

"Monsieur Chabert gave me a strange drink, which helped with the process." She touched her abdomen, her nose wrinkling. "It was terribly bitter, but I was able to access a few lost memories."

"Ah! That explains your dilated pupils." Daventry scanned Chandos Street. He beckoned Gibbs, who was sitting atop the box of their carriage parked twenty yards away. "We shouldn't linger on the street. The chances of another attempted abduction are slim, but it pays to be cautious."

They climbed into the conveyance.

Daventry sat opposite them, a knowing look in his eyes. It was like being silently scrutinised by a parent who knew you'd crept into the kitchen to steal the freshly baked biscuits.

Daventry looked surprisingly tense. "As I mentioned, I bring vital news about the case." His sombre tone would make anyone nervous. He removed a folded note from his coat pocket and held it like it was their death warrant. "I've been working on a lead for two days. An important piece of the puzzle."

The hesitance in his voice raised the hairs on Dorian's nape. Daventry was used to delivering bad news. This was different.

"As Flynn suggested, I approached the case as if you were a missing person, Miss Chance. I'm happy to discuss my findings here, or we can return to my office in Hart Street if you prefer."

Delphine gripped the edge of the carriage seat. "Here will suffice. The anticipation is unbearable. I'm not sure I can wait a second longer."

Daventry took a moment to gather himself. Those few silent seconds were telling. "The Pulteney Hotel no longer has records dating as far back as 1814. Flynn urged me to search through the chest of old newspapers I keep in the basement at home. I found no mention of a missing child, not from the Pulteney Hotel or any other hotel."

"Perhaps I was never at the Pulteney Hotel," she said, a tad despondent. "I may have lived nearby or been in the area for another reason. I may have been there to pick the pockets of foreign dignitaries."

Such skills would explain why Mrs Haggert kept her for a year.

"I managed to find the old porter who tended the entrance to the Pulteney Hotel during the month you went missing." The flash of triumph in Daventry's eyes was short-lived.

While Dorian held his breath, Delphine sat forward. "Did he remember me?" Her lips trembled. "Does he know who I am? Was I a guest at the hotel?"

"He recalls a family living in Bolton Street and even directed me to the right address. He said he always remembers the"—Daventry swallowed deeply—"tragic tales."

Delphine hung on his every word now. "Tragic tales?"

Dorian could sense her rising panic. He slid his arm around her waist. How could he not offer comfort in her hour of need?

With a heavy sigh, Daventry handed her the folded note. He waited for her to peel back the folds and read the elegant script. "I'm as sure as I can be under the circumstances. You're Miss Caterina Chadwick. Your father was Oscar Chadwick. He was secretary to the Ambassador to Turkey. While working abroad, he met your mother, Sofia Silva, daughter of an Italian diplomat."

A stunned silence descended.

A knot tightened in his chest as he watched her

struggle to absorb the information. Her hands shook. Her throat worked tirelessly as her gaze fell to the names on the note. A plump tear landed on the paper, the sight ripping Dorian's heart in two.

"They loved you dearly," Daventry said, a croak in his voice. "By all accounts, you were a walking image of your mother. I'm certain the same is true now."

They were the words Delphine had longed to hear, yet they were the ones that broke her spirit. The grief she had been unknowingly holding inside all these years escaped in one long, mournful cry.

Her shoulders sagged. The life seemed to drain from her limbs. Before he could haul her into his arms, she collapsed to the carriage floor and sobbed. Sobbed like the innocent girl snatched from the arms of her beloved parents.

Chapter Fifteen

Delphine woke to find a man sitting at her bedside, his head bowed, his strong, calloused hand wrapped around her cold fingers.

It wasn't Dorian. Her body didn't react to the smell of his cologne. His touch didn't send tingles dancing down her spine. And though the man she loved had a physique that made her mouth water, the sheer power emanating from this man would send Satan scurrying for cover.

"Aaron?" She realised she was still dressed when she reached out to stroke his hair. "Are you awake?"

Slivers of daylight sliced through the gaps in the drawn curtains, though she had no idea of the time or how long she had been dozing in bed. The sweet smell of stewed apples and cinnamon reached her nostrils. She had slept long enough for Mrs Maloney to bake her favourite fruit pie.

Aaron stirred. He raised his head slowly, his tortured gaze settling on her face as if she were a stranger. "I don't know what to call you," he said, his voice filled with despair. "I don't know how to make this right or make amends. All I can do is say I'm sorry. I'm sorry you've had to wait this long to learn the truth."

That's when she recalled Mr Daventry's confession.

They loved you dearly.

You were a walking image of your mother.

Those simple facts had squeezed the last breath from her lungs. She'd collapsed to the carriage floor, a sobbing wreck. The vision of an idyllic family scene was too excruciating to bear.

"You're the last person who needs to apologise." She pushed an errant lock of raven hair from his brow. This rare glimpse of vulnerability was a blessing.

Women would sell their souls to be alone in a bedchamber with Aaron. Yet thoughts of failure would send him slinking further into the shadows. There'd be no hope of a happy ending for him.

"I blame myself." They were the words she had been expecting to hear. "I saw no reason to believe Mrs Haggert had lied. Who would leave you alone on the streets? You were so delicate and dainty and—"

She pressed her fingers to his lips to silence him. "It's not your fault. You were young. You had three brothers to feed, and still you took me under your wing. I'm not sure why. It would have been easier to leave me at an orphanage."

Silence stretched between them.

Talk of the past was taboo.

Now he was more amiable, she had to know everything.

"Why did you risk your life to save me?" If she closed

her eyes, she would be back in Mrs Maloney's bedchamber, staring at the blood gushing from Aaron's stab wound, her sixteen-year-old protector fighting to survive.

Aaron swallowed hard.

"Please tell me," she begged him. "I need to know."

An internal battle played through his strained expression.

"Because no one tried to save me," he confessed. "Because I'd felt the fear I saw in your innocent eyes. A fear my father knocked out of me at the tender age of twelve." His bitter tone belied the flash of raw emotion in his eyes. "During those terrifying nights on the streets, when I was forced to stay awake to protect my brothers, no one put a strong arm around my shoulder. No one assured me everything would be all right."

Tears filled her eyes.

She clasped his hand, grateful he had opened the secret door to his heart. "I didn't know what love was until everything fell apart. Our lessons are entwined, Aaron. We had very different lives before we found each other. But if there is one thing I know amongst all this confusion, it's that you will always be my brother."

"I can't call you Caterina. I mean no disrespect to your parents or the life you had with them. But that's not who you are to me."

She took a moment to process the maelstrom of feelings inside. She couldn't change the past. Nor could she predict the future, but she had power over the present.

"I'm Delphine Chance," she said, because she would probably be dead or working in a backstreet brothel had Aaron not come to her rescue. "Never forget it." She paused, allowing the force of those words to penetrate his steely reserve. "That said, some things have changed."

"Oh?" Every muscle in his face tensed.

"When I return to Fortune's Den, I mean to purchase a membership to The Burnished Jade. I would like to visit Miss Lovelace's club. I like her." There was no question Aaron secretly liked her, too. "I think we could be friends."

She should have chuckled at that, but she looked around the pretty pink bedchamber and knew it would break her heart to leave Mile End.

Who knew what would happen with Dorian? Would this be a whirlwind affair? Two people seeking comfort during a difficult time? While the past was no longer a complete blur, the future was an utter mystery.

Aaron clicked his tongue. "You'd be bored within an hour. You detest dull conversations."

"I spend a ridiculous amount of time tidying my armoire. It's the epitome of dull." Though now she understood the thrill of a passionate affair. She knew what it was to love a man desperately. Dorian had awakened a hunger inside her, an insatiable zest for life.

"I imagine it's a damn sight more interesting than the mindless activities that take place at The Burnished Jade," he said.

Aaron spent a lot of time staring at the club. He fought against his admiration for the proprietor with the strength of a heathen army.

"Miss Lovelace is versatile and caters to all her members' needs. She led a discussion on Marcus Aurelius' stoicism. The ladies received lessons in the art of self-defence in case they encounter footpads."

Aaron scoffed. "Next, she'll be wearing trousers, smoking cheroots and lobbying parliament."

"Miss Lovelace is all alone in the world. She has no choice but to be strong and independent. Make no mistake. She is every bit a woman."

A muscle in Aaron's cheek twitched. He'd either developed a tic or was busy imagining the lady's feminine attributes. It was undoubtedly the latter because he was quick to change the subject.

"I want you to come home today." He sat back in the chair, relaxing a little while she strived to ignore the heaviness in her chest. "Theo is much improved and needs to keep busy before he wastes away in that damned bed."

He was right. They could not remain at Mile End forever, and Theo's recovery was paramount.

But to leave Dorian?

To not feel his presence all around her?

It would break her heart in two.

"We're still no closer to finding the person who shot him," she said, trying to sound practical, not desperate. They needed to locate Nora Adkins and the mysterious Tobias Trigg. Gather evidence from Mr Powell before tackling the wicked Mrs Haggert. "We're safe here. At least for the time being."

"Damn it all, Delphine. I've spent my life taking care of you. I don't need other men fighting my battles. Daventry and Flynn can go to hell."

"Yet Mr Daventry is the one who discovered my true identity. Mr Flynn has helped me unlock hidden memories.

That's how we know Mrs Haggert lied." They were close to finding the answers she craved. She could feel it in her bones. And to spend one more night with Dorian would be a dream beyond measure. "A day or two is all we need. Then I shall return home. I give you my word."

Aaron's intense gaze searched her face. "Very well. You'll come home tomorrow, though you'll not visit Mrs Haggert without me." His expression hardened. "I'll make that wretch pay for her vicious lies."

A vision of Mrs Haggert burst into her mind, a firm hand dragging her from the shrubbery in Green Park. Did she know Oscar and Sofia Chadwick? Was she responsible for their demise?

"Did Mr Daventry tell you the tragic tale of my parents?"

She remembered little after the man's grand revelation. It was as if her mind had shut down to protect her from the heartache.

Aaron frowned. "Flynn told me when I arrived. He sent for me because you were inconsolable. I suppose I should be grateful for that. Perhaps your mother died—"

"Stop! I'm not ready to hear how they perished." There was no telling if the story was true, and she wanted to live with the image of a happy family, just for a while longer.

Giving a curt nod, Aaron stood. "I imagine Flynn will be glad to have the house to himself. I'm told he's days away from announcing his betrothal to the Marquess of Bexley's by-blow."

The remark hit her like a punch to the gut.

She tried to smile, but jealousy had her in its talon-like grip. "Yes, I saw Miss Montague the other day. She's everything a man could want in a woman. Beautiful. Intelligent. Wealthy."

The corners of Aaron's mouth curled in disgust. "I pity Flynn. Who wants to be shackled to an insipid creature for the rest of his days? I took him for a man with more sense."

"One cannot help who they fall in love with." Though she was quite certain Dorian did not love Miss Montague.

"Love? His father has no legitimate heir. Bexley has the King's ear. No doubt Flynn will find himself with a title. The nobility bend the rules to protect their own." Aaron's diatribe against the aristocracy did not stop there, but she became lost in thoughts of Dorian.

There was one thing worse than neglect.

Being exploited by a selfish parent.

Keen to make a hasty retreat, she pulled back the bedclothes and stood. "On the subject of Mr Flynn, I should find him and apologise for spoiling the plans today."

Her skirts were creased. Her hair was a tangle of knots. But it didn't matter. The need to see Dorian was like the magnetic pull of a compass seeking its true north. It wasn't their failure to visit Bethlem that left her dejected, but the hour they'd hoped to spend alone in his quaint bedchamber above the Old Swan.

"Flynn isn't here," Aaron said. "He left when I arrived."

"Oh?" She tried not to look deflated.

"The mesmerist gave him an address for a man named Trigg. He went with Gibbs to see what he could learn about the strange fellow."

She smiled, though the needle on her inner compass would shake erratically until Dorian walked through the door. "While I wait, I shall hunt out Mrs Maloney and beg for a piece of apple pie. I might look through Nora Adkins' file and see if we missed anything."

"I'll help you. You know I hate feeling useless."

The offer chased away the chill of disappointment. Having Aaron's undivided attention was a gift in itself. "Are you sure? It must be getting late."

"Aramis is opening the club tonight. Flynn insisted I remain here in his absence."

She crossed the room and threaded her arm through his. "I have a better plan. I'll steal the whole pie and hide in Mr Flynn's study. You find the cream and the cutlery and meet me there."

Amusement flashed in his eyes. "You recall what happened when we crept into the kitchen and stole Mrs Maloney's bread pudding?"

"She made us eat every morsel. You cast up your accounts in a bucket." It should be a horrid memory, but she had felt so close to Aaron while they'd paid their penance. "This time, we have a weapon in our arsenal."

"We do?"

"Yes, Mrs Maloney would pardon the devil for a bottle of Garvey's sherry."

It was approaching midnight when Dorian returned to Mile End. After visiting Seven Dials and Bethlem Hospital, he'd stopped at the Old Swan to settle his weekly account with the landlord. Then he'd climbed the stairs to his chamber to collect a few papers and had a brief rest on the bed.

He'd done more than rest—he'd reminisced. Like a lovesick fool, he'd inhaled the traces of Delphine's perfume on his pillow, captivated by her alluring scent.

Watching her collapse to the carriage floor had roused the devil in him. The need to end her suffering had him tearing around town, determined to find the bastard with the ruby stick.

He had found Tobias Trigg.

Buried six feet under in Cripplegate Churchyard.

His home for the last sixteen years.

Someone had stabbed the mesmerist through the heart and stolen his precious walking cane. All within walking distance of Mrs Haggert's den of thieves in Monmouth Court.

In a fit of frustration, Dorian headed to Bethlem to throttle the truth from the Superintendent only to find the halfwit had gone home. So, he took advantage of Dr Collins' affable nature and stole the visitors' book while sending him on a false errand.

Indeed, he clutched the book as he stepped down from the vehicle and surveyed his home. But for the faint glow of candlelight in the study window, Mile End stood in darkness.

A pang of excitement led to lustful musings as he pictured Delphine sitting on his desk. He'd enter the room, throw the book on the chair and kiss her like there was no tomorrow.

"Do you need to go out again, Mr Flynn?"

Gibbs' question broke his reverie.

"Not tonight."

He needed to drive deep into the body of the woman he loved. Then he remembered Aaron Chance was visiting. Hellfire! The Chance brothers were probably up playing cards and knocking back Dorian's best brandy.

There was no sign of Theo Chance when Dorian entered his study. Aaron sat perched behind the desk, sifting through a pile of papers. The room smelled of cinnamon and cooked apples, not liquor.

Aaron finished reading something before raising his gaze. "While you were away, we've been studying the notes on Nora Adkins." With a sigh, he gestured to the wad of illegible scribblings. "There's nothing here, only evidence to prove a case of neglect. Though I suspect some documents are missing."

Dorian noted Delphine's absence but said nothing. "I had some success tonight." He prayed his luck wasn't over. "Tobias Trigg is dead. He was murdered sixteen years ago in Seven Dials."

He relayed the evidence in the order it had unfolded, the gossip from two shopkeepers, the epitaph on the tombstone, confirmation from an old sergeant at Bow Street.

"I'll wager Mrs Haggert got rid of him," Aaron said.

"It would seem that way. No one was ever charged with the crime."

"Mrs Haggert knows how to cover her tracks."

Dorian might have mentioned what he'd noticed in the visitors' book he'd stolen from Bethlem, but he'd not give Aaron a reason to remain at Mile End. "We plan to question the hag tomorrow, though I doubt we'll get a confession."

Aaron stood abruptly. "Theo and Delphine are grateful for your hospitality but will return to Fortune's Den tomorrow."

"So soon?" Did his tone betray the heavy ache in his chest? Did his stance mirror the sudden turbulence he felt at the thought of Delphine leaving?

"It's not healthy for Theo to lounge in bed. And I insist on being present when you question Mrs Haggert." Aaron's stone-like expression said he would not be denied. "I almost died because of that evil witch. I intend to look her in the eye and call her a liar."

Dorian shifted uneasily. "There's still so much we don't know."

He needed to call on Meldrum. The lord rarely set foot in the hospital. That changed three weeks ago when he began visiting daily.

"Meldrum is hiding something."

Aaron nodded. "He wants to elope with Delphine."

"Elope?" Dorian swallowed to quell his rising anger.

"I received his letter earlier today. He's persistent, which is a surprising quality in a coward. Daventry thinks we should use Delphine to trap the lord. To discover what he's hiding."

"Good God! Tell me you refused."

"I told Daventry what he could do with his plan."

The rush of relief was almost euphoric. "We'll discuss

what to do with Meldrum once we've learned more from Mrs Haggert."

"Agreed."

The hall clock chimed the midnight hour.

A stark reminder it was too late for him to wake Delphine.

"Well, there's much to do tomorrow," Dorian continued, prompting Aaron to leave. "We should retire if we're to make an early start in the morning."

Aaron looked at him like only children and the infirm needed sleep. "I shall rouse my coachman and leave you in peace."

"You're welcome to stay the night." He groaned inwardly as the words left his lips. He wanted rid of the Chance brothers. If Delphine was leaving in the morning, he hoped to catch her alone before breakfast. "Mrs James has prepared a room."

Aaron snorted. "Aramis enjoys wrestling with reprobates. I should return to Fortune's Den before he murders everyone in the club."

They arranged a time to meet tomorrow, and Aaron left.

Dorian remained in his study, his conscience preventing him from rousing Delphine. He relaxed on the chaise, wishing he was lying amid a mass of clothes on the orangery floor, the raven-haired beauty straddling his lap. He downed a glass of port, wishing it was champagne and Delphine was a little tipsy.

All was quiet in the house when he finally mounted the stairs to his chamber. Although he told himself solitude was the thing he coveted most, there was a reason he kept a room in a rowdy tavern. He simply chose not to acknowledge that all men needed company to some degree.

It was dark in his chamber, but seconds after he'd closed the door, he caught a whiff of a familiar scent. Delphine's exotic perfume assaulted his senses as he moved deeper into the vast room.

The sinful rogue inside him grinned.

He peered into the blackness. Where was she?

Keen to play the game, he checked behind the dressing screen and started stripping off his clothes. She wasn't hiding behind the curtains nor crouched in his armoire. The enchantress was already in his bed.

He moved closer, his cock a persistent ache in his trousers.

For a moment, he thought she was sleeping. Her hair was splayed over his pillow, her breathing slow and deep. He peeled back the bedcovers to find she was naked.

Mother of all saints!

The sight of her creamy skin left him ravenous.

Despite his obvious cockstand, he slipped into bed beside her and came up on his elbow, unable to do anything but stare. He liked the feeling of having her close. A warm welcome after a gruelling day. Someone who needed him as desperately as he needed her.

Tentatively, he reached to brush her hair from her brow.

Did she know she was leaving in the morning?

She opened her eyes, her smile hitting him deep in the pit of his stomach. "I missed you tonight." Her breath fanned his face like a prelude to a kiss. "I couldn't wait until the morning to see you."

The words pierced his soul.

He'd suffer a thousand lonely days just to feel the power of their undeniable bond. "You're all I've thought about tonight. The fact you're here, naked in my bed, is a gift beyond measure."

Her palm settled on his cheek. "I know we risk everything, but I need you, Dorian. I need you to kiss me and chase away the ghosts. I need you to hold me, make love to me."

"Love, your brother is asleep three doors down the hall."

She touched his bare chest, her hand sliding over the muscles in his abdomen to caress his hard cock. "He won't hear us."

A growl of approval left him as fast as his restraint. "God help me, you know how to tempt a man." He closed his eyes against the pleasure of her touch and the womanly scent that said she was equally aroused.

"I've not had to try too hard." Her fingers moulded around his shaft, and she pumped him in slow, teasing strokes. "It's pretty evident you want me."

"Want you?" He trailed his fingers over the curve of her hip. "I can't keep my damn hands off you, but we must be quiet. I'll need to move slowly."

"I just need you inside me."

"Let me see to your pleasure first."

"No." Her hand moved from his shaft to his waist, and she was parting her legs and dragging him on top of her sumptuous body. "I'm so empty without you. I've longed for this moment all day. Hurry."

The need to ease the ache, to feel her hugging his cock as he buried himself balls' deep, made him lose his head. He forgot where they were, that he had guests in the house, that they were unmarried, and he'd likely swing from the nearest bough if caught.

He forgot everything as he eased slowly into her, everything but how wet and warm and tight she was, everything except the urge to pound like a madman and the need to make her come apart beneath him.

"I'm so damn hard tonight," he growled. "I'm not hurting you?"

"No. It's divine."

She gripped his back, her fingers settling over his scars, making them the focus of his pleasure, not his pain. She raised her hips, encouraging him to banish thoughts of the past and push deep into the only place that felt like home.

"Oh, Dorian. I knew we were made for each other the moment I saw you. My life changed the moment you touched me."

By God, he was touching her now. He closed his eyes against the feel of her hot flesh hugging him like a glove. "Do you know how badly I want you? For days, all I could think about was tearing that gold gown off your shoulders and setting my mouth to your soft skin."

He'd taken himself in hand within an hour of leaving her … her image flooding his mind … her name breezing from his lips like fate's knowing whisper.

"I slept with your handkerchief." She sucked in a

breath as he plunged into her again. "Even the smell of your cologne left an indelible impression upon my senses."

Lord! He fought the desire to thrust, to rock into her so fast the bed would creak and take chunks out of the plaster. "Tonight, you'll sleep with me. We can make love again at dawn. I'll show you a different position. One that will benefit us both."

"Show me now."

"You need to be on top of me."

With surprising strength, she gripped his hips with her thighs and encouraged him to roll onto his back. He was still buried inside her, still pushing deep, holding her close, fighting against the knowledge she would be gone in the morning.

Then she eased out of his grip, rising above him like the goddess Venus. "Like this?" she hummed.

Merciful Lord, she was glorious.

He drank her in all at once—the long mane of ebony waves cascading over her pale shoulders. The soft bounce of her magnificent breasts, her rosy lips parting on a pant. Those dark, exotic eyes holding the lure of hidden treasures and mysterious adventures.

"You need to ride me, love. Do it quietly." He gripped her buttocks and helped her rock back and forth. "Imagine you're in the saddle. You once told me you were a gifted horsewoman."

Her eager smile melted his heart. "I'm a natural." She came up on her knees only to slide slowly down his cock, the sensation so hot and wet and exquisite he thought he might die from the pleasure.

He watched in awe as she claimed him, as she begged

him not to stop as he stroked her swollen bud. She came apart in a visual explosion of delights, shuddering as her inner muscles clamped around his shaft, her cheeks flushing, her eyes so glazed she looked drunk on love.

"Dorian!" A sweet cry escaped her.

"Hush, love." He should lock the door, but she leant over him to brace her hands on his pillow. Before he could rouse another thought, he was gripping her hips and thrusting hard and fast inside her.

Perhaps it was the way she angled herself or that he parted her buttocks and sank deep, but she came again, writhing on top of him and panting, "Yes. Yes. Dorian."

He flipped her onto her back, withdrew with nary a second to spare and spilled himself over her thigh.

Contentment, the likes of which he had never known, flowed through every cell in his body. Despite the absence of words or declarations, one emotion defined the connection between them.

Love.

The thought made him smile as he soaked a cloth in the washbowl and returned to wipe her clean.

She grabbed his wrist as he drew the cloth over her thigh. "I don't regret anything that's happened between us. What we have is magical. And when I've floated down from this cloud of euphoria, I'll make sure you know exactly what you mean to me."

"Stay with me." He couldn't bear the thought of her leaving him alone in bed, let alone her leaving tomorrow. The corridors would be cold again. The dining room silent. "Stay until dawn."

"I'll stay until the servants wake."

Stay forever.

He climbed into bed and drew her close, brushing his fingers gently over her back to lull her to sleep. He closed his eyes, too, happiness gripping his body in the form of lithe legs and dainty hands.

He didn't sleep deeply enough to dream. Why would he when he had everything he wanted right there in his arms? But when the creak of the door forced him to open his eyes, what he saw sent him hurtling into a living nightmare.

Theo Chance loomed in the doorway.

A murderous look in his baleful blue eyes.

Chapter Sixteen

The atmosphere crackled with tension. The silence stretched, sucking the oxygen from the air, making it hard to breathe. Theo's broad frame filled the doorway. His clenched fists hung at his sides. His face was a mask of fury. He looked every bit a dangerous devil.

Dorian held Theo's gaze, his heart thundering in his chest.

Their secret was exposed. The weight of judgement loomed. Fear would have most men pissing the bedsheets, but he was not afraid.

He loved Delphine.

Now he had to prove it to her brothers.

"Get dressed." Theo's ice-blue gaze could freeze a man's blood. His voice was a sinister whisper. "Do it quickly and quietly."

It was a command, not a request.

This was Dorian's damned house, but he deserved Theo's contempt.

Although he knew it would rile her brother, he pulled the blanket over Delphine's bare shoulders, stroked her hair and kissed her forehead—hopefully not for the last time.

Theo wouldn't kill him.

Dorian was more than a match for the man, and he was confident the Chance brothers wouldn't hurt Delphine. There would be a fight, punches thrown, blood spilled, bones broken, but he would live to see another day.

Without waking Delphine, Dorian slipped out of bed.

The sight of his naked body had Theo firming his jaw. "There's nothing more loathsome than a man who ruins an innocent."

"She's not ruined if I marry her." He yanked up his trousers and reached for his shirt, guilt sitting squarely in his chest.

The sight of the scars on his back had Theo inhaling sharply. He did not ask how Dorian came by them but muttered, "I see another disgruntled brother punished you for your sins."

Being born on the wrong side of the blanket was his only crime.

"Your comments say a lot about your character." Dorian pulled on his boots. "You're a man who makes careless assumptions."

"You were naked in bed with my sister. It's a fact, not a *bloody* assumption." Theo's hostile glare followed Dorian into the dim hall. He closed the door gently behind him and gestured to the stairs. "Summon your coachman. We're going on a journey. Be warned. It may be your last."

"Do I need duelling pistols? I gave you my best pair."

"You don't need pistols." Theo marched him downstairs like a thief destined for the gallows. "We'll fight like men, not pampered dandies."

So, it was to be a bare-knuckle brawl.

Luckily, Dorian was skilled in the art of pugilism.

He summoned Briggs, though it took the man thirty minutes to dress and ready the carriage.

While Dorian stood wondering how the night would unfold, Theo whispered to Gibbs at the coach-house door before saying, loud enough for Dorian to hear, "Remain in the house. Protect Delphine with your life. Unlike some, I'm sure you mean to keep your vow."

They travelled two miles in silence, except for Theo's groans as he nursed his wounded shoulder and cursed Dorian to the devil. When they left the Newington Road, it was clear they were heading towards London Bridge and most probably Aldgate.

"You're taking me to Fortune's Den." It was a statement, not a question. Theo would not be his opponent. Dorian would take a beating from the King of Clubs. A man feared by many and unrivalled when fighting with his fists.

"Damn right. Aaron suspected something was amiss when Delphine insisted she stay one more night. As did I when her eyes turned dreamy at the mention of your blasted name."

Delphine!

Dorian knew that soft, faraway gaze, as compelling as the dance of sunlight on the sea. He lost himself in those soulful brown pools, found himself the moment he pushed deep into Delphine's welcoming body. When they were together, the world around them disappeared. Protecting their undeniable bond was all that mattered. Nothing these men could do would ruin his future plans.

Theo shook his head and uttered, "Devious bastard."

"Have you ever been in love?"

The question took Theo by surprise. His haunted gaze shifted to the window as if a monument to heartbreak and humiliation could be found there. "Love is a conjurer's trick. Nature's ploy to force men to procreate. A device to secure the survival of our species."

"I was just as cynical once." He'd believed love was a weapon. Now he knew true love healed. It did not maim. "If you think that's all love is, then you have never wanted a woman the way I want Delphine."

Theo slapped his hand on the seat. "You've no right to speak her given name." Anger emanated from every fibre of his being. He was within his rights to throttle Dorian, but there was no doubt the mention of love had opened old wounds. "If you'd kept your cock in your trousers, I might believe you."

"I want to marry her."

Mile End had never felt like home. Delphine brought warmth to every cold corridor. She brought chaos and laughter and a deep sense of belonging.

"As if we'd let—"

"I'm going to marry her." He'd never been more certain of anything in his life. Woe betide anyone who tried to stop him.

Lady Gambit

Theo gestured to Dorian's mussed hair and crumpled clothes. "And you think this is how to seek her family's approval?"

"I don't need your approval, but I'll do what's necessary to earn it." He would fight all four Chance brothers if need be. "I'm in love with Delphine, and I'm damn sure she's in love with me. You should have woken her. She's not a child and deserves the right to speak for herself."

Theo might have hurled more insults, but the carriage stopped outside Fortune's Den in Aldgate Street. It was the early hours of the morning, but candlelight flickered in a downstairs window.

Moments later, Aaron Chance appeared at the front door, his shirt sleeves rolled to his elbows, revealing the muscular forearms that made men quiver. He looked at Dorian's lack of respectable attire and knew why Theo had dragged him across town.

"You'd better come in." Aaron's gaze moved beyond Dorian to the building across the street. A blonde woman stood watching from an upper window. "I'll not have all and sundry knowing my business."

Dorian stopped to stroke the lucky horseshoe above the gaming hell door, then followed Aaron into his study. Much like the man himself, it was a dark, domineering space.

"Sit down, Flynn." Aaron spoke with a measure of calm as he drew out a chair near his desk. He waited for Dorian to sit before settling into his black throne and turning his attention to Theo. "I trust you left Delphine asleep in bed?"

Theo nodded. "I did as you asked and waited an hour after Flynn climbed the stairs before checking both chambers. I found them in Flynn's bed."

Aaron's nostrils flared. His fiery gaze could sear a man's soul. "I assume this isn't the first time you've had intimate relations with my sister."

Dorian was careful not to use arrogance as a crutch. "No. It might pain you to hear this, but I doubt it will be the last."

Aaron slammed his clenched fist on his desk. "You've got a damn nerve. Most men would scramble to save their sorry necks, not look for ways to provoke me."

"Those men are not in love with Delphine."

Aaron's dark eyes narrowed. "How do you know you are?"

He did not need to search his heart for the answer. "Life is perfect when we're together. She understands me like no one else. She's my friend, lover, the person I trust most." The reasons he loved her were endless. "She's kind, loyal, so beautiful inside she steals my breath. I know I'm in love with her because I would fight every one of you for the right to claim her hand."

They would have to kill him to prevent him from pursuing her.

Aaron was not swayed by his rhetoric. "Your fight is with me, no one else. If you last one round, I'll be impressed."

"Do what you must."

When a boy lay trembling in bed at night, waiting for his enemies to strike with a torrent of abuse and a hail-

Lady Gambit

storm of punches, he did not fear fighting one man. Even if it was the indomitable Aaron Chance.

"Have you no thought for Miss Montague?" Aaron said.

Dorian squared his shoulders. "I'm not in love with Miss Montague. Any comments about a match stem from my father's ambitions, not mine."

He had not dishonoured the lady.

He had made his intentions clear.

A glimmer of curiosity lit Aaron's eyes. "You'd forsake a chance to join the upper ranks? The King might grant you a title. Your father wants to leave you his legacy. You need never work again."

The list of privileges would be endless.

"It means nothing without Delphine."

A mocking chuckle burst from Aaron Chance's lips. He relaxed back in his throne and steepled his fingers. "Did you hear that, Theo? Flynn would rather be related to you than the Marquess of Bexley."

"If only we'd made a wager to that effect," Theo replied. "Though I must say, you're taking the fact Flynn ruined our sister quite well."

"I admire any man willing to die for his cause," Aaron countered. "And I anticipated the chime of wedding bells when Daventry persuaded me to let Delphine remain at Mile End. Either Daventry is London's best necromancer, and he receives predictions from beyond the grave, or he's a mesmerist who has us all in a damned trance."

For the first time since he'd opened his eyes and found Theo lurking in the doorway, Dorian breathed a little easier. "Then I have your permission to ask for her hand?"

"I need to see the evidence of this love for myself." Aaron's provoking tone said Dorian had just sat through the preliminary interrogation. The real test was about to begin. "Delphine has suffered a great deal. Let us pray she sees you as more than a distraction, or there'll be the devil to pay."

Dorian realised he had walked into a trap.

Aaron confirmed as much when he examined his pocket watch. "Gibbs should have woken Mrs Maloney and explained your sudden absence. Wishing to help Delphine, Mrs Maloney will race to your bedchamber and deliver the dreadful news."

"The question is, will Delphine come to your aid?" Theo said. "Or will she realise you're nothing but a temporary distraction?"

Annoyed that his life was being manipulated by men other than his father, Dorian stood abruptly. "This is my life. It's not a game."

"No, but I'll not force Delphine into a loveless marriage," Aaron snapped. "Aren't you curious to know if her feelings are genuine?"

He would stake his life they were genuine. Love lived in every lingering smile, in every tender touch. Though he probably didn't deserve her esteem, she made him feel like a god amongst men.

"So you mean to stage a fight in the hope she comes running?" Dorian countered, thankful Gibbs was at Mile End and Delphine wasn't left to make the journey alone.

"Stage a fight?" Aaron sounded offended by the suggestion. "We'll not be prancing around like popinjays.

Lady Gambit

In an effort to keep your affair a secret, you have forgotten an important fact."

"And what is that?"

Aaron stood and braced his hands on the desk, his gaze hard and black like obsidian. "You gave me your word you would treat my sister with respect. No man reneges on a promise made to me. No man! You will face me in the pit. There, you will pay the price for your betrayal."

Chapter Seventeen

"Delphine! Wake up! What on earth is wrong with you? Have you been drinking? Can you hear me? Oh, what's a woman to do?"

The irate questions invaded Delphine's peaceful slumber. She was snuggled beneath the sheets in Dorian's bed, bathing in the warm afterglow of their lovemaking. Oh, he had been magnificent tonight. Pure sweat-soaked muscle in a body made for sin.

"Delphine!"

"Hmm?"

Cold air breezed over her bare skin as the blanket slipped off her shoulder. The sudden chill raised gooseflesh to her arms. The persistent prodding brought her back to reality with a bump.

"What is it?" A little annoyed, she opened her eyes to find Mrs Maloney dragging the blankets off the bed. "Good Lord!" Aware of her nakedness, she used her hands to cover her modesty. "Mrs Maloncy? What are you doing?" Then she remembered she was in Dorian's bed, and panic crushed her chest in its relentless vice. "Wait. Let me explain."

"There's no time for idle chatter. Get up, dear, before your brothers murder the man you love. Hurry, or you'll be mourning the husband that never was."

"Murder? Mourning? What do you mean?"

Still dazed and groggy, she gathered the blanket to her breasts and sat up. She was alone in bed. A quick scan of the room confirmed Dorian's clothes were not on the chair where he left them. His boots were missing, too.

She tried to fire her logical brain into action, but fear left her irrational. "Is Aaron here? What has he done? Has he hurt—"

"No. Will you listen?" Mrs Maloney was flapping her hands now. "Theo came looking for you and found you in Mr Flynn's bed. He's dragged him away to Fortune's Den. If you don't hurry, there'll be a trial with no jury."

"Fortune's Den!"

Good Lord! Aaron would demand Dorian join him in the fighting pit in the basement. For every stolen kiss, her brother would deliver a deadly blow.

"Why didn't they wake me?" She shot out of bed and snatched her nightdress from beneath her pillow. "If they hurt a hair on Dorian's head, I'll never forgive them."

"Men are barbarians when it comes to honour. Aaron will see this as a personal slight. If you want Mr Flynn, you'll have to fight for him."

"Fight? In the pit?" Delphine dragged her nightdress over her head.

"No, you goose." Mrs Maloney helped her thrust her arms into the garment. "You'll have to face your brothers and tell them how you feel about Mr Flynn. Remember, this is your life. Make them listen."

She gripped Mrs Maloney's wrinkled hands. "I love Dorian. I don't want to be without him, but my brothers will always have an opinion. What man would tolerate their interference?"

Certainly not one who longed for a peaceful existence.

Oh, she would be a spinster until the end of her days.

"A man who loves you. A man who isn't afraid to hit Aaron." Mrs Maloney handed her a silk dressing gown, her eyes shining with warmth and kindness. "Someone who's spent a lifetime alone. Someone who would thrive in a family of like-minded men."

An image of Dorian attending their daily meeting flashed into her mind. Mrs Maloney was right. He was strong enough to tolerate Aaron's scrutiny. He wasn't afraid to voice his opinion.

The question was, would Aaron let her go?

Their family home was emptying slowly.

How would Aaron cope when left alone with his memories?

"Hurry now." With nimble fingers, Mrs Maloney tied the belt on Delphine's dressing gown. "They're only half an hour ahead. Go get your boots. Mr Gibbs is waiting downstairs with the carriage."

"Mr Gibbs is still here?"

Thank the Lord! The man drove like wolves chased his heels.

"He's tasked with protecting you. If there's one thing I know about Mr Gibbs, the King himself couldn't deter him from his mission."

Lady Gambit

A sudden wave of relief had her tugging Mrs Maloney's hand. "Come. We should not delay." She noticed Mrs Maloney was still in her nightdress. "We need to fetch your coat. It's cold out, and—"

"You're going alone, dear. This is your battle, not mine." Mrs Maloney pulled an ornate iron key from her pocket and thrust it into Delphine's hand. "Take this. Aaron gave it to me in case there was trouble in the bookshop. With luck, you'll reach Fortune's Den before he throws the first punch."

That was wishful thinking.

Dorian's carriage was parked on the street outside Fortune's Den, and Briggs was snoozing atop the box. The gaming hell door was locked. The soft glow of candlelight spilled from the window in Aaron's study, but she peered inside and found the room deserted.

She hammered on the front door and tugged the iron bell pull. Using the key was a last resort. When encountering a figure in the dark corridors, Sigmund was trained to hit first and ask questions later.

Where was their man-of-all work? He was always the last to retire, which meant only one thing. He was in the basement.

Her hand shook as she slipped the key into the lock. Once inside, she hurried through the lavish red hall. The scent of aromatic oils disguised the stench of stale tobacco but did little to settle her nerves.

The basement door was ajar, and Aaron's devilish taunts echoed from the vast room below.

"I'm impressed, Flynn. Few men manage to land a punch, let alone last a round. The key to success is believing you can win. You certainly have faith in your own ability. I admire that."

"This is one fight I can't afford to lose," Dorian countered.

Her heart skittered upon hearing Dorian's confident voice. She raced down the stone staircase into the candlelit cellar.

Both men stood in the sunken circular pit resembling a small gladiatorial arena. Their elbows and knees were flexed, their clenched fists raised like human mallets. They had stripped to their trousers. A sheen of sweat coated their foreheads and bare chests. While Dorian's scars littered his broad back, Aaron's covered his muscular torso.

Theo and Sigmund were the only spectators. Both sat on a wooden bench, drinking brandy and goading the contenders.

"If he was fighting any other man, I'd put my money on Flynn," Sigmund said before downing a mouthful of liquor. "Happen if he shifted his stance, he might give Mr Chance a good crack on the chin."

"Aaron is merely toying with him," Theo countered.

"Stop this nonsense!" she cried.

All four men looked at her. No one appeared shocked by her sudden arrival. Dorian's gaze slid over her loose hair and nightclothes, a smile touching his lips.

It was evident she'd been in a hurry to reach him.

When a lady promised to protect a man, she meant it.

She descended the three small steps into the ring, strode over to Aaron and braced her hands on her hips. "Your argument is with me, not Mr Flynn. If you must blame anyone, blame me. I kissed him first."

Lady Gambit

"I was a heartbeat away from kissing you," Dorian replied.

She turned to him, her temper easing as she noted his determined expression and the sheer power emanating from his toned body.

Her chest hurt to think of how much she loved him.

She would lay down her life for him, stand strong and take every blow.

"We were drawn to each other," she confessed, her arms stretched between the men while she played referee. "I couldn't have denied myself the pleasure even if I'd tried. If I could return to that moment, I would kiss you on the count of one."

Dorian grinned. "I wouldn't bother counting at all."

That's when she saw the blood coating his lip.

That's when her temper escaped like a caged beast and went on a rampage. She flew at Aaron, prodding him in the chest. "If you lay another hand on him, I'll never forgive you. Do you hear me?"

"So you do care about him?" Aaron said, unperturbed by her threat. "I told Flynn if you loved him, you'd come. And here you are, rushing to his aid."

"You prize fool! Do you think I would give my virtue to any man?"

"That's the first time you've ever called me a fool."

"I shall call you one again if you throw another punch."

"Delphine," Dorian said, a pleading tone to his voice. "You'll never be mine if I can't show Aaron I can protect you. This is about more than me breaking my oath. I need to pay my dues. I need to prove I'm worthy of your esteem."

"Of course you're worthy. This is absurd."

"It's what men do," Theo called.

"Then you should all be in Bethlem. Nora Adkins' cell is empty."

"Flynn lied to me." Aaron drew his hand across his damp brow and resumed a fighting stance. "He ruined any trust I had in him. He'll go three rounds if he wants to make amends."

"What poppycock!" She threw up her hands in protest but knew nothing would dissuade Aaron from proving a point. He had learned hard lessons while surviving in the rookeries. Trust was worth more to him than all the gold in the King's vault.

Still, she'd be damned if she'd sit idly and watch the men fight.

That's when an idea struck her.

When she realised there was only one way to disarm Aaron.

"So be it," she said, marching towards the stairs. She had a weapon in her arsenal and wasn't afraid to use it. "I'll be in my bedchamber. Come find me once you've settled your differences."

She did not go to her bedchamber but hurried across the street and knocked on the door of The Burnished Jade. Candlelight in the upper window brought a wave of hope.

It took Miss Lovelace no time to answer. "Miss Chance?" Her gaze dipped to Delphine's nightclothes, and she peered out into the street. "Good Lord. Is everything all right?"

Delphine suppressed a triumphant grin. Miss Lovelace's golden curls hung in glorious waves over her shoulders. The lady's silk dressing gown clung to her womanly curves. One look at the delightful Miss Scrumptious would bring Aaron crashing to his knees.

"Forgive me. I know it's late, but I need your help. Aaron won't listen." She pointed to Fortune's Den. "I'm in love with Mr Flynn, and Aaron means to test his worth in the fighting pit." She grasped the lady's hands. "Please come before someone gets hurt."

Miss Lovelace glanced at Fortune's Den like it was the entrance to the netherworld. "What can I do? He never listens to me, either."

"You're the only person who unnerves him."

"I am?" A mix of confusion and pride flashed in Miss Lovelace's pretty blue eyes. "Well, if you think I can help, I'll be glad of an opportunity to try. Come inside while I fetch my boots and coat."

"There's no time. They have fought one round already." Delphine tugged the lady's hand. Aaron needed to see her looking like the goddess Venus. "A punch from Aaron can be deadly. I can't lose Mr Flynn."

"Very well. At least let me lock the door."

Miss Lovelace secured the premises. She raised the hem of her nightwear and tiptoed barefoot over the cobblestones.

Mr Gibbs watched with a curious frown from atop his box.

"This way. They're in the basement." Delphine led the lady through the club. "Please. Make him see that violence is not the answer."

Miss Lovelace sighed like she knew it was an impossible task. "I shall do my best. However, I find it difficult to control my temper around him. Mr Chance is a strain upon my sanity. I told myself it's best to stay away."

No!

Little did the lady know, but she was the key to Aaron's future happiness. No one affected him the way she did. No one!

The second Aaron saw Miss Lovelace descending the stairs into the basement, he froze. He stood like a stone statue hit by Medusa's deadly glare, except his nemesis was beauty personified.

All eyes were upon them as they reached the ring.

"Good grief! You didn't tell me he was practically naked," the lady whispered through gritted teeth. "He'll be furious."

"Yes, but he will listen to you. I'm sure of it."

With a doubtful nod, the lady marched into the ring. "Good evening, Mr Chance. Or should I say good morning? I believe we're approaching the witching hour."

Aaron's gaze moved slowly over her loose hair. His eyes closed briefly and swayed like the sight of her left him a little drunk. "Go home, madam. This is none of your concern."

"I was invited here."

"I'm uninviting you."

"You're frightening your sister." Through stormy blue eyes, she scanned Aaron's muscled torso and gulped. "Judging by the scars littering your chest, perhaps you're looking to add another to your collection."

His Adam's apple bobbed. "What if I am?"

Lady Gambit

"Punching this gentleman won't settle your dispute." Her gaze dipped to his rippling abdominal muscles, and she struggled to form the next word. "W-w-would it not be better to sit and discuss the problem like grown men? You have an intelligent mind. Why not use it?"

"I am. My intelligent mind is the only thing stopping me from throwing you over my shoulder and carrying you back to The Burnished Jade. Leave, madam, before you're mauled by a monster."

"It would seem violence is the only thing you know."

"These fists are the reason I'm alive." He inhaled deeply, though must have caught a whiff of the lady's scent because he shook his head and muttered a curse. "Don't come here looking like you've fallen from heaven and expect me to abide by your command."

Miss Lovelace stared at him. "What did you just say?"

He groaned. "I said these fists—"

"No, the part about heaven."

Realising his error, he jerked as if reeling from a punch but gathered himself quickly. "Only a fool goads the devil."

"You're not the devil. I saw you carrying Mrs Maloney into your carriage two weeks ago when she hurt her ankle."

"Are you spying on me?"

"I live across the street. It's hardly spying." The lady arched a challenging brow. "You moved your desk so you could watch my premises."

If Aaron was shocked that she'd noticed, one could not tell. "I'm observing my competitor. It's considered good business acumen."

"You were at the window long after my club closed." The lady smiled before offering another damning piece of evidence. "When that drunken buffoon hammered on my door last Friday, you were there in seconds, dragging him away by the scruff of his coat."

Annoyed his secret had been exposed to all, Aaron captured Miss Lovelace by the elbow. "We'll resume the last round in a moment, Flynn," he said, guiding the lady towards the stairs. "Once Miss Lovelace has learned I'm not as patient when I'm half-naked."

Delphine would apologise to Miss Lovelace tomorrow.

For now, she took advantage of the distraction to inspect the cut on Dorian's lip. She hoped to steal a kiss, but fate had other plans.

Mr Gibbs appeared at the top of the stairs, blocking Aaron's retreat. "You've a trespasser. I caught her slinking through the darkness like a wraith." He dragged a woman forward by her arm. "She says she's here to see Caterina. Says she ain't leaving until she does."

"Get off me, you brute." The white-haired woman tried to wrestle her scrawny arm free while muttering gibberish. "Caterina!"

Dorian slid a comforting arm around Delphine's waist and pulled her close. "There's no need to look for Nora Adkins. It appears she has found us."

Chapter Eighteen

Delphine stared at the thin, emaciated woman dwarfed by Mr Gibbs. Nora's lank white hair covered half of her face, but not the ugly gash on her forehead. Her dress hung off her bony shoulders like it belonged to someone twice her size.

Like the day she visited Bethlem with Aramis, Nora's eyes found Delphine's in the crowd. "Caterina!" she called, the cry disturbing in its desperation. "Oh, Caterina! I've found you."

Dorian firmed his grip on her waist. "Proceed with caution until we establish her motive. Remember, if she was sane when she entered Bethlem, she may be deranged now."

"Most people are insane to some degree. You'd know if you'd ever tried to steal a biscuit from Aramis." She tore her gaze from Nora and looked into Dorian's warm brown eyes before noticing the cut on his lip. "I'm sorry Aaron did this to you. There's no excuse for his brutish behaviour."

"Aaron did what any protective brother would do under the circumstances." He brushed the backs of his fingers softly over her cheek. "He's not the enemy."

She breathed a sigh. "I know."

Nora's screech stole their attention. In a dazed fit, the absconder tried to tug her arm free from Mr Gibbs before kicking his shin.

"I'm not sure I want to hear what Nora has to say." How could she trust the woman's word? "I'm not sure I can bear more bad news."

"The truth is never easy to hear, but it may set you free."

What if the truth was a poison in the water, destroying everything in its wake? What if it ate away at her, and all she felt was bitter regret?

"I'm not sure Nora has a grasp on reality. How can I trust her to tell me who I am and why she was locked in Bethlem?"

Aaron intervened then. "I assume you're Nora Adkins." He stood at the bottom of the stairs like a human shield.

Nora's eyes bulged as she scanned his physique. "Well, ain't you a fine gent? It's been an age since I've seen a man without his shirt."

"What do you want with my sister?"

"Sister?" Nora hopped from one foot to the other as if standing on hot coals. "Caterina is an only child. She's like a precious pearl found in the ocean. That's what her mother used to say when she tucked her up in bed at night and sang her a sweet lullaby."

The vision brought a sharp pain to Delphine's throat, a

deep ache to her heart. She hugged herself to stop a tidal wave of emotions surfacing. "How do you know my mother?"

"I'm cold to my bones, and the rumble in my belly ain't thunder. I'll need a plate full of sustenance and somewhere warm to sit. Be quick now. It won't be long before them beggars find me."

"How did *you* find us?" Aaron said, his words laden with suspicion.

"I pecked and pecked and followed the crumbs." Nora chuckled and said, "He told me where to come. Happen he was tired of my squawking."

Aaron gritted his teeth. "Who told you?"

Nora rubbed her belly. "I'll be grateful for your hospitality first."

Aaron began barking orders. He had Sigmund race upstairs and secure the premises. He demanded Miss Lovelace stay until they'd established a few facts. As Cook had left for the night, Theo was sent to the kitchen to prepare a cold platter.

Aaron mounted the stairs, beckoning them to follow. "We'll retire to my study. The fire is lit there."

Delphine would have been hot on Aaron's heels, but Dorian caught her arm to stall her. He leant closer and whispered, "From the few words Nora said, I suspect Powell released her and gave her your direction. It's evident he doesn't want us prying into his affairs."

"I agree. Mr Powell must have helped her abscond." Neither of them believed Nora had escaped of her own volition.

They moved to follow everyone upstairs.

Dorian stopped to grab his shirt off the bench. He winced as he dragged the garment over his head. "Your brother delivered a punishing blow to my ribs. The man is as swift as a bolting steed."

Keen to touch him, she helped pull the fine lawn down over his torso.

Their eyes met.

Desire coiled low in her belly.

Just like it had hours earlier when he moved deep inside her.

But something else held her enthralled. A feeling too strong to contain.

"I love you." She slipped her fingers under his shirt to touch his bare skin. "I'm so in love with you, Dorian. I don't care to hear what Nora has to say. I'm yours. I'll leave with you tonight. We could run away somewhere. A place no one would find us."

He cradled her throat and kissed her, his tongue skimming her open lips before plunging deep into her mouth. The hunger, the sheer dominance of the action, made her want to tear off his shirt and rain kisses over his magnificent body.

"I love you," he growled, tearing his mouth from hers. "I'm so in love with you, I'd travel to the ends of the earth to please you."

She sensed his hesitation. "But?"

He grasped her cheeks and kissed her again as if unable to stop. "I've spent my whole life relegated to the shadows. A nobody. One of the misbegotten. A person whose feelings don't matter."

"They matter to me."

Lady Gambit

Her reply earned her another kiss.

"From the moment we met, I've been unable to refuse you anything. Don't ask me to hide away like I should be ashamed. I want the world to know what we mean to each other."

By world, he meant his father.

The man who could ruin everything.

Fear crept into her heart.

Run, run, my darling!

What if her life was meant to be marred by tragedy? What if happiness was never part of the plan? Now that she understood the power of love, did fate have other cruel lessons in store?

"We could go far from here where the truth cannot hurt us," she said. "Leave the demons of the past behind."

He entwined his fingers with hers as if nothing could tear them apart. "We must face the truth together. I shall be beside you every step of the way. I'll help you cope with every harrowing detail. Even if it takes a lifetime."

They might have kissed again, but Aaron appeared, poking his head around the door jamb. "Delphine! I need you upstairs. You'll not leave me alone with that mad woman."

"We don't know Nora is mad."

"I'm not talking about Nora. Miss Lovelace hasn't stopped staring at me since I gave her a piece of string and told her to tie back her hair."

Though Aaron had thrown on his crumpled shirt, it was open to the navel, revealing the toned physique that had made the lady's mouth water.

"Miss Lovelace is her own mistress," she said, moving

towards the stairs. "She's not used to a man telling her what to do. She will be annoyed you gave her no choice."

Aaron frowned. "And some devil could be parked on the street waiting to pounce. I need to question the loon, not worry about Miss Lovelace."

He was worried about Miss Lovelace?

What an astonishing revelation.

"As I'm acting on behalf of Bow Street, I'll question Nora Adkins," Dorian countered.

Aaron arched a brow and gestured to the hall. "Be my guest. Had you put the case before your amorous liaisons with my sister, we wouldn't be in this predicament."

They joined Aaron in his study.

Nora was seated in a wooden chair by the fire, warming her stocking feet and tucking into a selection of cold meats and cheese. Miss Lovelace stood in the corner like a disobedient child, out of Aaron's line of sight. She'd fastened her hair in a loose braid and held a plaid blanket around her shoulders, though the room was stifling hot.

"Your brother has an issue with my attire." The lady pulled the blanket firmly across her chest while meeting Delphine's gaze. "I had the choice of this or Sigmund's greatcoat."

Delphine inwardly smiled. Though she felt guilty for involving Miss Lovelace in her personal problems, these unexpected encounters weakened Aaron's resolve. To make amends, she would become a member of The Burnished Jade.

Dorian approached Nora Adkins, who shoved food into her mouth quicker than she could swallow. "How do you know Caterina?" he said, using the name belonging to the girl who would always be lost in the night.

Nora looked up through wild eyes and wiped her mouth with the back of her hand. "What's it to you?"

"Unless you want to sleep in a dank cell for the next sixteen years, I suggest you answer my questions."

The woman laughed. "*He* won't take me back. He needs rid of me before them governors start poking into his affairs."

"You speak of the Superintendent, Mr Powell?"

"No!" Nora looked at Dorian like he was as mad as a rat in a trap. "The toff with the face of an angel and the heart of a beast. He's the one who had Powell set me free."

Delphine stepped forward. "Lord Meldrum freed you? We were told you hit the doctor with a bottle of castor oil and snatched his keys."

"I did. We had to make it look like a real escape." She touched her fingers to the cut on her head and blenched. "Though I reckon Powell enjoyed giving me a good old thwack."

Dorian frowned. "I can think of only one reason Meldrum wants you roaming the streets. You're a witness to his duplicity. The only hold the blackmailer has over him. Perhaps he believes the contract would become void if you escaped and were found dead in the Thames."

Clearly, Aaron thought the theory had merit. "Meldrum wouldn't want her dying in Bethlem. He'd not risk an enquiry."

Nora stuffed a piece of bread into her mouth. Crumbs fell onto her lap when she spoke. "His men were waiting outside the hospital gates. They'd have done me in good and proper, but I escaped through the garden and over the back wall."

Delphine wondered if they were the same men who'd tried to abduct her outside Miss Darrow's shop. It made sense. Lord Meldrum was weak and lacked moral character. If he married her and killed Nora, his life would no longer be a shambles. Except that his man had shot Theo and ruined the plan.

"He knew I'd come looking for you, Caterina," Nora added. "He has one of his thugs across the road watching this house. I slipped inside when he went to relieve himself in Golden Fleece Alley." She cackled. "Or should I say, Golden Sprinkle Alley?"

Aaron was at the window in a second. He peered into the darkness before turning to Miss Lovelace. "Now do you see why I suggested you remain here?"

The lady looked angry, not thankful. "I'll not stay the night."

"Rest assured. You'll be gone at the first opportunity. Sigmund will escort you home once I'm certain this thug poses no threat." He scanned the street again before sending Theo and Sigmund out to hunt for the blackguard. "Bring him here. He'll tell me who hired him, or I'll cut out his tongue and feed it to the dogs."

Dorian had other matters on his mind, namely dragging answers from the irrational Nora Adkins. "What makes you think Miss Chance is Caterina? Why are you looking for her?"

Nora held up her plate. She'd gobbled the food like it was her last supper. "Any more cheese? And I'll want bread to squirrel away to eat later. When I leave here, I'm heading to the coast. Don't suppose you can spare a few coins for my purse?"

"Who tied you up and left you for the previous Lord Meldrum to find?" Dorian persisted. His scowl said he was nearing the end of his tether. "You'll answer all my questions before you get another morsel."

Nora glowered at him. "I ain't eaten in days. How can a woman think when her stomach growls like an injured bear?"

"You've managed thus far."

The woman looked at Delphine, though her hard eyes did not soften. "She's the image of her mother. Now, can I have more cheese? Got any pickled cabbage?"

"You'll get nothing more until you co-operate."

Nora huffed and rested her plate on the grate. "I told you when you came to pick my mind before. Big black hat. Big shiny shoes. One ruby eye on a stick. That's the devil what made me dizzy."

"Why? What had you done?"

"Done?" Nora's eyes bulged. "Nothing. Happen I knew too much. Those devils stole Caterina off the street. It took me months to find her. Then I saw the poor lamb picking pockets on West Street."

Picking pockets!

"You speak of Mrs Haggert?" Delphine said.

"Who else? She stole you right from under your mother's nose."

Aaron turned from the window, his temper barely contained. "Did I not say Mrs Haggert is the devil incarnate? I'll take great pleasure in making her pay for what she's done to this family."

A memory slid into Delphine's mind. That of Mrs Haggert gripping her wrist so tightly it left a bruise, tugging hard and dragging her from the shrubbery.

We need to get her away from here and quickly.

Other memories fought for supremacy.

She was staring into a basket of flower petals, too scared to put her hand inside and scatter them as instructed. A woman beside her was crying, begging the maid for help.

What did it mean?

Perhaps it was time Dorian explained how her parents had died. It might be a valuable piece of the puzzle. It might spark an important memory. But first, she had to learn everything she could from Nora Adkins.

"How did you know my mother?" she said firmly.

"I worked at your house in Bolton Street. I know everything that went on there. I know what they did." Nora glanced at Dorian and Aaron and snarled. "But I'll not tell you in front of these blighters. I'll hang for what I know. Happen you wouldn't want to tarnish your mother's memory."

Beyond desperate for answers, she turned to Aaron. "Leave us for a moment. I want to speak to Nora alone."

"Like hell," both men echoed.

Dorian's hand slid around her arm. "I'll not leave you with her. We'll find the answers we need another way." He met Aaron's gaze. "Have Sigmund fetch the watchman. I'm sure Nora is missing her cell at Bethlem. And we need Daventry to get a warrant for Powell's arrest."

Perhaps Dorian was right to air his concern.

He'd been distrusting of Nora since she arrived.

Indeed, Nora shot to her feet and made a hullabaloo. "I ain't going back to that hellish place. And I ain't meeting my maker until I've brought death to the devil who put me there." She grabbed her scuffed boots from the hearth. "I came here of my own free will, and I'll leave the same way."

"There's nowhere to go." Dorian sounded like a constable from Bow Street. "The man you mean to murder is dead. And you won't get within a hundred yards of Mrs Haggert."

If Nora wasn't mad before, she was now. She stamped the floor and shook her head and swore like a dockside lout. Without warning, she lunged at Dorian, hard and fast, pushing him in the chest with all her might. "Stay back, you wretch!"

He stumbled in shock, giving Nora the valuable seconds needed to thrust her hand into her boot and draw a small pistol.

Everyone gasped.

"No one move," Nora cried, cocking the hammer and aiming the gun at Delphine. "Don't test my patience. I'll shoot her. Make no mistake."

Nora's eyes flitted about though her hand remained steady. Every facial muscle conveyed a determination to carry out her threat.

Was the woman unhinged?

Was this merely a last bid for freedom?

"I'm sure you don't want to hurt me." Delphine raised her hands in surrender. "I'm sure this is a simple misunderstanding." How did one reason with a maniac?

"This ain't no misunderstanding. Say your prayers now."

Dorian's face was a white mask of fear.

"Please don't shoot," she pleaded, crossing her arms over her body to protect her heart. "We can resolve the problem. You can leave. Don't you want to find Mrs Haggert and punish her for putting you in Bethlem?"

Nora pressed forward, forcing Delphine to shuffle back towards the open study door. "Have no fear. I'll find that crone soon enough. I'm here to put a ball in your false heart."

"Mine?" Good Lord! Why?

"Step back!" Nora yelled to Aaron. "Flinch, and I'll shoot."

Both men froze, afraid to make a wrong move.

Attempting to make sense of Nora's motive for murder, Delphine said, "But I was a child when you knew me. What did I do to you?"

"You're the one who put me there. If it weren't for your loose tongue, the deed would be done, and we'd all be happier for it."

"I don't remember. You're not making any sense."

"Happen you'd remember if you'd spent sixteen years in a cell."

Confused, Delphine glanced at Aaron, but she'd never seen him look so afraid. As they shuffled slowly past Miss Lovelace, the lady caught Delphine's eye. She splayed her hand on her chest, three fingers visible. Slowly, three fingers became two, then one, then her gaze dipped to the floor.

"Kill the chick and blame the hen," Nora sang in a childlike voice, "and the wolf will set me free."

Delphine ignored the woman's mad ramblings and studied Miss Lovelace's fingers, waiting for the signal. She knew instinctively what to do and prayed the plan would work.

Three. Two. One, Miss Lovelace mouthed.

Delphine said a silent prayer and dropped to her knees.

She wasn't sure what happened next, but Aaron swore and Dorian gasped.

Nora screamed in pain and collapsed to the floor, writhing as she cradled her arm. "Evil wench. You've snapped my wrist in two."

Delphine shot to her feet, as dazed as the day Monsieur Chabert brought her out of a trance. She looked at Miss Lovelace, thankful she'd had the foresight to knock on her door. The lady had one hand clasped to her chest, the other wrapped around the small pistol.

"I've only practised the move twice but was assured it works to disarm a villain." With shaky fingers, she gave Aaron the pistol.

Aaron's chest heaved as he struggled to catch his breath. He gawped at Miss Lovelace. Either he was about to murder the lady for her interference or carry her upstairs and ravage her senseless.

"That was stupid," he said, "and ingenious."

"I'm not sure I'd want to do it again."

"There's sherry in the drawing room. Pour yourself a glass."

The lady nodded and left them to deal with Nora.

Despite looking as pale as a ghost, Dorian crossed the room. He stepped over Nora and hauled Delphine into his arms.

He didn't care that Aaron stood watching them. He kissed her, a long, lingering kiss that spoke of relief.

"I'll not fail you again." Dorian brushed her hair from her face, cradled her cheeks and kissed her deeply. "You might have died had it not been for the intrepid owner of The Burnished Jade."

"It's not your fault. None of us expected Nora to draw a pistol from her boot." Though she would suffer Nora's threats again if it meant Miss Lovelace could prove her worth.

"The hellcat must have hidden it on her person and slipped it into her boot." Aaron hauled Nora up by her good arm, though the woman wailed like a hungry babe. "You didn't escape Bethlem with a loaded pistol. Who gave you the gun?"

Nora shook her head, her pain forgotten, and started dancing like a witch at a cauldron. "*Diddly de, diddly dum.*"

Dorian faced the woman. "Tell me! Was it Powell?"

"It had to be Mr Powell," Delphine interjected.

"Not necessarily. According to the visitors' book, Meldrum entered Bethlem a few hours before Nora absconded. He could have easily passed the weapon through the bars."

"Why would Lord Meldrum want me dead?" It made no sense.

"I don't know," Dorian admitted. "But I know someone who might."

"Mrs Haggert?" she suggested. Who else could it be?

"Indeed. We'll visit that cunning devil first thing tomorrow."

Chapter Nineteen

Seven Dials
St Giles

"Mrs Haggert ain't seeing anyone today." The boy guarding the alley leading to Mrs Haggert's premises shoved the calling card back into Dorian's hand and doffed his cap. "Be on your way, gov'nor."

The arrogant swine!

"I'm not leaving without seeing Mrs Haggert." Dorian thrust his calling card back at the boy. "We can do this the polite way, or I can storm the house and arrest everyone inside."

Dorian raised his trouser leg, showing the hilt of the hunter's blade peeking from the sheath strapped to his shin. He parted his coat to reveal the pistol in the leather holster fastened across his body.

The boys looked at each other, their arrogant grins fading.

Delphine stepped closer. "We're all armed and quite

Lady Gambit

prepared to die today." She gestured to her brother, whose only weapon was his baleful mood. "Mrs Haggert will answer our questions, or she will be arrested."

One boy scurried away and returned with a burly guard. The hulking fellow looked at Aaron Chance and his eyes almost popped out of their sockets.

"We're not leaving," Aaron said, his tone dangerously unsettling.

After a brief conversation with his mistress, the guard led them into Mrs Haggert's drawing room and told them to wait.

"We must remain calm," Dorian said as he sat patiently on the sofa. "Discovering the truth is our primary goal. Too many people know of her involvement. She'll not lie her way out of trouble this time."

Delphine turned to Aaron. "We can't hurl accusations without proof. We can't rile her before we get the answers we seek."

Aaron sat forward in the wing chair, one arm resting on his knee. "I have my own gripe with the woman, but we'll do this Flynn's way, as we agreed."

Tempers were frayed.

Emotions ran high.

They had barely slept since Daventry left Fortune's Den with the magistrate. They'd watched two *peelers* wrestle Nora Adkins into the prison wagon, the woman scratching their faces and screaming like a banshee. An hour later—while Dorian was away fetching clothes from his room above the Old Swan—they received word that Powell had been arrested. Once they'd dealt with Mrs

Haggert, they were heading to Bow Street to interrogate the Superintendent.

Tense minutes passed.

They heard whispers in the hall before Mrs Haggert entered.

She wore a red dress with modish sleeves and a bell-shaped skirt. Her expression was hard to read, but she sounded resigned to her fate when she said, "They say red is the colour of vengeance. The day of retribution has come, though I prayed it never would."

"Why?" Aaron scoffed, his hatred like a malevolent spirit climbing the walls. "Because you want people to think you're a woman of your word when we both know you're a liar."

Dorian inwardly cursed.

So much for following the plan.

Mrs Haggert's hooded eyes darkened. "I did what was best, all things considered. Yes, you've a right to be angry, but you got the better end of the bargain. You got to keep the jewel in the crown."

"You wanted me dead."

"That ain't true." Mrs Haggert raised her hands in silent apology. "I needed you alive. I didn't know the fool would pull a knife. I didn't know he'd be a sore loser and take his shame out on you. You were too clever for your own good back then. I never expected you to grace my door, wanting to know where she came from."

"Wait," Dorian interrupted, before Aaron released a tirade of abuse and had them all thrown out. He shot Aaron an irate glare. "We're racing ahead of ourselves. We're here because—"

"Nora Adkins escaped Bethlem and tried to shoot Caterina last night." Mrs Haggert's thin lips curled in amusement, though the memory chilled Dorian's blood. "It pays to have *friends* at Bow Street, Mr Flynn."

He was impressed, though not surprised. Only a handful of men were on the take, but greed was an incurable disease and often contagious. "How do you know Nora Adkins?"

"I don't." Mrs Haggert lowered herself into the chair. "I've never spoken to her myself."

"How do you know Tobias Trigg?"

Silence ensued.

"I went to see a mesmerist," Delphine confessed. "He helped me access lost memories. Monsieur Chabert said I may need more sessions to unlock all the secrets of the past, but I remembered seeing you in Green Park."

The news had Mrs Haggert trembling. She covered her mouth with her hand, taking a moment to regain her composure. "Trust me. Those memories are best left buried. No good will come from resurrecting the dead. It's a mistake, Caterina."

Delphine remained resolute in her quest for answers. "We have every reason to believe you're to blame for what happened to my parents. That you stole me away and murdered them in cold blood."

Although Delphine had sobbed this morning when Dorian held her close and explained how her parents had died, she did not shed a tear now.

"Then the devil has done a good job of making you believe his lies. Search your heart, Caterina. You know I ain't to blame. If you could remember the time you spent here, you'd know I ain't never hurt you."

Instinct said there was truth to those words, but Dorian was quick to prove her wrong. "Nora said she found Caterina picking pockets on West Street."

"That's a lie. Nora saw Tobias on West Street. She recognised him because he refused to get rid of that ruby stick. She never found us. He died keeping our secret."

"What secret?" Delphine darted from the chair and fell to her knees at Mrs Haggert's feet. "Be honest with me. Please. I deserve to know the truth, however ugly it may be. I need justice, justice for my parents." She reached for Mrs Haggert's gnarled hand and gripped it tightly. "Something tells me I can trust you. Don't forsake me now."

The woman's rheumy eyes settled on Delphine. She surprised everyone by saying, "I'd have kept you if it weren't for Nora Adkins. I'd have raised you as my own daughter, said goodbye to this life and bought us a cottage on the coast somewhere."

Delphine looked more confused than ever.

"You need to tell me everything," she begged.

The weight of the past had Mrs Haggert slumping in the chair. "I've kept the secrets for so long, I ain't got a clue where to start."

Dorian helped matters by relaying the facts.

"Monsieur Chabert believes someone tampered with Miss Chance's mind when she was a child. That man was Tobias Trigg. He was there the night you took Miss Chance from Green Park. He left Nora bound and gagged in a warehouse not far from here. The timing suggests he was murdered sometime after that."

"He was murdered the same night," the woman barked. "They never caught the devil, but Nora had been blabbing to someone." Mrs Haggert dabbed a tear from her eye. "It's why I had to let Caterina go. It's why I had the name Delphine sewn into her dress and arranged for Aaron Chance to find her."

Aaron shot to his feet. "She's lying. It was a chance meeting. We've always joked about it because of our surname. She's inventing a story to suit her purpose."

Mrs Haggert laughed. "It weren't no chance meeting. You went to look at lodgings on Phoenix Street. That's where you found each other."

Delphine looked at Aaron, her eyes wide. "I remember now. I was told to wait in Phoenix Street, to sleep in the baker's shop doorway."

"Course, I couldn't have you living so close to the hen house," Mrs Haggert continued. "So I arranged for you to fight Maguire. I made a sizeable donation to the purse. That's how you could afford the room above Mrs Maloney's bookshop. I knew she'd take one look at you all and gather you under her wing."

Aaron dropped into the chair, dumbfounded.

"The rest you've done on your own," Mrs Haggert said proudly.

"How did I hurt my head?" Delphine was still holding Mrs Haggert's hand. "I thought that was the cause of my memory loss."

"You tripped over a loose cobblestone. It's as Flynn said. Tobias helped you to suppress your memories. It was a trick he'd learned in Vienna. He left for the continent the night we took you, but the fool made the mistake of returning to town." She sounded exasperated, as if her pleas had fallen on deaf ears. "That's when he happened upon Nora. That's when the plan fell to pieces."

Delphine's jaw dropped. "But I don't remember my time here, either."

"Tobias locked them memories away the night he lured Nora to the warehouse. Escaping the hen house was the one chance you had to make a new life for yourself."

"One chance," she whispered, gazing fondly at her brother. "How apt. The day I met Aaron changed my life."

"You mention the night you took her from Green Park." Dorian was keen to know why Delphine's parents died. It was the key to the puzzle. It had to be the reason Nora had tried to kill her. The reason someone had hired thugs to abduct her off the street. "How did you know where to find her? And why would you steal a child from her parents?"

Perhaps her parents were already dead.

Mrs Haggert looked like she would rather lose a limb than repeat what happened that night. She shifted in her seat and stared at Aaron. "If the wrong people learn about this, she might hang."

Delphine tugged Mrs Haggert's hand to get her attention. "It has something to do with me scattering flower petals. They were going to kill my mother if I refused."

He came for the Jubilee and got lost in the whispers.
Happen he meant for me to stay at the Pulteney Hotel.

Nora's crazed words flitted through Dorian's mind. Every foolish thing the woman said had a ring of truth to it. It was just a case of piecing the fragments together.

"He came for the Jubilee and stayed at the Pulteney

Hotel. It's on the corner of Bolton Street, where Delphine lived with her parents. The hotel is near Green Park, where she was told to wait for you."

Mrs Haggert nodded and hung her head.

She wept for a minute or more.

But what the devil did it have to do with scattering flowers?

Then a thought struck him.

"Lots of foreign dignitaries came for the celebration. Many stayed at the Pulteney. There were processions. Some children were invited to sit with Queen Charlotte in the flotilla of boats parading along the Thames. With her father being secretary to the ambassador, Delphine was one of them."

Mrs Haggert wiped away her tears. "Her father tried to stop it, but they had footpads rob him and throw him off Vauxhall Bridge."

Stop what?

And why would the truth place Delphine in danger?

The Grand Jubilee of 1814 marked the 100th anniversary of Hanoverian rule. It was also a means of celebrating the end of the Napoleonic Wars. Whispers of assassination attempts were rife. London received an influx of Napoleon sympathisers. Hence they came up with the idea of having children sit with Queen Charlotte in the royal barge.

An icy chill rippled down Dorian's spine.

While Delphine and Aaron looked confused, he said, "She was meant to carry something other than petals in her basket. Delphine was meant to carry the weapon someone planned to use to assassinate the Queen."

Delphine shook her head. "That can't be true."

Mrs Haggert's sigh carried the weight of her burden. "They were going to kill her mother if she didn't. Sofia confided in a maid. The maid's brother worked for me, and together, we made a plan."

A mournful stillness filled the room.

The weight of unspoken grief hung heavily in the air.

"You were right to hire Flynn," Aaron said dolefully. "But I've never been as afraid as I am right now. Someone killed to keep this secret. They'll not rest until they've silenced you, Delphine."

Dorian's stomach churned. "We'll find the people responsible."

He'd not lose Delphine.

He couldn't lose Delphine.

"They're faceless men," Mrs Haggert said, reminding Dorian of the many times Delphine had used those exact words. "There were four of them. Strange that three Frenchmen died in a blaze the night after we rescued Caterina. Nora is the only one who can identify the ringleader. That's why I hid her in Bethlem instead of hanging her from Blackfriars Bridge."

The news brought a chorus of gasps.

"So *you* blackmailed Lord Meldrum?" Dorian said.

Mrs Haggert smiled. "I had to find someone who had some clout at the hospital. I had to get Nora off the streets so she couldn't find Caterina. All this time, I've let Aaron think he had to keep Caterina safe from me. It worked a treat for the best part of sixteen years."

Aaron cursed. "You never told me her name was Caterina."

"Now you know why."

Lady Gambit

Dorian took a moment to consider the next step in the investigation. All evidence pointed to the current Lord Meldrum being a key player. He visited Nora in Bethlem. He freed her from the hospital and gave her the pistol. But he would have been fourteen years old at the time of the Jubilee.

"Picking the old Lord Meldrum may have been a mistake," he said. "Lucky for you, he had no idea who was blackmailing him. But it's possible he was the ringleader, and now his son is left trying to hide the evidence of his crimes."

The lord's desperation to marry Delphine stemmed from more than a need to clear his debts. What's the betting she would drown in the lake at Farnworth Park or suffer some other accident a month after they'd wed?

Mrs Haggert shuffled to the edge of the seat. "Then you'd better arrest the bugger, Mr Flynn. Caterina ain't safe until you do."

"You're not safe either." He recalled what had been said in front of Nora last night. "Nora knows you were with Tobias in Green Park. We inadvertently named you as being complicit in the crime." They needed to put a man outside Bow Street to monitor all visitors.

Mrs Haggert shrugged. "Death comes to us all, but I hope I'm in the crowd when they hang the beast who shot Sofia."

What sort of heartless beast shot an unarmed woman in the back? Still, the nature of Sofia's death left one unanswered question.

He touched Delphine's arm. "Isn't there something you want to ask Mrs Haggert? Something about your mother?"

She glanced at him over her shoulder, her bottom lip trembling. "Will you ask for me? I'm not sure I have the strength to say the words."

He nodded, and she came to sit beside him on the sofa, threading her arm through his and resting her head against his shoulder.

Aaron looked but said nothing.

Mrs Haggert merely smiled.

"We learnt that Sofia Chadwick died in the Belle Sauvage Inn, Ludgate Hill." Daventry had been quite thorough in his investigation. "A witness statement said she had a child with her when she took a room, but the child disappeared."

Mrs Haggert sighed. "I'd rather tell you the combination to my vault than repeat the words you need to hear, Caterina." She rubbed her eyes and inhaled a deep breath. "But there ain't no point you leaving here without knowing how much your mother loved you."

The comment brought an image of Dorian's mother crashing into his mind. There were many words to describe the woman who had given birth to him. Selfish. Vain. Cold.

But all men were not born equal.

One day they would depart this world, and the confusing elements of life would read like a chapter in a book. Every page would make perfect sense.

"I let Sofia take one of my boys," Mrs Haggert began. "She dressed him in a hooded cloak and bought tickets for the stage to St Austell."

Delphine slid her arm around Dorian's waist, holding him tightly. "Was she running away?"

"No, gal! She was trying to fool the devil. It was the night we took you from Green Park. She was trying to lure him across town. Except she didn't know Nora had turned with the tide."

They all sat solemnly for a few seconds.

"We got away." Mrs Haggert's hand came to rest on her heart. "But in the shadow of the majestic St Paul's, with its bells tolling loudly, Sofia was shot in the back."

Delphine cried then.

She buried her face in Dorian's coat and wept.

He made a promise to himself as he held her close and watched her sob. He couldn't promise their life would be unmarred by tragic events, but he would ensure the days between were glorious.

Mrs Haggert's discreet cough stole their attention. "Happen the question you need to ask yourself is why now? What stirred the hornet's nest?"

Delphine raised her head and dashed tears from her eyes. "It all began after my visit to Bethlem when Nora called me by my mother's name."

"Did it? Nora is mad. Why would anyone give a hoot about the nonsense she spouts? The only person it would mean anything to is the devil who killed your parents."

It was clear the guards at Bethlem thought Nora was deranged.

Anything she said would be dismissed as lunacy.

"It began after my visit." Dorian would never forget Powell's hostility and his reluctance to answer questions. "The Superintendent must have told Lord Meldrum that I interviewed Nora."

"Probably because he feared you'd learn the truth of

how Nora came to be there," Aaron said. "Meldrum doesn't want anyone to know he's being blackmailed."

"No one knows he's being blackmailed," Mrs Haggert countered. "I ain't told a soul, and I trust my men. I can't see the Superintendent blabbing. His neck would be for the chopping block."

One piece of evidence cast doubt over the extent of Meldrum's involvement. Dorian had struggled to understand why Meldrum would free Nora and give her a pistol. He had to know it would bring trouble to his door.

Delphine must have read his mind because she said, "One other person knows Lord Meldrum is being blackmailed. His friend, Bertie."

"Who?" Mrs Haggert said.

"Gerald Bertram," Dorian added. The man had practically begged them to help Meldrum and find the blackmailer. Perhaps he had a personal interest in the outcome. "He met Lord Meldrum while on a Grand Tour. I found it odd that they were abroad the same year. I imagine Bertie is approaching forty."

Aaron sat forward. "I make it my business to know all the men of the *ton*. I know the names of their relatives and close friends. I've never heard of Gerald Bertram."

"Happen that's because he don't exist," Mrs Haggert said, "though there's only one way to know for sure. Question Meldrum on his own. Aaron can scare the devil into confessing."

Dorian considered the plan. "Invite Meldrum to Fortune's Den. Say it's to discuss his mounting debts and his marriage proposal. We can take matters from there."

Though he hated to admit it, the safest place for Delphine was at her brothers' club.

"If you need help, I've men at my disposal." Mrs Haggert was keen to be part of the solution. Her desire to find the man who'd shot Sofia was there in her determined expression.

"I heard they arrested Harold Haggert for highway robbery." Aaron scoffed. "Why would I trust your men when they lack the courage to pull the trigger?"

Mrs Haggert laughed. "Do you remember what I told you to do when there's a tough choice to make, Caterina?"

Delphine looked at her blankly.

"The decisions we make today shape our future. Why would I hang for that blackguard when I can stand in the crowd, sip gin from a flask and watch him dangle?"

Dorian admired the sentiment. Every decision they made now, every thought and deed, laid the foundations for Delphine's future.

He just prayed they didn't make a mistake.

He prayed the faceless man wasn't one step ahead.

Chapter Twenty

Fortune's Den
Aldgate Street

Mr Daventry sat at the dining table, listening as Dorian relayed the information they'd gained from Mrs Haggert. His gaze moved from his cut of veal to the mantel clock. "Her account is logical and far too accurate to be anything but the truth."

Aaron tossed back half a glass of burgundy before grumbling under his breath. "While I'm happy Delphine has clarity, knowing that woman had a hand in helping us off the street makes my blood boil."

"At least we know why she kept the secret." Delphine did not wish to defend Mrs Haggert's actions, but the woman had come to her mother's aid, and for that, she would always be grateful.

Daventry raised his glass in salute. "Nothing is ever as it seems. It's impossible to know another person's motives. It's a lesson for us all."

"I know the damn lesson," Aaron snapped. He'd been agitated since Lord Meldrum agreed to visit Fortune's Den tonight. His dark eyes flicked to the clock. The incessant ticking bothered him, too. "I'll rest easier when this business is behind us, and the culprit is in Newgate."

They all fell silent as they ate their meal.

No one mentioned the plan.

If Lord Meldrum confessed, they could all rest easily.

If Bertie was the faceless man, someone would die tonight.

Dorian glanced at her across the table, his heart-stopping smile making her stomach flip. She wanted done with this dreaded business, too. She wanted to spend the rest of her life in his bed. Spend forever simply loving him.

"Has Miss Darrow returned to her modiste shop?" Daventry said, an air of intrigue to his tone as he addressed Theo. "She must have lost a substantial amount of work while caring for you. I'm surprised she stayed at Mile End so long."

The change of subject brought light relief, though it roused the same curious questions about the modiste.

"I'm the King of Hearts. Perhaps she finds me irresistible." Theo's teasing was sweet music to Delphine's ears. "In truth, I spent most of the time asleep while she busied about in her sewing box. Miss Darrow hugged the thing like it was a beloved pet."

Delphine had noticed the modiste's preoccupation with the box. Miss Darrow had brought it to Theo's room every day.

Aramis snorted. "You're losing your appeal, Theo. I

wouldn't admit that a lady preferred the feel of thread on her lips to those of the half-naked man in bed."

Theo grinned. "Why do you think I stole the box and brought it home? It won't take Miss Darrow long to realise it's not at Mile End. Then I shall play a little game with her. It will be her reward for mopping my brow. Her punishment for being a liar."

Aware of the importance of raising Theo's spirits, Aramis continued goading their brother. "Miss Darrow strikes me as a resourceful woman. Let's make a wager on how long it takes her to reclaim the box."

The subtle storm behind Theo's eyes dissipated, leaving a ray of excitement in its wake. "Very well. State your bet and the sum you wish to stake."

While the men debated how long Theo could keep Miss Darrow's box, Delphine excused herself and headed upstairs. She needed a moment alone to gather her wits before Lord Meldrum arrived. A moment to consider all that had transpired since her initial meeting with Dorian Flynn.

Everything in her bedchamber was as she left it, yet she was not the same woman who had idled away hours reading or brushing her hair. She noted the half-read book on the nightstand, the pretty combs on her dressing table, the ream of blank paper at her escritoire.

Who should I write to, Mr Flynn?

Besides Miss Darrow, you're my only friend.

Dorian was more than her friend. He was the warmth that kept the coldness away. He was her guiding light in the darkness. He was faith, hope, the strength she needed to get through the day. He was heaven here on earth.

Tears filled her eyes as she glanced around the room. Loneliness clung to every corner. The memory of the time spent staring at her reflection brought a chill to her bones.

Who am I?

The woman gazing back always asked the same daunting question. Inventing stories had filled the time, but never the cavernous hole in her chest. Never the feeling that part of her was out in the world somewhere, desperately trying to find her way home.

The light knock on the door brought Dorian.

He looked anxious. "I came to see if you needed anything. Meldrum will be here in half an hour. You don't have to come down. I can speak on your behalf."

A pang in her gut said Lord Meldrum was an imbecile, not a murderer. Both Mr Powell and Mr Bertram were old enough to know her parents. Old enough to be part of a posse who sought to make a political statement by killing Queen Charlotte.

"I wish to hear what Lord Meldrum has to say, and he needs to believe he's coming to discuss his proposal." She beckoned Dorian inside and urged him to close the door. "I thought I might change into a warmer dress." Clothes had always been her armour. "Will you help me with the buttons?"

She opened the armoire doors and gazed at the neatly folded garments, but having Dorian in her chamber played havoc with her senses. Like the way his rampant hands had moved over her body two nights ago, his eyes were everywhere, devouring every inch of her personal space.

"There's something you're not telling me." He came to

stand behind her, his strong fingers gripping her waist, his hot mouth against her ear. "A secret you've not shared."

His body was a masculine wall of virility at her back. His potent scent roused desirous thoughts, wicked thoughts, thoughts that left her breasts heavy, her nipples hard, her sex pulsing. Silent calls only he could answer.

Bend me over.

Take me here, Dorian. Take me now.

"I suspect Lord Meldrum is innocent." She raised her skirts as if preparing to remove her stockings. "I fear we will need a cunning plan if we mean to catch the true culprit."

"Instinct tells me you're right." The slight hitch in his breath confirmed his thoughts were of an amorous nature, too. His lips brushed the shell of her ear. "If only we had time to explore the possibilities. Cunning plans are your forte."

She closed her eyes, savouring his touch.

"Perhaps swift action is needed." She needed to feel him moving inside her, feel complete and utter bliss. "We could reach a conclusion in minutes, indulge in hours of rigorous scrutiny tonight."

He moved the fraction needed for her to feel the ridge of his erection against her buttocks. "Trust me, love. The way you affect me, I can reach a conclusion in seconds."

She raised her skirts past her thighs. "Consider this a prelude to the deep and meaningful discussion we'll have later. Take me like this, Dorian. Take me now. I need you. I can't wait."

He growled as he fiddled with his trousers. "After a

Lady Gambit

fistfight with Aaron, one would think I'd learnt my lesson. But I'm powerless to resist your charms. Bend over, love. Grip the shelf."

A shiver of need ran through her when he tossed her skirts over her back. He smoothed his hands over her bare buttocks and groaned like he'd never seen such a glorious sight.

"You'll be the death of me, woman." He slid his manhood back and forth over her sex before breaching her entrance. "Minx. You're so wet. I might think you planned this all along."

Everything about this man was divine. Everything about this moment was sublime. As he stretched her wide and pushed deep, she knew exactly who she was ... a passionate woman who would risk her life for love.

"I love you," she panted as his manhood thickened inside her. "I want you every minute of every day. Now take me hard and quick. But whatever you do, be quiet."

"I'll show you how much I love you later. I shall strip you naked and worship every beautiful inch, stare at you as I make you come. For now, I mean to remind you how good we are together."

He slid his hand over her hip to her sex, his long fingers teasing her bud while he sank his hot flesh into her. He pumped long and deep, the rustle of silk doing little to disguise the erotic sound of their bodies slapping.

"Yes, don't stop, Dorian."

She was so aroused, desire licked her body like flames. As her climax tore through her, Dorian gripped her hips and rode her harder.

Seconds later, his guttural moan preceded his own release.

He withdrew, spilling the evidence of their love over her buttocks.

She was still holding onto the armoire shelf, sated and happy, while Dorian cleaned her with his handkerchief.

"I'll never think of this room in quite the same way." She stared at her clothes, remembering the times she'd felt detached from life, so numb. Now love filled her heart and flowed through every cell.

"Delphine!" The stern sound of Aaron's voice echoed from the stairs below, which meant time had run out, and Lord Meldrum was moments from arriving.

"We should return to the dining room," she said, straightening her skirts and turning to face the man she loved.

Passion gleamed in his eyes. "I never expected to meet anyone like you." He leaned closer and kissed her, holding her face in his hands as his tongue swept through her lips. "You've turned my world upside down in a way I never thought possible."

She smiled while fighting the need to make love again. "You're the love of my life, Dorian. Never forget that. Never forget how much I adore you."

"Is it too late to run?" he teased.

"Why would I run when you promised to remain beside me forever?" Doubt slithered into her heart. Danger loomed. She felt the coldness of it in her blood. "Let us deal with the devil who would tear us asunder. I'm Delphine Chance. I shall fight to the death to protect what we have."

Lady Gambit

Aaron hammered on the bedchamber door. "I need you both downstairs. The show is about to begin."

With the hour nearing seven, they hurried to the study and took their seats with Aaron and Mr Daventry.

Sigmund hung a sign on the front door confirming the club was closed. Aramis, Christian and Theo were waiting in a carriage at the end of the street, keen to ensure Lord Meldrum came alone.

Aaron settled into his throne. He cracked his knuckles and cricked his neck, though this was to be a battle of words, not fists. Thankfully, he didn't ask what they'd been doing upstairs.

Lord Meldrum arrived five minutes later. He wore a green coat with excessive padding and an ugly blue waistcoat that clung to his narrow waist like a strangling vine.

He handed Sigmund his hat as he strode into the room but came skidding to a halt when he noticed the crowd. "What the blazes? Your letter said this would be a private affair."

Aaron kept calm. "It is a private affair." He gestured to the other men in the room. "Flynn is conducting a criminal investigation, and the Home Secretary placed Daventry in charge of the case. Before I agree to anything, I need to know you're not a murderer."

"A murderer?" Lord Meldrum looked aghast.

Aaron's nod prompted Sigmund to close the door and turn the key in the lock, which only added to the lord's agitation.

"What the devil is going on here?"

"Who knows I summoned you to Fortune's Den?" Aaron barked.

"What? No one."

"Who knows?" Aaron yelled.

"No one." The lord spun on his heel and met Dorian's gaze. "What's this about, Flynn? Did you find the blackmailer, is that it? Has the devil accused me of a crime? If so, it's a ploy to make me look like the villain."

Delphine stood and urged the men to remain seated. The lord would likely expire of heart failure if he didn't calm down. She gripped Lord Meldrum's arm and led him to a seat.

"We know the identity of your blackmailer." She kept a pacifying hand on his shoulder. "The person no longer has a reason to demand Nora Adkins remains at Bethlem and releases you from any obligation."

Lord Meldrum was not appeased. His face twisted in anger as he captured her hand. "Who is it? That swine almost drove me to the brink of insanity. I demand to know my tormentor's name."

The blind rage in his eyes made her falter. "I—"

"Your father stole money meant for the hospital's relocation," Dorian said, his gaze meeting hers in silent reassurance. "If you want to draw attention to that fact, then we'll prosecute the blackmailer, and you can have your day in court."

Lord Meldrum paled.

"While you're considering your position," Dorian continued, his furious glare fixed on their joined hands, "you will release Miss Chance before I break your fingers."

Noting Dorian's vehemence, the lord turned to Aaron. "If you've caught the blackmailer, then why the hostility? I had nothing to do with the attack on your family. What else can I do to persuade you I'm innocent?"

Aaron's dark gaze sent a chill through the room. "You can answer Flynn's questions. The mounting evidence suggests you've plotted to have my sister killed. If you want to leave here alive, cease with the bravado and tell the damn truth."

Silence descended.

The lord sat, shaking his head in confusion.

Dorian rose and perched on the corner of Aaron's imposing desk. "Who knows you're being blackmailed?"

The lord swallowed. "No one. Well, perhaps my butler, though he wouldn't dare disgrace the household."

"And Bertie," Delphine said.

"Yes, and Bertie, but I trust him implicitly."

"How long have you been friends?" She supposed it must be almost a decade if they met on Lord Meldrum's Grand Tour.

"Nine years." He frowned, clearly wondering why it was relevant. "We met in Geneva and again in Turin. I remember remarking it was strange, not strange we visited the same destinations, but that we'd chosen the same hotels. We exchanged letters while he travelled the Continent, but he returned to London when my father died."

"That was three years ago," Mr Daventry said from a shadowed corner of the room. "I presume he didn't remain in town."

"No, Bertie rarely stays in one place for long." Tired of answering what he surely perceived were pointless questions, he said, "What has my friendship with Bertie got to do with anything? You said there's evidence to suggest I'm guilty of a crime."

"Nora Adkins came here last night." Dorian folded his arms across his chest. "She said you released her from Bethlem, that you gave her the pistol she used to threaten Miss Chance. According to the records, you've visited Nora's cell frequently the last few weeks."

"That makes you an accessory to attempted murder," Daventry added. "Worse still, Nora was part of an assassination plot, so I suppose we could charge you with a crime against the Crown."

Lord Meldrum shot off the chair. "No!"

Fearing what he would do, Dorian grabbed the lord by his cravat. "I suggest you start talking. Even a peer can hang for treason."

"Wait! Wait!" Lord Meldrum raised his hands, his breath coming in shallow pants. "There's been a misunderstanding. Allow me to explain."

Dorian threw the devil back in the seat. "Did you conspire with Powell to free Nora from Bethlem?"

"Yes, but the woman is mad." He scrubbed his face with his hand. "I presumed she'd be dead within a day, and then I'd be free from the blackmailer. Bertie said I needed to deal with the matter swiftly, and Powell feared the board would learn he'd been taking bribes."

"So you gave her a weapon?" Aaron said incredulously.

"It was Bertie's idea. He said she would most likely shoot herself, or she'd wave it about in the street and come a cropper."

One look at this pathetic fool made Delphine glad her

brothers were rogues. She looked at Dorian, butterflies fluttering in her belly. There was something attractive about a man who knew his own mind.

"Do you do everything Mr Bertram says?"

"I trust his advice."

"Did he ever go with you to Bethlem?" she said.

He hesitated before saying, "Twice. We let him talk to Nora, hoping she'd tell him why someone wanted her kept locked away."

"His name isn't in the visitors' book," Dorian snapped.

"He used an alias."

For long, drawn-out seconds, no one spoke.

One could almost hear the cogs turning in everyone's mind.

Something Lord Meldrum said earlier roused her interest. "You said Mr Powell has been taking bribes. What did you mean?"

The lord shrugged. "Powell said the blackmailer contacted him directly. He threatened to report him to the board if he didn't keep Nora's incarceration a secret. Powell was to inform him if she had any visitors or mentioned any names."

After confessing all today, Mrs Haggert would have told them if she had written to Mr Powell.

"Did you ever check the letters Mr Powell received against the letters from the blackmailer?"

The lord shook his head. "Why would I? No one else knew I was being blackmailed. It's obviously the same person."

For a man of thirty, Lord Meldrum was stupid and naive.

Could he not see that Bertie had been using him?

"What else did Bertie tell you to do?" she said before raising a hand to stall him. "Let me guess. He advised you to elope with me. He urged you to write to my brother."

Lord Meldrum's cheeks flushed. "Well, yes. He said it was the most logical solution to my problems. Indeed, why would you not want to marry a peer?"

"Because she's marrying me," Dorian said, resolute.

"You haven't asked me yet, Mr Flynn." She would marry him in a heartbeat. "I suggest you find the courage soon." Before an accident occurred and she found herself with child.

"I've courage abound, madam. As you've recently been made aware." Was he referring to their illicit encounter upstairs or his fight with Aaron?

Mr Daventry stood suddenly and took centre stage. "There is another solution to your problems, Meldrum. One that would persuade Aaron Chance to wipe your debts to the club and ensure this blackmail business never surfaces."

Lord Meldrum clasped his hands together in prayer. "I'll do anything you ask of me. I mean to clear my name and make a new life. Bertie suggests visiting India for—"

"For goodness sake, man," Aaron cried. "Bertram is the damn problem. He murdered Delphine's parents. He's the reason you're being blackmailed. I'll wager he's the one who wrote to Powell."

Lord Meldrum frowned. "It can't be Bertie. In the absence of family, he's to inherit my house in Mayfair along with any personal effects. Why would he encourage me to marry Miss Chance if he'd benefit from my death?"

"Because he wants you to clear your debts before he murders you and your wife," Mr Daventry said calmly. "Allow us to prove it to you." He waited for the peer to nod before continuing. "Do you agree to abide by the plan?"

"What is the plan?"

"You must send a note to Bertram telling him that you're leaving London with Miss Chance. Say you're staying at the Belle Sauvage in Ludgate Hill tonight and heading to Scotland in the morning. Say you had to act quickly before Aaron Chance changed his mind. Mention Miss Chance has her own room, but you hope to consummate your union tonight."

Dorian turned his head sharply as if reeling from a slap.

"But I'm not really going to Scotland?"

"No!" Aaron muttered a curse. "We'll wait for him to arrive. I assure you, he will come if he thinks Delphine is in a room alone."

Dorian wasn't convinced. "Someone needs to remain here and ensure Miss Chance is safe. Bertram might guess it's a trap and come looking for her at Fortune's Den."

Mr Daventry looked at Dorian and gave an amused snort. "If Bertram smells a rat, he will be on the next boat to Madras. No. Miss Chance will be waiting in the room at the Belle Sauvage. We can't risk anything going wrong."

Aaron and Dorian jumped to attention, their protests so loud she could hardly hear herself think.

"I will do as Mr Daventry asks," she cried, silencing the men. "I will lure Mr Bertram to the Belle Sauvage. I owe it to my parents to see this matter through to the bitter end."

She would ensure Mr Bertram never forgot the name Caterina Chadwick. The child he tried to use so cruelly had returned to have her vengeance. Though if she survived the night, she would take a new identity. A name that was destined to be hers. She just had to pray she lived long enough to become Delphine Flynn.

Chapter Twenty-One

The Belle Sauvage Inn
Ludgate Hill

Dorian sat in the parked carriage in the outer courtyard of the Belle Sauvage Inn. Part of him wished he was still the man who ambled through the lonely corridors of his manor house, not a man so in love he was about to suffer a seizure.

"Gerald Bertram should be here by now." Three hours had passed since Meldrum and Delphine entered the Belle Sauvage's busy inner courtyard. They'd shared supper and retired to their respective rooms, where they remained like sitting ducks. "Why the hell did you suggest this place? It will be impossible to identify Bertram in the crowd."

With stabling for a hundred horses and an inner courtyard large enough to accommodate ten carriages, the inn was a hive of activity, even at this late hour.

"We must be patient." Daventry watched as more carriages trundled past and couples on foot came to drink in the taproom and rent a bed for the night. "We need Bertram to believe he can kill a woman here and escape unnoticed."

Bile stung Dorian's throat. "You could kill five people and no one would hear the screams. Besides, the son of a devil has done it before."

Why the hell wasn't Daventry panicking?

"We've men stationed on the street. The Chance brothers are positioned in a room on the upper gallery. Gibbs is in the yard assessing all new arrivals. He'll give the signal once there's a confirmed sighting."

"Gibbs has never seen the villain and has no means of identifying him other than from the brief description I gave him." No one had spent long enough with Bertram to point him out with any accuracy.

"Gibbs is as shrewd as they come. I trust he will alert us the moment he sees something suspicious. But if it will settle your fears, I'll enter the taproom and assess the situation there."

Daventry's sangfroid used to be a quality Dorian admired—not anymore. "I'm certain you wouldn't be so composed if your wife was upstairs, waiting for someone to shoot her in the back."

"Probably not," Daventry said, his remark feeding Dorian's growing apprehension. "But Miss Chance is armed, and we've eyes and ears everywhere."

"What makes you so sure Bertram will come? He'll know it's a trap."

Daventry's grin said he'd dealt with enough fiends to understand their motives. "Why do you think I chose the inn where Miss Chance's mother was shot? Revisiting the scene to finish the job will be too tempting for Bertram to resist."

Dorian cursed.

He was one breath away from ruining the plan, from leaping out of the carriage and charging to Delphine's room, but the comment she made as he kissed her goodbye kept echoing in his mind.

There's no proof Mr Bertram has committed a crime.

Meldrum would be blamed.

Nora was mad.

Mrs Haggert was the blackmailer.

All evidence against Bertram was circumstantial.

My only hope of gaining justice for my parents is to force him out of the shadows. And I can't live a happy life if I'm always looking over my shoulder.

Dorian scrubbed his face with his hand and sighed. "The wait is killing me. It's the worst form of torture."

"That is the nature of love. To love someone so completely is not without risk or hardship. But I know how this ends. And it's nothing like the bleak image you paint in your mind."

He tried to banish his fears and imagine them strolling through the gardens at Mile End, slipping into the orangery to make love. He couldn't be without her. She brought meaning to his empty existence. She brought hope where there had been despair.

"There is something I've not told her," Daventry said as he peered into the dim courtyard and observed those entering the inn on foot. "I feared it would distract her from her course."

Dorian's stomach churned. Another sad story would be

one too many. "Does it relate to her parents? I'm not sure she can cope with hearing more depressing tales."

"It relates to her life before she became Delphine Chance. This is good news. Oscar Chadwick's father is alive and living in Chichester."

Dorian sat forward, shock and anger waging war. "Good Lord! Her grandfather is alive, and you've not told her? Does Aaron know?"

"No. I had to be certain of the facts. I'd not raise her hopes only to dash them again." Daventry narrowed his gaze as a carriage rattled by. "Tonight, I need her to focus on catching Bertram."

Dorian studied the vehicle. The groom's familiar green livery raised his pulse another notch.

The sudden bang on the window added to the mounting tension, too.

"Something about this don't feel right," Gibbs said as soon as Dorian lowered the window. He scanned the cobbled lane leading to the inner courtyard. "We're like trout nibbling the bait. This cove is cunning. And he's playing us for fools."

Daventry fell silent for a moment—lost in thought.

That's when a figure marched towards them, jabbing a finger at Gibbs. "You! You there! I recognise you from the Old Swan."

Saints and sinners!

What was the Earl of Retford doing at the Belle Sauvage?

Dorian's father strode up to Gibbs. "I assume my son is here. Fetch him before I raze this damn place to the ground."

"Fetch him yourself. I ain't your lackey." Gibbs shooed the earl away. "I don't care who you are. I answer to no one but my maker."

Affronted, the earl looked like he might thump Gibbs, but he caught sight of Dorian sitting in the carriage, and a row erupted.

"Of all the rotten schemes your mother invented to hold me to ransom, this one takes the biscuit." The earl stamped his foot on the cobblestones. "I thought you were cut from a different cloth. Evidently, I was mistaken."

The devil's own fury burned in Dorian's chest, but he kept his tone even. "Go home, Father. I'm tired of watching you act like a fool."

The earl yanked the carriage door open. "There's only one fool here. I offer you the world, and you throw it back in my face. What son does that? A thankless one, I say. Now, get out of this vehicle."

Dorian noted a few bystanders watching from the entrance to the inner courtyard. Bertram could be amongst them. A diversion would give him the perfect moment to strike.

Indeed, he needed to get rid of his father and quickly.

With his temper rearing like an untamed stallion, Dorian vaulted to the ground and faced his father. "You reap what you sow. You had no interest in me when I was a boy. I'm not interested in you now."

The earl's face ballooned, his glower conveying the depth of his displeasure. "I'm warning you. Marry that strumpet, and you'll not get another penny from me."

Strumpet? Was he referring to Delphine?

How had the earl known where to find him? And how

had he learned of Dorian's intention to marry her? No one but her family knew—and Lord Meldrum. But he'd been hiding in a rented room for two hours.

"I don't need your money. I've never drawn my allowance."

"No, because you're happy to live in a hovel."

"Flynn owns a large manor house south of the Thames," Daventry said as he rounded the carriage. "He uses the room above the Swan while working in town. Presently, he's investigating a matter on behalf of the Home Secretary. Some men are made for idleness. Some lead the country to greatness."

Dorian glanced at Daventry with untold respect. They were kindred spirits—the illegitimate sons of heartless men and devious women.

The earl blinked and stuttered in shock, but he picked his arrogance off the floor and dusted it down quickly. "You're nothing without me."

Dorian squared his shoulders. "I'll never be your puppet. Had you taken the time to nurture a relationship, I may have followed you to the ends of the earth. As it is, I wouldn't piss in your chamber pot."

Before the earl could respond, Daventry said, "We're acting on behalf of the Crown, and you're hindering an investigation. How did you know Flynn was here?"

"I don't have to tell you anything," the earl said, stony-faced.

Daventry's eyes darkened, and he looked like a panther on the prowl. "If our client dies because you failed to reveal a crucial piece of evidence, I shall take the matter to the highest authority."

Lady Gambit

"I'll answer to no one but the King."

"I'm sure the King will be keen to hear of your failings."

Dorian stepped forward, his face mere inches from his father's. "If you care for me at all, you will help me save my betrothed from a devious villain. This is your only chance to prove I mean something to you. How did you know to come here?"

The earl failed to answer.

"You're wasting your breath," Daventry said in disgust.

Dorian was wrong to say he felt nothing. His father's silence brought the same crushing inadequacy he had felt as a child. It was hard to rise above it, hard to accept he was the better man, and move on.

"My father had me followed." Dorian turned his back on his kin and focused on his future. "How else could he know I was here? The important question is, how does he know I plan to marry Delphine?"

A frown marred Daventry's brow. "I don't know, but Bertram is devious. He's skilled at hiding in the darkness. He's always one step ahead."

Above the racket of those drinking in the taproom, the earl coughed to get their attention. "A penny boy brought a letter to my club. I was told my son planned to marry some nameless chit, and they were staying here before eloping in the morning."

Dorian's pulse pounded in his throat. "The bastard knows we're here and still means to kill Delphine. It's not about keeping his secret. It's about punishing her for ruining his plans. He's determined to settle a personal score. Wait here. Let no one pass."

He took to his heels and darted along the cobblestones, through the inner courtyard and up the stairs to the upper gallery. He hammered on Delphine's door, relieved to see her face at the window.

"Dorian?" She frowned as she peered around the jamb. "What are you doing here? Have you found Mr Bertram? Has he confessed to killing my parents?"

"No, but I needed to know you were safe before I tore this place apart." He reached for her, gripping her hand to quell his raging fear. "Lock the door. Don't answer it again until I return."

She nodded, her mouth drawn into a tense line. "Hurry back."

He waited to hear the lock click, then raced to Meldrum's room and thumped the door with his clenched fist.

Aaron Chance appeared on the landing. "Have you lost your mind? What the hell are you doing up here? You'll ruin the plan."

Though breathless, Dorian quickly explained his fears. "Meldrum must have sent a secret message when his coachman delivered the letter to Bertram." They had read the letter before Meldrum sealed it. Everything seemed above board. "Or Bertram knew to expect a trap."

Aaron's head shot in the direction of Delphine's room.

"She's safe." Dorian kicked Meldrum's door this time. "But I'll not stand helplessly and wait for the bastard to strike. I intend to hunt him down. Deal with him in a manner I see fit."

"Agreed." Aaron flexed his fingers as he scoured the darkness. "I'll fetch my brothers. We'll get justice for Delphine our way."

Tired of getting no response from Meldrum and wondering if the lord might be dead, Dorian barged the rickety door with his shoulder.

Meldrum was asleep on the bed, holding an empty silver flask.

Dorian dragged the lord by the waistcoat, forcing him to stand. "Bertram knows we're here. You told him of our plan. How, I cannot fathom. So if you want to live to see sunrise, start talking."

Meldrum blinked sleep from his eyes. "Y-you saw the letter. I wrote exactly what you told me, not a word more."

"What the devil did you say to your coachman? You gave him a message to relay to Bertie."

Meldrum's breathing quickened. "I told him to deliver the note, that's all. I need Aaron Chance to clear my debts to Fortune's Den. Why would I risk his wrath?"

"Because you're in love with your beloved Bertie."

Meldrum blanched. "I assure you, I am not."

"I've been watching the entrance for three *bloody* hours, and there's been no sign of him." Had Bertram donned a disguise and sauntered past them unnoticed? If so, where was he, and how did he mean to murder Delphine? "He knows I'm here because he sent a note to Boodle's, alerting my father."

"Bertie is an intelligent man. He will have anticipated your move. He'll not risk his neck. Besides, I don't believe he's responsible for the things you claim. In barking up the wrong tree, you've let the real villain escape."

Dorian took less than a second to consider the suggestion.

"Bertram killed Delphine's parents." He felt the truth of it to the marrow of his bones. "He cannot afford for her to regain her memory." She had to know something about the man, something that would make him risk everything to silence her.

Meldrum refused to believe his friend was culpable. "Perhaps Bertie came here to wish me well. Perhaps he saw you and thought it odd."

"I'd have seen him pass through the entrance."

"Perhaps he was supping in the taproom and saw us arrive."

Releasing the fop, Dorian exhaled in exasperation. If the lord had an ounce of sense, he would be dangerous. "It would have been impossible for Bertram to travel from Nelson Square and arrive before we did."

"Nelson Square?" Meldrum looked confused.

"You said he was staying with you in Southwark."

"Yes, but his mistress has a house in Warwick Square. He called there last night. I told my coachman to try that address before venturing to Southwark."

Dorian's blood froze in his veins. "Warwick Square is less than a five-minute walk from here."

"That's what I'm trying to tell you. If Bertie was guilty, he would have been here by now." Meldrum sat on the bed. "The fellow never stays in the same place for long. He certainly wouldn't wait in the darkness for hours."

No, not unless it was part of the plan.

Dorian scoured his mind for answers.

The best solution to Bertie's problem was to blame

Lady Gambit

Meldrum for Delphine's murder. Perhaps he meant to wait until the morning before launching an attack. He might hold them up on the road, make murder look like a highway robbery gone awry.

No.

Wicked men often revisited the scenes of their crimes.

Arrogant men liked to outwit their opponents.

Bertram would do the deed tonight under cover of darkness, which meant Delphine would need a reason to visit Meldrum's room or vice versa.

"Have you spoken to anyone since you entered this room?"

Meldrum shook his head and gestured to the crumpled bedclothes. "I've not moved from the bed. Well, except to read the note from Aaron Chance. It's on top of the chest of drawers."

Dorian's hands shook as he peeled back the folds and read the brief missive. Aaron advised Meldrum to check on his sister hourly.

"I'd have gone but fell asleep," Meldrum said.

"This letter isn't from Aaron Chance." They'd agreed not to veer from the plan. He was suddenly glad Meldrum had slept. Had he gone to Delphine's room, they would both be dead.

Still, they were missing something crucial.

Dorian was considering the possibility that Bertram had abandoned his plan when Daventry burst into Meldrum's room. "You're not going to like this. I'm unsure how to proceed, but I know where Bertram is hiding."

"Where?" Dorian said, fear lancing through him as he

realised there was only one place Bertram could hide without them spotting him. A place he could achieve his goal without worrying about witnesses.

"The woman manning the counter in the taproom said a man arrived twenty minutes before us. He paid for Miss Chance to have her favourite room, said he was her brother and it was a surprise. The point is, it's the only one with a hidden cupboard."

Dorian didn't need to ask Daventry what that meant.

Bertram had been lurking inside Delphine's room for hours.

The devil was merely waiting for the right moment to attack.

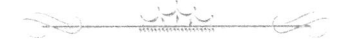

Delphine peered through the dusty windowpane into the dim courtyard below. Her heart thundered so fast she could hardly breathe. A murderer lingered in the darkness, waiting for her to make a mistake.

Was this how her mother had spent her last night?

Had she known a monster lay in wait?

Sofia must have known something was wrong. She was found face down on the cobbled walkway. Bertram had waited until the toll of the bells to shoot, hitting her in the back as one did a fox fleeing a hen house.

For the third time in as many minutes, she checked the door was locked and moved to sit on the bed.

Her leg hadn't stopped shaking since Dorian left.

Lady Gambit

But she was safe in the room. Her brothers had taken one close by and would watch the door like a hawk did prey.

Nerves forced her to the window again. Dorian had gone tearing after the villain, risking his neck to ensure she could live the rest of her life in peace. Love wasn't about gifts or nice outings. Love wasn't about reaching a climax while locked in a warm embrace. Love was a selfless act. A sacrifice made for the good of another.

There was no question her mother had loved her.

There was no doubt Dorian loved her, too.

Perhaps that's why she felt so afraid.

Unable to settle, she retrieved the pistol from under her pillow and placed it on the nightstand. Lewd sounds emanated from the room next door. The earlier argument was now a catalogue of deep groans, incessant banging and the occasional high-pitched squeal.

"This place is the devil's haunt," she uttered.

"You should have stayed at the Pulteney," came the ghostly whispers of a masculine voice from somewhere deep in the gloom. "They have a better clientele."

Her heart stopped for a beat or more.

Someone was in her room.

Yet she had sat watching the door for hours.

"W-who's there?"

"A faceless man has no name, Caterina."

The pulse of fear in her throat became a pounding drum. She squinted, gazing into the far corner of the room. Perhaps her addled mind was playing tricks because it looked like the wall was opening up and a demon was climbing out of the eaves.

She might have darted for the door, but Gerald Bertram rose before her, wearing a wicked grin and brandishing a pistol.

She gulped, unable to move or form a word.

"It's been many years since I hid in this room." He prowled towards her, the dim candlelight casting ominous shadows over his face. "Your mother thought she had escaped me. Though I admit, I was convinced you were here with her." He breathed a strange sigh. "She died because she refused to tell me where you were."

Anger rose like a tempest inside her. "You would have killed my mother either way. Had I agreed to carry the basket onto the Queen's barge, you would have killed us all when the deed was done."

Mr Bertram came to a halt at the end of the bed. "I cannot argue with that. Once I'm done here, I shall have no choice but to dispose of the men you've trusted. Starting with a terrible fire at Fortune's Den. When Flynn dies in a blaze at the Old Swan, London will mourn the loss of one of its oldest taverns."

The thought of losing everyone she loved might have cleaved her soul in two. But this fiend thought he was clever. He was not, or he would know of Dorian's Mile End abode.

Emboldened and keen to wipe the smirk from his face, she said, "Vengeance has been your constant companion all these years. It's been mine, too, though I've been blissfully unaware of it until now. Still, you've underestimated my family. You won't escape this place alive. And if you do, know I've written to Thomas Erskine of the King's

Lady Gambit

Counsel, informing him of your plot to kill the King's mother during the Jubilee."

Unperturbed by the threat, Mr Bertram laughed.

"Who am I?" he said. "No one."

Those words had echoed in her mind many times over the years. No matter how hard she tried, the answer never came to her. Yet now, it was like a locked door in the corridor had creaked slowly open, inviting her to peer inside.

"I can disappear into the mist, and no one will ever find me." He stroked his thick side whiskers. "You'd be surprised how different a man looks when he's clean-shaven, not that you will need to concern yourself with that thought again. Once Meldrum knocks on that door, you'll both meet your maker."

Though the threat left every muscle in her body stiff, she had to edge closer to the nightstand and retrieve her pistol.

If only there was a way to unsettle Mr Bertram.

When your life's on the line, you remember what I told you.

Mrs Haggert's comment seemed pertinent now.

Oddly, she didn't have to look beyond the door in the corridor to know what secrets lay inside the room.

"You're Samuel Stern. You're wanted in connection with other murders." So many confusing names and facts filled her head, but she was compelled to reveal them. "You killed the Comte de Croze and his wife on British soil two years before the Jubilee. Their servant was hanged for the crime."

All colour drained from the man's face.

The slight tremor in his hand said she had hit the mark.

"It was thought Napoleon ordered their execution." How she knew proved baffling, but the information poured from her mouth like water from a fountain. "They were killed with an unusual dagger you purchased from Mason & Sons on Ludgate Hill. Indeed, your sister lives in Warwick Square, a short distance from here."

The man's temper erupted. "So you were there that night, listening at the door like a filthy little mouse."

She had no memory of the event, only a list of facts she'd been conditioned to repeat when necessary. "I remember everything," she lied. "If you kill me, your sister will be arrested."

Mr Bertram dragged his hand down his face.

His breath turned raspy.

But a sudden knock on the door made him firm his grip on his weapon. "Ask who it is," he whispered through gritted teeth.

"Who is it?" she called.

"I've brought the extra blanket you wanted," came a woman's apologetic voice. "I'd have come sooner, but I've only just been told."

"Leave it outside," she said, per Mr Bertram's mouthed instructions. She didn't recall asking for a blanket, but perhaps Dorian knew Mr Bertram was lurking in her room.

"I ain't leaving it out here for some bugger to steal." The woman persisted in knocking again. "How long does it take to open the door?"

Mr Bertram moved to the window and peered around the shabby curtain. Whatever he saw must have instilled confidence in him because he gestured for her to open the door.

Say nothing, he mouthed. *Or I'll shoot you where you stand.*

Delphine nodded. This was her one chance to escape.

Mr Bertram cocked the hammer and aimed the pistol at her head. "I'm an excellent shot," he muttered.

Shaking to the tips of her toes, she opened the door ajar and glanced at the woman standing on the dim landing. "I'll take the blanket."

"I have to place it on the bed. Some buggers ask for extra bedding and filch it away with their luggage." There was something familiar about the large eyes peering out from beneath the white cap. "I'll only be a minute, ducky."

"I'm afraid I can't let you in," she said, though mouthed, *Help!*

"I'll be in the workhouse if I can't keep this job. Move aside."

When the woman pushed open the door, Delphine realised it was Mrs Haggert. She knew by the woman's determined chin and the slight limp as she dragged her left leg.

Mr Bertram hid the pistol behind his back. "Be quick, woman."

Mrs Haggert winked at him. "I understand, sir. Happen you want the lady all to yourself. I'll just sort out the blanket and be on my way."

While Delphine held her breath, and Mr Bertram stood with murderous intent in his evil eyes, Mrs Haggert hummed a little ditty before shaking out the blanket.

Of course, she stumbled a little during the action and whipped Mr Bertram in the eye with one rough corner.

"Stupid witch!"

Mrs Haggert hurried over but offered no words to atone for her mistake. She pulled a blade from her pocket and drove it deep into Mr Bertram's chest.

"That's for Sofia," she snarled as the pistol fell from Mr Bertram's hand and the chill of death chased over his face. She twisted the knife, ignoring the man's shrill scream. "And that's for trying to hurt Caterina."

Chapter Twenty-Two

Dorian sat at a table in the Belle Sauvage's sombre taproom, answering the magistrate's questions. All guests were confined to their rooms while the coroner examined Bertram's body and his men sketched the wound that had finished the devil off for good.

Mrs Haggert had been taken to Bow Street.

Lord Meldrum bumbled his way through his interview. The fool admitted to freeing Nora and giving her a pistol. He shocked them by revealing Bertie had hired the thugs to kidnap Delphine. "Bertie never meant for them to shoot Theodore Chance. It was supposed to be a way of helping to clear my debts."

Judging by the thunderous look on Aaron's face, it was a good job Bertram was dead. Meldrum would need to flee the country or Aaron would hunt him down and make him pay.

"Do you understand how incredulous the tale sounds?" Sir Malcolm Langley asked Dorian while the constable beside him took notes.

"All events can be corroborated." He had named Miss Lovelace and Miss Darrow as witnesses. They already had Nora and Powell in custody. And two constables had fetched Bertram's sister from her home in Warwick Square, hoping she could identify the body.

"By Jove, when the King hears about this, you'll all be knighted."

A shiver of dread ran down Dorian's spine. A title was the last thing he wanted. "I don't need a knighthood. I need to know we've been exonerated. That none of us will hang for murder."

Daventry returned with a man no one knew. The tall, elegant fellow spoke privately with the magistrate, and as quick as a wink, the constables left with Lord Meldrum in tow.

Daventry drew Dorian to a dim corner of the room. "We're all free to leave, though speak of this to no one. The King fears the news may bring public unrest. The monarchy cannot afford to look weak."

"I pray no charges will be brought against Mrs Haggert."

The woman had appeared in their darkest hour with a plan Dorian felt sure would work. He had stood a few feet away on the gallery, his heart lodged in his throat, waiting to charge inside when Mrs Haggert gave the signal.

Daventry glanced around the taproom before saying, "Mrs Haggert parades as a vigilante but is part of a secret government organisation. None of her boys were hanged. It's a ruse. They're being trained to work as spies abroad. Though we're not permitted to discuss that either."

"That explains how she happened to be here tonight.

She has eyes and ears everywhere." It also explained how she managed to avoid prosecution as the leader of a pickpocketing gang. "Although nothing surprises me after the hell we've been through."

Daventry laughed, but something akin to pride passed over his face. "I always knew you would succeed." His gaze drifted to Delphine, who sat drinking ale in a booth with her brothers. "However painful, Miss Chance deserved to know the truth. My wife will be glad to know you earned your fee."

Dorian had almost forgotten he'd been paid to help Delphine. While solving the case, he'd earned something more precious than gold. "Based on what I know now, I would have offered my services for free."

Daventry grinned. "I shall tell my wife to expect a refund."

"Tell your wife I owe her a debt that can never be repaid."

Daventry gave him a brotherly pat on the back. "Miss Chance hasn't taken her eyes off you since we began talking. After all she's been through, I suggest you take her home. Meet me at Bow Street at noon tomorrow, and we'll help Sir Malcolm with his reports."

Within seconds of Daventry departing, Delphine darted from the booth and hurried past the empty tables, heading in Dorian's direction.

He'd not held her since he'd burst into the bedchamber and found Bertram dead on the floor. Perhaps that's why they were running towards each other now.

She threw herself into his embrace. "Dorian."

He lifted her off the floor, wrapping his arms around

her so tightly he feared he'd squeeze the breath from her lungs. "You're safe now."

Love filled his heart.

He closed his eyes and inhaled the lilac scent of her hair. He let the heat of her body warm him. Beautiful dreams of their future flitted through his mind, as soothing as a summer breeze.

"I don't want to be without you," she uttered against his neck.

They'd come so close to losing everything.

No doubt the same thought plagued Delphine, too.

"I'll never leave you again. You're my love, my life, my everything."

As she drew back, their gazes locked with a power that defied the heavens. "I love you. My life is with you now." A smile touched her lips as she brushed his hair from his brow. "Take me home."

"To Fortune's Den?" He'd have to fight Aaron again because he wasn't letting her out of his sight, not even for a second.

Her hand came to rest gently on his bristled jaw. "Home is wherever you are. Home is where you decide to sleep tonight. Take me there."

His heart constricted.

"Home is Mile End. It's where we'll spend our married life and raise our children. Tonight, I'll take you to the Old Swan." It was but half a mile to Long Lane, and they were desperate to be alone. "We can continue that deep, meaningful conversation we started earlier."

She flashed a coy grin. "I doubt we'll reach a quick conclusion."

Lady Gambit

"We'll still be conversing madly when the first rays of dawn breach the horizon."

She kissed him tenderly on the lips. "There's one important factor you've neglected to mention, Mr Flynn."

He knew she spoke of marriage. "I thought I might propose in Miss Darrow's yard. It's where you swept into my life in a swathe of gold silk and teased me with talk of your undergarments."

"If only you'd known what a terrible burden I would be."

"Yes, I'd have doubled my fee." He kissed her quickly and patted her discreetly on the bottom. "Say goodbye to your brothers. I'll not have them bursting into the Old Swan and dragging me to the fighting pit." He sensed the men enjoyed brawling amongst themselves. If he married Delphine, he'd have to join the ranks and become a rogue. "Tell Aaron I'll visit him tomorrow to discuss our plans."

She giggled as she left him.

The sight brought a rush of relief. Then he turned and saw his father sitting at an oak table in a darkened corner of the old taproom, and his good mood soured.

Steeling himself—the last thing he wanted was an argument—he approached the man he tried hard to despise. "I thought you'd left two hours ago."

The earl looked up through weary eyes. "You may have been arrested. I'll not sit by and watch them throw my son in gaol."

"A traitor is dead. I'm more likely to get an invitation to the palace than suffer the walk to the gallows."

"Still, someone needed to be here for you."

An awkward silence ensued.

The earl stared into his tankard.

"I'm thirty years old," Dorian said, keeping his frustration at bay. "You sired me, but you don't own me. As your illegitimate son, I will never belong to the aristocracy. The sooner you accept it, the better. Marrying Miss Montague won't change the nature of my birth."

"No." His father glanced at Delphine standing at her brothers' table, laughing at something Aramis said. "You love her. It's plain to see. I pray it lasts. There's nothing worse than knowing you've failed someone dear to you."

He might pity the man, but his pity dried up years ago, along with his tears and the wounds on his back. "I'll do everything I can to love her as she deserves."

"Then I wish you luck. It's evident you belong with these people."

These people? He didn't remind his father that Daventry was the bastard son of a duke. He didn't mention the Chance brothers were nephews to the current Earl of Berridge.

Relationships shouldn't be this difficult.

His father could change it all with a simple word or gesture.

"You mean to marry her, then?" His father nodded to Delphine.

"At the first opportunity."

"I see." The earl tossed back the contents of his tankard and slammed the vessel on the table as he stood. "If you require help with a special licence, I can write to the archbishop."

Dorian stared, a little shocked his father had offered an olive branch. "I'd be grateful for your assistance."

"You have it. I'll deliver the letter personally."

His father rounded the table. He didn't bid Dorian farewell or pat his arm affectionately. "You proved what sort of man you are today. You put us idle men to shame." And with those parting words, he left.

Evidently, it was to be a night of surprises.

Though Dorian spent the short journey to Long Lane locked in a passionate clinch with Delphine, the landlord of the Old Swan scuppered any plans to race upstairs and tear off their clothes.

"Mr Flynn!" Simpson rounded the counter in the empty tavern, drying his hands on a cloth. "That gent was here again. He waited for three hours but had to leave London tonight."

"Oh?" he said, wondering if they would ever get a minute's peace.

"He left this." Simpson drew a sealed letter from his apron pocket and gave it to Dorian. "The poor devil has gone back to Winchester but said all the details are in the note."

"Winchester?" Dorian examined the paper and scanned the wax seal. "Did he mention the nature of his business?"

"No, he just said you were a beneficiary."

A beneficiary?

It did not take Aristotle's logic to solve the puzzle.

He thanked Simpson, clasped Delphine's hand and led her upstairs to his bedchamber. He locked the door, lit the lamp and closed the curtains.

"It's chilly in here." He turned to find her studying him intently.

"I'm sure we'll be warm soon." She glanced at the

letter he'd placed on the nightstand. "Aren't you going to open it?"

"Tomorrow." He reached for her hands and drew them to his lips in turn. He wanted to make love and discuss marriage, not deal with a flurry of old emotions. "I don't want to think about anything but us and our future."

Amusement danced in her eyes. "When we make love tonight, it will be a new beginning. A time to focus on ourselves. To make happiness our priority. Let's deal with any unanswered questions now."

It wasn't the letter that bothered him so much as the need to tell her about her grandfather. But she was right.

He reached for the letter and tore open the seal. A quick read revealed a pleasant surprise. "Good Lord."

She touched his chest. "I trust it's good news."

"Do you remember I mentioned my old tutor? Mr Brown taught Classical Studies. We read philosophy and played chess together on the occasions I was left at school."

"I remember. You credit him with your love of Aristotle. Did he leave you his library?"

Dorian reread the letter, somewhat shocked. "Yes, along with his house in Winchester."

"His house?"

He knew Mr Brown had no family—there'd been but a handful of people at his funeral—but the gift brought a tear to his eye. "It will mean a trip to Winchester."

She slipped her arms around him. "When do we leave?"

"As soon as we're married."

"You haven't asked me. I might refuse."

"Like hell you will." He captured her chin and poured everything of himself into a toe-curling kiss. "Your mouth betrays you. You can't wait to have me in your bed every night."

"Our bed," she corrected. "I'll not sleep in separate rooms."

"I fear we might not sleep at all." The secret he'd been keeping pushed to the forefront of his mind. "When we visit Winchester, we might venture to Chichester, then tour the south coast. Make a honeymoon of it."

Love lived in her beaming smile. "How could I refuse an opportunity to have you all to myself? Though why Chichester?"

He threw the letter onto the bed and captured her face in his hands. "Daventry told me something tonight." He paused, knowing nothing he said would make his job easier. "Your paternal grandfather is alive and living in Chichester. I thought you might like to visit."

Her throat worked tirelessly as she absorbed the information, though no words left her lips. Tears gathered in her eyes, and she buried her head in his chest and wept like the sound came from her soul.

When she found the strength to look at him, she said, "Does he know I survived? Did he ever try to find me?"

He dried her cheeks with his thumbs. "We can ask Daventry tomorrow. I'm certain he has your grandfather's address."

Lost in thought, she nibbled her lip. "What if he doesn't want to see me? What if he can't bear to relive the painful memories?"

"Why would he not want to see you? You're beautiful in every way. You're intelligent and funny and kind."

She kissed him, the salty evidence of her tears on her lips. "You're biased. No one has ever loved me like you do."

"Marry me."

"In a heartbeat."

"You may want to take time to consider my proposal. Someone I love madly once told me marriage was worse than death." She'd been quite adamant during their first meeting in Miss Darrow's yard.

"I didn't know a love like this was possible. Besides, you said you'd prefer a swift death to a life spent shackled to a woman."

"You're no ordinary woman."

"No, I have a host of aliases."

"Soon, you'll be Mrs Flynn. Yet one name encompasses them all. I'm sure everyone who knows you would agree." He thought of the monikers her brothers used. He'd never been a gambling man, but luck was on his side the day they met. "You taught me the true meaning of love, Delphine. You're the Queen of Hearts. The undisputed ruler of mine."

Chapter Twenty-Three

Mile End Manor
Walworth

They were married five days later by special licence in St Peter's Church in Walworth near Mile End. Miss Darrow graciously lent her a stunning ivory silk dress featuring a two-tiered skirt and ruche sleeves, a style fashionable in Paris.

The guests congregated in the front pews, although Aaron did his utmost to avoid looking at Miss Lovelace. Miss Darrow sat beside Theo, playfully nudging him twice in the ribs during the ceremony.

The Earl of Retford entered the church late and slipped silently into a back pew. He left when the vicar proclaimed them husband and wife and warned *those whom God has joined together let no one put asunder*.

Mrs James looked as proud as a peacock when they returned to Mile End for the wedding breakfast. "Everything changed the moment you walked through the door, ma'am. I knew from the way the master looked at you he was smitten."

Dorian's hand came to rest on Delphine's back. "I was smitten when she insisted a dislike of mussels might help me solve the case, Mrs James." He pressed his mouth to her ear and whispered, "And when you slipped your tongue over mine while your brother slept twenty feet away."

Delphine gently nudged him to be quiet. "When I saw him, I knew we were destined to be more than friends."

She had spent many lonely hours conjuring an image of her future husband. Now she knew he was tall and broad, with a smile that would melt any woman's heart.

Indeed, she was still staring at Dorian when the guests gathered in the drawing room to converse and drink champagne. Mrs Maloney's remark must have been amusing because Dorian shook his head and erupted into laughter.

Heavens! He was so handsome. He looked so happy and carefree. And to think she would wake to his sinful grin each morning.

Everyone seemed to be avoiding talk of Mrs Maloney's male companion. Keen to protect the woman dear to all their hearts, Aramis had drawn the elderly gentleman into a quiet corner of the room to speak privately. Perhaps Mrs Maloney's love interest was hoping for a proper introduction because he glanced at Delphine three times during the conversation.

"Delphine?" Miss Darrow cleared her throat and tapped Delphine's arm to get her attention. "Are you well? I called you so many times I feared you were still in the mesmerist's trance."

"Forgive me. I was so lost in my thoughts I didn't hear you." In truth, she couldn't wait until all the guests had left so she could meet Dorian in the orangery for a romantic rendezvous.

Miss Darrow smiled. "You had the same faraway look in your eyes the first time you saw Mr Flynn."

"I did?" So much had happened since then. "Perhaps our meeting was fated. Some things are written in the stars. How strange Theo accompanied me that day, and you were on hand to nurse him."

Miss Darrow grumbled under her breath. "Trust me. There is nothing fated about our meeting. If Theodore Chance is the King of Hearts, all maidens are doomed."

"I've always found his playful manner endearing."

Miss Darrow's grimace said she disagreed. "By any chance, have you come across my wooden sewing box?" She gripped her sherry glass between firm fingers, probably wishing the stem was Theo's neck. "While I'm at Mile End, would you mind if I searched upstairs? It may have slipped behind the bed."

As mistress of the house, Delphine was happy to oblige her. "Of course not. You should ask Theo for help. He may remember where you left it. I presume the box holds some sentimental value."

Why else would the modiste be so desperate to find it?

"Erm ... yes. It belonged to my grandmother."

That was clearly a lie. Miss Darrow's eyes darted about in their sockets. She had been jittery all day, though Theo didn't help matters. He watched the modiste over the rim of his glass, his angelic blue eyes hiding wicked intentions.

The lady hurried away when Aaron joined them.

"It comes as a relief to know I have such a negative effect on women." As if controlled by the power of the tides, Aaron's traitorous gaze drifted to Miss Lovelace. "Your husband has made a wager with Aramis. He'll lose, of course."

"Dorian is remarkably astute." She looked at the magnificent man she'd married, lust's coil tightening in her stomach at the thought of them making love tonight. "What was the wager?"

"Based on the fact Daventry is encouraging Theo's game with Miss Darrow, I wagered he'd be married by the autumn. Doubtless they'll both drag us to hell and back first. Lord knows what the woman is hiding."

"What did Dorian wager?" she said, feigning ignorance.

Dorian had mentioned his prediction days ago, which is why she had argued with Aaron and insisted Miss Lovelace receive a wedding invitation.

"Flynn thinks I'll be married by Christmas." Aaron gave a cynical snort. "Do I look like a man who would tolerate a wife? I'll not have a woman in my home, disturbing my sanity. Perhaps it's time I took a mistress."

"No!" She coughed to hide the rising panic. Taking a mistress would ruin any hope of him making an alliance with Miss Lovelace. "How would you have time? You rarely leave Fortune's Den and swore you'd never mix business with pleasure."

"I need a way of wiping the arrogant grin off your husband's face. Perhaps I'll find a reason to fight him in the ring."

"Lay a hand on him again and I shall put a toad in your bed."

"A toad?" Aaron laughed, the rare sound capturing Miss Lovelace's attention. "You're not twelve, Delphine. Besides, I happen to like toads. Almost as much as I like your husband. Flynn is the sensible brother I never had."

Aaron never praised anyone.

The compliment proved promising.

"Dorian has had quite a lonely life," she said, her heart so full of love it might burst. "Being part of a large family will be good for him."

Aaron knocked back his champagne. "I saw his father enter the church. I'm surprised he's not here, dominating the conversation."

So was she.

Thus, she had sent Briggs to Mayfair with a note.

"Healing past wounds is a lengthy process." They had to focus on taking one step at a time. "Neither knows how best to proceed, but it's important to move in the right direction."

"Some wounds never heal," he said gravely.

"The right ointment can work wonders." She hoped Miss Lovelace was the salve Aaron needed to put the past behind him. Overcoming his stubborn streak was the first hurdle to lasting happiness.

Kingsley appeared. The butler cleared his throat and said quietly, "You have a visitor, ma'am. I took the liberty of asking his lordship to wait in the library."

Her heart shot to her throat. The earl had come? Now she had to find the strength to confront him with the truth. "Thank you, Kingsley. I shall be right there."

"Good luck," Aaron teased. "I believe you'll need it."

"I watched a lunatic creep out of a cupboard and point a pistol at my face. I can cope with the earl's gruff temper. Say nothing to Dorian. I don't want to dash his hopes."

She left Aaron and slipped out into the hall. After taking a few calming breaths, she stole into the library to find the Earl of Retford admiring a painting of a racehorse.

"My lord." She dropped into a demure curtsey. "I trust you received my note. Forgive me, had you remained at the church, I would have extended an invitation."

The earl's cheeks coloured. "I wasn't sure I'd be welcome." He glanced at the plush furnishings and shelves of leather-bound books. "If my son wanted me here, he would have given me his address years ago."

She smiled, hoping it looked sincere. "May I speak openly?"

"By all means." He gestured for her to continue.

"Dorian is the best of men. If you want his love and respect, you'll have to fight to earn it." She imagined the earl in Aaron's pit and had to bite back a grin. "If that is beyond your capabilities, then you should leave. Dorian has suffered enough."

The earl arched a bushy brow. "Are you always this frank, madam?"

"Time is precious. Why waste it on ambiguity?"

The earl's amused snort surprised her.

"If you cannot raise a toast to your son on his wedding day, there's no hope of a reconciliation. If you agree, I shall fetch my husband." She prayed Dorian wasn't angry and the earl didn't spoil this golden opportunity to make amends.

"I agree, though do not wish to ruin his wedding day."

"I'm certain you won't." She curtsied again before adding, "Let us be clear. Hurt him, and I shall make you suffer in ways you cannot begin to imagine. The men in my life are loving and loyal. I pray you won't disappoint."

She left the earl pondering that thought and went in search of Dorian. As soon as she entered the drawing room, Mrs Maloney's companion took to staring at her strangely again.

Dorian spotted her and drew her aside. "I missed you." His hand at her elbow sent a tingle down her spine. "Give me fair warning next time you sneak out of the room. We might have an interlude in the understairs cupboard."

"I'm sure we will spend endless days exploring all the hidden corners in this house." She swallowed past her nerves, hoping he wouldn't be angry. "I have some important news to share. You may be furious, but consider it a wedding gift that keeps on giving."

He drew his thumb across his bottom lip. "Now I'm intrigued."

"Don't raise your hopes." Out of the corner of her eye, she spotted the elderly gentleman gawping. Maybe he was desperate for her approval, too. "I invited your father to spend a few hours with us. I left him waiting in the library in case you disapprove and wish to throw him out, though he seems amiable."

Dorian straightened, his shock short-lived because his gaze moved to Mrs Maloney's male companion. "I know I'm supposed to be the most important man in your life, particularly on our wedding day, but I fear someone else deserves your attention today."

Confused, she followed his gaze to the white-haired fellow with a penchant for grinning. "You speak of Mrs Maloney's companion? Why would—"

"That man is your grandfather. He stayed with Mrs Maloney last night. He wouldn't let me tell you because he didn't want his arrival to overshadow our celebrations. Aaron went to fetch him from Chichester. It seems your brother insists on vetting every man in your life."

Delphine froze.

She turned slowly, but her grandfather's beaming smile suddenly made everything right. Now she knew why he hadn't stopped shaking Aaron's hand, why he had spent time alone with all her brothers.

Her throat tightened. It was like having her parents with her on her wedding day. A comforting feeling of unity and enduring love enveloped her.

"Go to him," Dorian whispered. "He has been waiting hours to speak to you." His hand skimmed her hip, a sensual caress that carried the promise of something illicit. "I'll attempt to be civil to my father, though I shall be counting the minutes until we're alone tonight."

She cupped his cheek and kissed him quickly. "Meet me in the orangery at eight. I'll be waiting."

He moistened his lips. "I'll bring the champagne."

It was nine o'clock when their guests left and they had the house to themselves. Her sisters-in-law had decorated the orangery. They'd draped chiffon around the windows and had Kingsley bring the chaise from the library. Lit candles glowed in hanging lanterns, giving an ethereal charm. The warmth of the summer night and the sweet scent of garden roses cast a seductive spell over the room.

Lady Gambit

She watched Dorian descend the terrace steps, her stomach doing somersaults because she would never tire of making love to him. Wearing loose black trousers, an open white shirt and nothing on his feet, he looked utterly sinful tonight.

He entered the orangery, took one look at her pale pink nightgown and nearly dropped the bottle of champagne. "And they say once you've exchanged vows, married life is a downward spiral."

Suppressing a grin was impossible. "I used to hide behind clothes until I met you. Now I feel free to express my true self."

Dorian swallowed as his gaze slid over the diaphanous material that left little to the imagination. "You've never hidden yourself from me. The first time we met, you revealed more than your bare shoulders. I saw everything."

"Everything?" Keen to learn more, she moved towards him at a slow, sensual pace. "What exactly did you see?"

It wasn't just her nightgown that was transparent. From the needy purr in her voice, surely he knew how badly she desired him.

"I saw my loneliness reflected in your eyes. It was there when you clung to me and cried. It lived like an ache in my heart when you sent me away."

She recalled their second meeting and the tug in her gut when he left Miss Darrow's yard. Had Theo not been shot, she would not have seen Dorian again. The thought was enough to make her weep.

"Fate had other plans for us."

He placed the bottle on the floor, rubbed his hands

together to warm them and closed the gap between them. "Who knew I craved chaos?"

"Who knew that a man so reserved could seduce a woman in her brother's bedchamber?"

He stood so close now, she felt his warm breath on her lips. "You kissed me first," he said, his velvet voice stroking her senses.

"The madness of love is the greatest of heaven's blessings."

He smiled as he tugged the ribbon on her nightgown to reveal the deep valley between her breasts. "I never understood the power of love until we were alone in the Old Swan."

"Lust had us in its intemperate grip."

And every moment had been glorious.

"It was more than lust." He cupped her cheek, his gaze moving from her hair to her lips. "I loved you then. Lust I could have fought, but the power of our love is like a tempest—a raging passion no human force can control."

He brushed his thumb over her lips, down the column of her throat to circle her nipple through the filmy pink silk. It hardened, anticipating the moist flick of his tongue.

But Dorian took her hand and drew her to the chaise. "Lie down."

She obliged him, practically drooling as he dragged his shirt over his head and tossed it to the floor. His trousers followed.

She would never tire of looking at his muscular physique. She would always gasp at the size of his engorged manhood.

He straddled the chaise, hooking her legs over his thighs before sliding her nightgown slowly up to her waist.

"What do you mean to do?"

"I'm the lowly Knave of Hearts." Carnal heat flared in his warm brown eyes as he moistened his lips and gazed at her sex. "I'm preparing to worship my queen."

She laughed, but he set his mouth to her aching womanhood. Every hot swipe of his tongue had her writhing with pleasure. It was no surprise that she came quickly—she'd been desperate to have him all day. The shivers of delight as he entered her said she would climax many times before they left their garden hideaway tonight.

"There's nothing lowly about the knave." She gripped his firm buttocks as he pushed so deep inside her she moaned. The knave was loyal and brave beyond compare—her hero. "He's a passionate and generous lover."

"He is?"

"Hmm."

"Then prepare yourself for a night to remember. As the queen of my heart, you'll get all I have to give."

I hope you enjoyed reading *Lady Gambit.*

What is so special about Miss Darrow's box? Will the lady wage war in a bid to reclaim it? When will Theo realise that his game has put both their lives in danger?

Find out in …

My Kind of Scoundrel
Rogues of Fortune's Den - Book 4

More titles by Adele Clee

Gentlemen of the Order

Dauntless

Raven

Valiant

Dark Angel

Ladies of the Order

The Devereaux Affair

More than a Masquerade

Mine at Midnight

Your Scarred Heart

No Life for a Lady

Scandal Sheet Survivors

More than Tempted

Not so Wicked

Never a Duchess

No One's Bride

Rogues of Fortune's Den

A Little Bit Dangerous

Temptress in Disguise

Lady Gambit

My Kind of Scoundrel